P9-EDN-092

WITHDRAWN
UTSA LIBRARIES

WITHDRAWN
UTSA LIBRARIES

Books by Brock Brower

The Late Great Creature 1971

Other Loyalties 1968

Debris 1967

The Late Great Creature

Brock Brower

New York Atheneum 1972

The
Late Great
Creature

LIBRARY
The University of Texas
At San Antonio

Copyright © 1971 by Brock Brower
All rights reserved
Library of Congress catalog card number 72–168255
Published simultaneously in Canada by McClelland and Stewart Ltd.
Manufactured in the United States of America by H. Wolff, New York
Designed by Harry Ford
First Edition

For All Five

The Late Great Creature

I. *From a Self-Addressed Envelope*

A clown isn't funny in the moonlight.

LON CHANEY

INITIAL SELF-IMPOSITION: put down everything I failed to tell them at the Breadloaf Writers Conference this past August about writing my piece for *Esquire* on Simon Moro. The slipshod omissions, the more practiced lacunae, the big, deliberate gaps, everything. That far down on my knees for starters. However: even in contrition, small credit where credit is due. Yes. My talk—no, it was higher rhetoric than that—my *lecture* at Breadloaf didn't go so badly. Obviously curious, most of them, about Moro. Comfortable chair creaks, i.e., stirrings of a deep, dogged nostalgia. Could remember him from as far back as, say, a triple-feature Halloween horror show in the late thirties. Or, slightly later, from some gothically patriotic, anti-Nazi, Defense-Bond-rally chiller they might have thought had Karloff in it too. (Not so. Karloff and Moro never did a picture together, and if you think about it, they really are incompatible evils.) Or maybe from right after the war, a bad, really awful Abbott and Costello, one of those abortions where Bud and Lou "meet" the enfeebled wraith of this or that bygone creature. But, even that bad, still a subject of intriguing, if ephemeral, interest. Or is it that any subject that intrigues nowadays also self-destructs, ephemerates? Anyhow, most to my credit: even that death row of lady English teachers who come every year to Breadloaf—a slough of slumped corduroy from one rump end to the other—perked up a little during my remarks, bless them. Though they must believe— must *have* to believe—that Moro is some kind of depredation. A foul smirch on the literary purity of their most beloved teaching aid, Edgar Allan Poe. Sensed that when I began talking about Moro's work on *Raven*, could see the disapproval in their faces, like trowel marks in sad, old stucco. And it goes a long way back, that disapproval. If only *they'd* been around when that spindly Poe boy, the one well-read, sensitive lad in a classroom full of upstart Virginia farm girls, reached for his first, fatal glass of cooking sherry. . . .

Also: the gist of what I had to say was straight cold tur-key, a good Puritan sermon for would-be writers on a drizzly, devil-damp Vermont evening. "*Why* There Is Only a *How* to Article Writing." Final self-appraisal of lecture: semi-enlightening, damn near close to candid, wittily self-deprecatory, but, in the end—since this manila envelope has got to be some kind of four-cornered hell, nor am I out of it—in the end, diligently self-preserving. Yes, a large cut of self kept in reserve, or if that self isn't always too sure a thing these days, maybe only a large cut of reserve kept in reserve. Single biggest fudge: gave audience distinct im-pression that I was letting them in on a sure thing, a lead article that would Soon Appear in a leading national maga-zine. Chances not too good of that happening, right now. Legitimate excuse: didn't quite know that then, hadn't really even finished writing the article yet, but, on the other hand, how was this stark truth recently ascertained? By breaking the very first rule I laid down for them at Bread-loaf. *Never call an editor.* I gave them that one, chiseled in porphyry. Such restraint, I elaborated, (1) allows editor to make up his sluggish mind more leisurely, hence, more fa-vorably, and (2) allows writer to maintain his ineffable dig-nity, hence, his top price. So, this morning, I didn't call. No. After four long weeks of not hearing, I got on the 9:10 A.M. bus to New York City, arrived at Port Authority Bus Ter-minal around 10:25 A.M., walked over to Forty-second Street. Noticed that none of his old movies were showing along there any more—bad sign—then checked the pop poster in the first dirty-books-store window, a big, scaly one of Moro as Gila Man. A true believer had scrawled "Gila Man Lives!" across the window in some new blood type of murderous lipstick, but inside, the poster's edges were start-ing to curl, rolling up under the streaked glass, tight, like a creeping shroud. Another bad sign. Got a taxi over to 488

Madison, driver still for Wallace, took elevator to fourth
floor, slipped in side door, Staff Only—"After all," told myself, "I used to work here"—and since Connie wasn't at her
desk, walked right in on Harold.

"Hel-lo there, Warner." Cheery, no surprise. "Glad you
came by. I was just going to call you."

"Got a lunch date?"

He even bothered to swivel up and frown at his desk cal-
endar. "Sorry. Can't break it. Sit down, sit down."

I sat. We sat. And we talked, or I talked. I talked about
how far along I was on my novel, I wanted him to see it first
when I had enough to show, then in a tight, familiar way
about the Names I have to admit are bigger than mine—
Tom (Wolfe) and Jimmy (Breslin) and Joan (Didion) and
Dan (Wakefield)—and in a friendly, distant way about the
ones that are still smaller, that you have to give in full. All
the time establishing my own size, of course. But the anxiety-
brewing thing was I couldn't tell if Harold was really agree-
ing with me on size. He wasn't saying much, making me feel
almost like a full name myself. Finally I had to say, "When
are you going to run my piece?"

"Well now, Warner, we've got a little problem here."

How many times have I heard Harold say that, with the
same little pebble-and-rill, good-old-So'thern-boy chuckle.
But never to me, never to me. How do I dump thee? Let me
count the ways. *Nota bene:* chuckle runs much swifter, a
lot more Rebel, coming at you.

"You're late on this already," I got right back at him.
"You wait any longer, with your lead time, it's all going to
be over. These things peak, then they plummet."

All Harold did was nod.

So I reversed wisdom.

"Look. Everything Moro's doing—I don't care how bad it
looks—it's all working for him."

"He's gone too far."

"You can't go too far any more, Harold. There's no such place."

"You don't think so?"

"If there is, we've been there and back."

"You've heard the word on the picture?"

"You seen a screening?"

"Wouldn't bother."

"He's great, Harold. I'm not saying anything about the picture, but if you want to see a performance."

"I've seen his performance. How can you miss it?"

"They're trying to calm him down."

"Who is?"

"Terry's here. I'm seeing him for cocktails."

"Who he?"

"The director. Read my piece."

I got a blink of credit for that twist, but then he swung around on me with that hard, black-eyed-pea stare of his. "You *saw* what he did on the *Tonight* show."

"I heard about it."

"You didn't see it?"

"No."

"Susan and I *saw* it."

"We were out that night."

"You know how he got that thing into his mouth? With his foot. Took off his damn sock and picked it up between his toes."

"That's an old trick of his."

"Oh come on, Warner!"

"No. Truth. From *The Unholy Circus*. Did it first with a spoon, then with a cigarette. He played this armless clown. Kind of a *Pagliacci* story." Can see now I was talking too much. "Clown used to be a trapeze artist but had both his arms amputated after he let this other acrobat fall. Remorse. But his wife is this high-wire artist, still the star, and she puts him down. Betrays him with the strong man, and Moro strangles her. Lil Dagover, I think."

"How?"

"What'd you mean?"

"*How?*"

"Oh. Between his knees."

We both started sort of shrugging at each other. "It was a silent," I tried to explain. "A very early German silent."

"What about the cawing?"

"He cawed?"

"Whatever the hell ravens do."

"His animal thing. I've got it in the piece."

"I guess ravens rave. He was raving, Warner."

"When he came to this country, he didn't have that much English, had to play it kind of Harpo Marx-y for a while, but he had all these gutturals. So he used them. Rolled them over into a lot of midnight-zoo sounds."

"He also flies, right?"

"Right."

"Straight at you, with this dried-up . . . *thing* still in his teeth."

"Did he?"

Could see it: exactly how Moro *would* go and do the Raven on TV. Live. Same way he did the Moth in 1935. Up close on camera, with a lot of wild, undulating motion, but always with something to deflect, rivet your attention, so you don't notice he isn't really off his feet. Could see the whole bit, could admire his moves, even smile, sorry I'd missed it.

Wrong facial gesture, at that particular moment.

"Wasn't funny. It was plain sick-grisly."

"Guess it depends on your sense of humor."

"Come on, Warner, he's a damn ghoul." Harold went after something in his manuscript pile. "Now where in here do you tell us that significant personal fact?"

He had my piece slap-down in front of him, with the green bucksheet paper-clipped on top of it. I couldn't read the comments, but I could see there were too many, all too long, to be favorable.

"You said you wanted a funny piece," I said.

"Not if he's not funny! Not if he's plain damn morbid!" Harold has this kind of low-key, rational, almost enumerative way of screaming at you. "You know he was fired out of Shakespeare in the Park. You know he's just damn lucky they didn't cut him off on TV. You know what he's been pulling over all this damn city. If you don't know, read the papers. The damn New York *Post* even had an editorial on what he pulled in Gramercy Park . . . or do you only see the *Times* out where you are?"

"You hold a piece this long, it's bound to date."

He laughed. "You know as well as I do." Not chuckled, laughed. "It's a whole different piece now."

I mentioned this type of situation to them at Breadloaf. I quoted, quote, "A friend of mine who writes a lot for *Life* once wrote: 'Such is the precipitancy of present-day events, denying that sparest consistency to human affairs upon which even the most ephemeral reporting must depend.'" Ponderous, but I wanted to sound respectable. The truth: I wanted to be asked back to Breadloaf. The truth behind that truth: you have to hedge your woes and master a knowing, rock-ribbed tone if you're going to hold your own with the would-be's for two solid weeks up there in the Green Mountains. They listen, do they ever listen, for the ring of self-fulfillment and proper remuneration and tacit immortality. Have to sound *simpatico* but always deeply laureate. Can't let any would-be know you might be a would-have-been. But, in sum, a propos that unmanageable quote: what he's saying, I'm facing.

"Harold," I try, "Moro used to be part of all our bad dreams. The good part. Maybe even the best part. Why else

this craze? He's only trying to stay in there as a going fig-
ment of the public imagination. These days it's terribly hard
to be a horror."

"Why didn't you write it that way?"

"That wasn't supposed to be the idea."

History of an Idea: Warner Williams, a middle-class indi-
gent, given, during times of nervous stress, to referring to
himself in the destitute third person—like a failed CIA
agent, babbling under a blown cover—quits his job at *Esquire* to take a contract with the *SatEvePost*. A move down
in the maso-fadistic careerism of the New York literary
scene, but what good is reputation if it can't buy you
money, what with four children and a superior wife. Far
superior. Above American letters, a Francophile; above anti-
biotics and chemical fertilizers and the Pill, a naturalist;
above money, perhaps even above marriage, a housewife.
During 1966–67, Williams manages to slip enough pieces by
Otto Friedrich to gain a little extra money, i.e., time, to
work on his novel—though he does not use that time to
work on his novel—and even survives one of those French-
Revolutionary editorial changes at the *SatEvePost*. From the
Committee of Public Safety to the Directorate. All the close-
in powers-that-were are trying, but it would really take
Thomas Carlyle to write the company history of Curtis
Publishing. But this past spring, he is given a crack at Richard M. Nixon during the primary campaign. The assignment
is the first one he has liked, not having been passionately
either for or against such as the Country's Leading Tree
Surgeon or the New, Rough-and-Tumble Patty Duke, Teen
Turned Trollop. He is, as an objective reporter, fanatic
against Nixon.

After following the candidate around for several weeks,
from White Plains, N.Y., to the Disneyland Hilton, and
watching Nixon slowly inch out of his shell to start slavishly
impersonating his own crowds, Williams begins to see a pos-

sible approach to the story. He is fascinated by the candidate's victory gesture, a borrowing from Eisenhower. Both Nixon arms shoot upward, and then the big Nixon hands hang limp from the Nixon wrists, index and middle fingers forming two loose, pudgy V's. Like waggling claws, and has nobody but Williams ever noticed that a lobster goes through exactly the same motions when you pick one up by its back and drop it into the pot? Williams' conception is now that Nixon is still in his shell, but has evolved into one of those shellfish that assume a more mobile life form. The Old Nixon was possibly a mollusk. The New Nixon is perhaps more like an Alaskan King Crab.

He is told by the *SatEvePost* that it's an *Esquire* idea, and besides, the staff is being cut again. Williams did not last into the Empire. Then again, nobody there turned out to be Napoleon either.

He and his wife then have a long, many-whiskeys talk and agree that free-lancing is no kind of life for them, that he hasn't gotten that much done on his novel anyhow, that he'd better ask for his old job back at *Esquire*.

Harold tells him his old job is gone, but would he like an assignment? In fact, a free trip to Hollywood. "Some schlock outfit is shooting *The Raven* again. Why don't you do Simon Moro for us?"

"Simon Moro? I thought he was Undead."

"That's what I mean. Could be a very funny piece."

Williams calls his wife to say he'll be home on the 6:00 P.M. to tell her all the news, meet him at the Junction, but she wants to know now.

"No," Williams finally admits, "but he has a great assignment for me."

Nothing.

"Simon Moro."

Nothing.

"I can do a fast job on it. It'll only take a couple of weeks, and then I can start looking around for a—"

"A couple of weeks where?"

"In Hollywood."

Nothing.

"He's paying me a thousand this time, and I can pick up a little on expenses by staying with the Dunnes."

"So you're still free."

"That's not it, honey."

"I wish I were free."

"Look. Alice Glaser has my old job."

"What's it feel like to be free, Warner?"

"I can finish it during July, and then we can both go up to Breadloaf together."

"I'm not going to Breadloaf. You're free to go if you want. Come and go, just as you please."

"It's not as I please. But we need—"

"Only it isn't really freedom. You know that, Warner? It's just absenteeism."

"You know we need the money."

"You're being marked absent, Warner. Get your mother to write you an excuse."

Williams also calls his agent, to tell her that Harold will call, to tell her . . . no, to have *her* tell *him* that it's all fine and grand and dandy. But she surprises him.

"Why are you doing this?"

Nothing.

"Why are you doing this, Warner?"

"The money, Candida."

"You know it's not the money."

Nothing.

"It's going to be the *Post* all over again, only for even less money."

"I *learn* from these trips, Candida. I'm using a kind of cinematic technique in my novel. These guys won't be D. W. Griffith out there, but that's just the point. I want this novel to have a sort of hand-held quality. It's going along nice and trashy now, and—"

"Then why would you want to do *this* instead of *it?*"

"I can't just starve."

"You've never starved, Warner. Except for things I guess you don't really have that much appetite for, do you?"

Addenda to History of an Idea: I was often asked two questions at Breadloaf. 1. *Do you think up the ideas, or do they?* "We sort of agree on them together." 2. *Does an agent do any good?* "Funny thing, but it's not so much the money, though an agent can obviously be very helpful there. It's much more the comfort, the relief."

Then there was a third question. *What happens if a magazine doesn't take an article?* "You mean, one they've assigned?" *Yes.* "Well, there's always a guarantee. . . ."

"We've already paid you the two-fifty, haven't we?" Harold began to wind up on me. "We'll forget about that. It's still a thousand, clear, if you want to do the rewrite. Keep the anecdotes. They're great. Same with the bio, but better check your facts. The researcher couldn't find half the stuff you've got in here."

"It's all from personal interview. Nobody ever asked him about his Vienna days before."

"Okay, okay. That's not the real problem anyhow. What you've got to tell us is why this new weird scene. Is he just playing to his own craze, like you say, or has he gone megalomaniac, like I say, or maybe back on drugs again?"

"That's out."

"You be sure."

"I am sure."

"All right. For all I know, he's seeing a Mad Scientist, but *something*'s freaky. That's where this piece falls down. You've got to tell us why this zombie walks. There's a title for you."

Maybe I should've said no, but Harold is another one of those people in my life who goes down on my Gunga Din List.

> *So I'll meet 'im later on*
> *At the place where 'e is gone—*
> *Where it's always Dull-Won't-Do and Please-Revise—*
> *'E'll be squattin' on the coals*
> *Givin' leads to poor damn souls,*
> *An' I'll write a piece in hell for Gunga Hayes!*
> > *Yes, Hayes! Hayes! Hayes!*
> > *You hickish, hacky, hambone Gunga Hayes!*
> > > *Though I've 'sulted you and 'trayed you,*
> > > *By the fashion mag that made you,*
> > *You're a better man than I am, Gunga Hayes!*

So, that's three in a row that have bounced on me. The Nixon piece. Then a commentary on the New Journalism I tried for *The American Scholar*. Admittedly a rewrite of "*Why* There Is Only a *How* to Article Writing," but since they didn't take it after Mary Moore Molony heard me up at Breadloaf and asked for it, I have to count it against me. And now this run-in with Harold. Maybe not quite strike three, but a barely audible foul tip.

Have to try to salvage this one. I'm at a point now where something, no matter how trivial, has got to go right for me. As far as Jane's concerned: the piece is sold, for some reason the check is late, I've told her Candida is seeing about that, and I'm back working on my novel again. We've got a few other matters to settle, e.g., the Hazel Rio Business—Incident? Affair? What was it, what short title covers it?—but I'm beginning to think the same rules hold for marriage that hold for fiction. Point of view. Don't state, indicate. Less is more. Et cetera. Maybe marriage *is* fiction.

But what I'm really doing is working back over my notes, putting down here every last nuance and gesture and movement of eyelash I can remember from my brief but still festering association with Simon Moro. I've got to do this before I start rewriting because (1) Harold is right, I missed on him somehow, and (2) that's all I have to work with. Moro won't see me again.

Met Terry for cocktails today at the Ground Floor. Hard to recognize him without his tennis shoes, but I guess he was dressing for the East. Underneath, still the same incorrigible M-G-M cheerleader-type: "All right now, evvvry-body, let's give a great big lion's roar for the mooo-vies!" He ordered a Gibson with four onions, which he nibbled off the toothpick like shashlik. Stagy implication: sorry, can't stay and drink, must eat and run.

"I don't want you to talk to him again. I don't mind telling you that because I happen to know he's not going to talk to you."

"Has he flipped out, or what?"

"Beats me. The trouble I had with him during shooting—you know, you saw it—was subtle trouble. A lot of scene-stealing, real cutie-pie and devious, like a pickpocket. You don't know your wallet's gone until you see the rushes. Fouled me up a little, but I edited most of it out. If you've seen the picture, you probably can tell, but the audience can't."

He was fishing, but I wasn't going to say I'd seen the picture because I didn't want to tell him what I thought of the picture—because I don't really *know* what I think. It's lousy, but not true-lousy. Ersatz-lousy, with Moro great. True-great, not phony-great. Nobody can cut into a Moro performance. They found that out in 1937 when they tried to butcher *Ghoulgantua*. And I happen to know Terry isn't allowed to edit his own pictures anyhow. "I'm waiting to see it with an audience," I said.

"You'll love it." (Cheer, cheer for old Notre Dame, let's hear it for the Hunchback. . . .) "It's a real coronary." He stopped to fight down the heat of an onion. "But this act he's pulling now. I don't dig. Plain fucking blatant. Like a mugging. That I can handle too. He's not gonna kill this picture, hard as he's trying. Too good a picture, and I'm gonna cut his balls off in broad daylight."

"Where?"

"At the premiere."

"Which is?"

"Wednesday, midnight. The Pentagonal."

"You're going into the Pentagonal?"

"You don't like the Pentagonal?"

"It's a good Broadway flophouse."

That, or the onions, got him finally to take a sip of his drink. "Okay. You get a few bug bites from the *Times* second-stringer, who reads? You still got your New York showing, and the drive-ins could care less." He sipped yet again. "But it just so happens I like, I want the Pentagonal. Big stage. For this personal appearance I'm gonna have him make."

"Can you trust him?"

"Got it fixed so I don't have to."

"What's up?"

"Stay close."

"I need to know for my story."

"All I can say now is that Wednesday will not be for those who are weak of heart. I'll leave you a freebie at the box office."

We talked about the Hazel Rio . . . File, I guess, and he said she was somewhere around New York, didn't know where to get hold of her, figured she'd show up Wednesday midnight. "Never gonna be in another picture of mine," he finished her. "Had to edit her as much as him. Too much titty-titty-bang-bang." A lot of help. He finished his skewer of onions and left the rest of his drink, bounced all the way out of there on nothing but the balls of his feet. Captain Ked. I stayed behind to pay the bill, then walked over to the Warwick and tried to call Moro on the house phone. He answered with what I thought was a hello, but when I said who I was, he began doing his animal sounds. The cougar scream, then the raven, the rabid dog, the hyena, and then that long, low hiss he once told me was a lizard lying in the hot desert sun with its throat cut. Vide, *Gila Man.* I think it was all a deliberate act, but couldn't swear to that in open court.

Where I stand now: waiting for Wednesday. Meanwhile, shoving manuscript into this envelope, which is going to go to only one person for consideration. He alone will decide whether it's right or not, whether it contains the "makings of an article." I've had enough of outside rejections. This is really an intricate, highly ulterior, who knows, maybe even counterproductive assignment: write a piece on Warner Williams doing a piece on Simon Moro. Write it for Warner Williams. Forget style. Just show whether Warner Williams, during this short disease, his career, still has a fighting chance, or has he finally fallen fatally nil, incurably slick?

THE RESEARCHER is a pain. I know her. A melancholiac about opinion, a paranoiac about facts. Considers Homer unreliable oral history and crosschecks dates like July 4, 1776, or the Ides of March, or December 25. "You research a piece until you meet yourself coming back the other way," I told them at Breadloaf. I failed to mention you might still have to meet up with her. Miss Clio, Vassar '62. "Unable to verify Moro's appearance as a robot in *Manmade Man*, 1927. Not included in any cast list."

Okay, okay, he was using a different name then. Maybe his own. Check cast list for Rudolph Eckmann. The film, of course, is lost. So, for that matter, is *The Unholy Circus*. Actually, we know them both only in synopsis, and then only in rather suspect translation, from their American publicity releases. (Cf. above, what I pitched to Harold yesterday could be pure potato pie.) All very dubious, Miss Clio, highly questionable sources, but it just so happens there also yet survive a few grainy stills from these Weimar epics, prominently featuring a gaunt, crook-necked, hump-beaked figure who is unmistakably, under all that metal casing, irrefutably, under all that clown paint, the early Simon Moro. Armored, then armless. Solid evidence, Miss Clio, right there before our very eyes, those matched and paired sensory orbs that so often team up to give us full retinal validation of the cinematographic experience whenever we drop round to the local nabe.

I guess I've seen all the rest of them. Wasn't that hard, what with the craze kicking up. I caught *Zeppelin* at the Strand in Lambertville, N.J., an arty nickelodeon, but very comfortable; owner yanked out every other row of seats so his patrons could stretch and slump, and when you drop a candy wrapper, it doesn't go into the dark, dark, dark, but lies right out there in the noon blaze of the EXIT signs.

However, to be serious, à la Sarris: few people apparently realize that *Zeppelin* was his first talkie. Berlin, Fritz Lang,

1930. Also significant that Moro played the part of Hans, the Westphalian infanticide, so close to his own physical characteristics. For the first time in his film career—and he was already a legend among cosmeticians—suddenly no disguise, and none of the contortionist. Only the ungarnished actor, the potentially great, remarkably pure actor who'd begun to work with Brecht. And even on the primitive sound track, you can hear *ab ovo* that reedy, alienating, Moro rasp that is actually as natural to him as it seems to be preternatural to others. I don't know German, but in voice quality, it's exactly how he sounds later on in English. As much off screen as on, though his ordinary voice tends to grate much more insidiously. All the modulations of predation, and also the gestures. He doesn't even really need that voice. He can indicate corruption with just the back of his neck. There is that famous sequence in *Zeppelin*, right after he's committed one of his atrocities, no, right *before*, when the camera focuses on nothing but his shaggy hairline, his seedy collar, two bony knobs of his spinal column. All he does is shift his shoulders, but the knobs swell, engorge. You never see his face, don't have to.

Much more chilling, convincing, for my money, than what's supposed to be the big scene, up in the zeppelin itself. Too Expressionistic, or maybe just too Germanic. Captain Kleist (Conrad Veidt) spots him running from the bushes in the band park where he's dragged the dead Heidi, swoops down, captures him on the fly, then carries him out over the North Sea. Just too goddamn God-like, and at this late date, it's hard to understand how come people got so hysterically frightened of zeppelins, vide William Butler Yeats. But Moro still lends it considerable realism. You almost believe he's maybe innocent—just stumbled onto the dead girl—after his long protestation to Captain Kleist. Then the breakdown. Kleist puts him in a bottomless cage out over the bomb bay and lets all these frolicsome *Kinder* run loose

around the bars. Shot so that Moro looks like this big furry
pet in a pen, right in the middle of a nursery school. He
plays it that way too, romping, wagging, gamboling, the big
St. Bernard, anything to fight down his impulses, pretend he
doesn't have this Reichian compulsion. Then he sees this little blonde girl, younger than the rest, another Heidi, and
that cracks him open. Close-ups of swirls of Viking-white
hair, and then every cut back to him shows another part of
his mind crumbling. Obsessive lava leaking through the thin
crust of normality. The lunge at the bars, and then the high,
scratchy scream as Kleist, having proven the psychiatric
case, opens the bomb bay, drops him down, down, down to
the ice floes, and that last great touch, the little girl crying,
Captain Kleist promising her another puppy.

That's his best role until *Ghoulgantua*. Some people think
a lot of *The Moth*, but I still didn't care much for it when I
saw it again at the Thalia. Too many cheap tricks. Moro told
me they were originally going to end up with the Moth
caught in a giant, electrified wire web, face to face with a
sort of Spider Lady (Fay Wray) who finally zaps him with
the current. But some Southern power company objected,
and besides they were way over budget, so they wrote in
that chintzy ring of medieval torches instead. Doesn't work.
He goes up much too fast, like a leaf pile. M. only went
through with the picture on a promise from the studio that
he could do his own version of *The Idiot* next. But *The
Moth* did lousy box office, deserved to, the studio backed off
a little on Moro, and he never got to play Prince Myshkin, a
shame because, stretching a point, but not that much, it's
like Dostoevski wrote it for him. The film's only interest
now lies in M.'s personal gymnastics: the terrific, fluttery
leaps he takes, made them look like flights, up against the
outsides of lit windows; his dark flapping over his smothered
victims with powdery, umbrageous wings; and his last desperate efforts to keep away from the flambeaux even as he

snaps and flits nearer and nearer their blazing allure. Also, his twittery hum, and the way, during close-ups, he curls his tongue around on itself, so that the tip becomes almost a scroll. True to nature, that bit, but more for butterflies than moths, and it didn't really carry much of the idea of blood lust.

No, *Ghoulgantua* is his masterpiece, 1937, and the fact that it's been unavailable for so long, amounting almost to a suppression, has got to be one of the all-time low points in film-distribution practices. A real pandering to public taste. Americans could take *Frankenstein*, but not this much more involuted and honest evocation of monstrosity. Some critics, even Pauline Kael, I think, tend to put Moro down for stealing so much from *Frankenstein*, but they miss the point. M. never thought of his borrowings as a theft. He was simply out to pillory the bourgeois decadence of *Frankenstein*.

"That's a good example of Brecht's influence on me, if you're still looking for one," I have M. down here saying in my notes. Then some jottings: *All art is public. No property rights in culture. Artist's duty to correct, revise, re-do previous artists.* "I went along with that nonsense, if it is nonsense. Very un-American of me." Then that toothsome grin, somehow as twinkly as it is skeletal. "But also very American of me. What the majors did for years."

Actually, odd bits of Brecht run all through the film, right from the opening scene with Dr. Dollfuss and Bruno out collecting the dead bodies. "Grave-robbing. What kind of a crime is that? What real social harm?" (Still quoting M., but these don't sound like his own ideas.) "Some poor beggar we see picking through trash—do we arrest him? But if the refuse is human, *was* human, picking through for a few bones and a brain is supposed to be an outrage. Stupid. No, I wanted to make the—let's give the religious their due—the resurrection of the bodies, I wanted that to have social import." Hence, the montage. The two caped figures skulk among the broached graves, Dr. Dollfuss with his hooded lamp held high, its slit of light swinging from time to time directly into the camera, blinding us with sudden, burnt-out vignettes, all reverse-negative. A Negro corpse twisting on a lynch rope, but the Negro white, the rope black. A striker falling under a murderous, but ghostly, charge of mounted policemen, on spectral steeds, wielding silvery nightsticks. A banker jumping from a high ledge on a building as pale as a pillar of salt. A wino slumped into frozen death on the cold steps of the New York Public Library, turned black as an Aztec altar. A trapped miner, his face dirty—but the dirt like lime, not soot—agonizing in silent throes. Even a shrouded, girlish body, presumably, from the few bleak instruments glowing like obsidian on the ashy sheet, an abortionist's victim. "What *kind* of bodies? What *nature* of death? That was the point." (Still M., but more like himself.) "They gave Frankenstein's monster—what? A madman's brain. *Carte blanche*. Freedom Now. To kill and maim, and still be loved. Sentimental slop. Truly. I didn't want sympathy for Ghoulgantua. I wanted justification. The dead rising in vengeance. For what has been done to them." This kind of thing is what eventually got M. called before HUAC, but I don't think people really caught much of the propaganda when they first saw the film. Certainly that wasn't why it disappeared. It was much more people's shock at how M. had realized the monster visually.

He's very good on that himself. "Talk to Boris sometime. I love Boris. A dear, sweet, old man." (F.Y.I., there is maybe thirteen years' difference in age between them.) "But ask him how they arrived at his make-up. He'll tell you. They spent days. 'A fortnight,' Boris will say, always the limey. The expanded forehead, the sutures, the contact points, putter, putter, putter. Then, what happens? When Jack Pierce is all done, Boris takes one look in the mirror and sees—what else?—the two bright eyes of an intelligent Englishman—

who else?—staring out at him from this subhuman face. 'The thing you always had to bear in mind'—I've heard him say this—'was that the monster was only five minutes old.' So Boris takes two little bits of putty and puts them on his eyelids, weights them down, the right even more than the left. For him I suppose it was right, but what did that produce? A squinter. A staggerer. A somnambulist. Mr. Mona Lisa.

"No. I didn't want a pitiful brain. I wanted an intellect. A vampire's keenness. The story has my brain being stolen bit by bit out of the crypt of a university chapel, and I used rubber bands. Tight. Back over my eyelids, you see, popping the eyes, squeezing them out. I was in tears, all the time, but since I couldn't blink them back, the tears bathed the eyes. Laved them, made them shine all the more. Like specimens. Boris loves to complain. The heat, the hours, the boredom. But mine. Mine was pure torture. That's what made it work. I really *was* in pain."

That comes through clearly on film, often overwhelmingly, but at the same time Moro was very careful not to trail off into mere masochism. He balanced his portrayal by adding that terroristic grin, which we first see through the clouds of steam as Dr. Dollfuss and Bruno together winch the fully-formed Ghoulgantua up out of the bubbling vat. N.B.: another triumph over *Frankenstein*, that vat—G. slowly steeping in the reeky elixirs of the moribund, until ripe—as opposed to Dr. F.'s rather sterile electrification process. Initially we take this grin at, so to speak, face value —as simply another ghastly sign of awakening life in the monster—but then we soon discover it signifies G.'s vampire lust. Long, splayed fangs in parched, bloodless lips almost rake open the bottom half of that skull-like face: unquenchable sanguivorousness. Better than *Nesferatu*, in my opinion. Actually, it was a gigantic denture that Moro had made for him, deliberately too large. "An Iron Maiden, taken orally," he used to joke about it, and that also heightened the look of excruciating blood-thirst. The only difficulty was that he couldn't talk with it in his mouth, and since he was really directing the film, despite a nominal credit to Tod Browning, this hampered him on set. When I saw *G.* recently at the Modern Museum—the uncut version, finally—I was struck with how much more woodenly the grin scenes come off than *G.*'s other rampages. But it was still an inspired guise. Nobody argues that. What controversy there is centers on the nudity. *M.* really did starve himself down to almost skin and bone, and then wore only this sort of mummy wrapping of a loin cloth. Watching very closely this time, I did catch several moments when it does definitely bulge, but it does not, as Louella Parsons kept writing in her column, ever slip. Like so many others, she missed Moro's intent, which wasn't at all exhibitionistic, and saw what she wanted to see. What was bothering *M.*, what he strongly opposed, was "putting the dead in civilian clothing," as he accused James Whale of having done in *F.*, "making the fruit of the grave dress just like you and I." He wanted to show the skin graftings, the putrefications all over *G.*'s white-horrid body, and not alone for their shock value either. "Perhaps I was thinking of your Herman Melville." *M.* is full of American literature. "There are variations in the skin tones. Pronounced variations. You can see them even in black and white, and they represent—if you don't mind a literary borrowing—they show that Ghoulgantua contains as much of humanity as the *Pequod.*"

My own guess is that he probably could still have gotten away with all this egregious horror, for whatever intellectual purposes, if he hadn't done the scene with the little girl. *Zeppelin* automatically comes to mind, but he was really still picking up from *Frankenstein* here, though perversely, since Universal had already cut that episode from *F.* after loud public outcry. Yet he went right ahead, and even made it worse. "Not worse," he insists when you get him on this. "More realistic. Psychologically." He gets really adamant, now that I remember. "They misunderstood at Universal. Completely. It isn't the little girl who gives the flower to the monster. That's daughter-father. It's the monster who gives the flower to the little girl. That's boy-girl."

Even at the Modern Museum, a pretty hip audience, I noticed a few people walked out when that came on screen. It really is pretty hard to take, and I think I now know why. Not because of the enticement. That's almost gentle, though maybe precursively stomach-turning since you begin to suspect what's coming next. Then the walk off into the woods together is an extreme long shot, can't really tell who's leading, who's following. All there is, actually, in the way of action consists of a twig snapping under G.'s hard, skeletal heel, extra loud, then a couple of shots of crushed wildflowers on the forest floor, small, look like violets, and then, suddenly, the violent swaying of branches, crashing together loud enough on the sound track so as to drown out any (implied) plaints or moans or maybe ecstasies. It gets to you, that scene, no question, cornball as it is, but not, I'm suggesting, through anything Ghoulgantua does. It's somehow much more the girl. There's something about her, for all her Shirley Temple ringlets, that's vaguely illicit. I get a slight Baby Le Roy vibration from her. . . .

But that's material I prefer to handle all in due course. And in fine detail, since I never did get M. to admit absolutely outright, total truth about her. Back to cinematographic history. My own critical judgment of G., having now seen it five times: still a masterpiece, one of those rare instances where the imitation is better than the original, much the way Hamlet outdistances Hieronymo. (Good way to put it, as a matter of fact, because, at bottom, *Ghoulgantua* is a Revenge Tragedy. Maybe a line to follow in revising article?) M. improved not only upon the Universal film but also, I think, upon Mary Shelley's original tale, which, despite its arctic denouement, has aspects that are too lakeside and summery, straight Lac Como. He kept all the gothicism, but enlarged upon the depredations, broadened them out into the modern world as we know it, and fear it. The startling disclosure, for instance, twenty minutes into the picture, that Dr. Dollfuss's medieval laboratory is really located in the sub-basement of a huge department store, i.e., symbolically, a level of alchemy that lies beneath all the bargain floors above where dross is truly turned to gold. This also allows G., following his feast upon his creator and the unfortunate Bruno, the use of an elevator.

From then on—and I think this is Moro's greatest achievement—the monster turns into an urban terror, a conception that was at least thirty years ahead of its time. G. strikes quickly, everywhere, with randomness and *anomie*. On the empty subway car, in the vacant hotel lobby, up the fire escape, more than once from a public comfort station. Even the little girl is one of those attacks in broad daylight that we so often read now in the park news. G. kills, consumes, at the febrile pace of the city itself. I have down here from M.: "I wanted to see the last of the monster as rural plodder."

The ending has sometimes been questioned, cf. Richard Schickel in *Commentary*, "Three Films That Go on Past 'Now' ": is it perhaps too urban, insufficiently gothic? But once a cinematic rhythm has been established, it has to be kept up. Besides, M. didn't want what he called "the excuse of garlic and crosses." "That's paraphernalia. What really destroys Ghoulgantua," he explained, "is Christmas. The way I sometimes feel it destroys us all." More than a light-hearted comment; M.'s scripting here amounts to a subtle philippic against commercialization of the Yuletide; says he himself is a Zoroastrian, i.e., belief in the Three Wisemen, the dignity of their mission, but not all the claims made by the Parent for the Child. At the height of the season, the store is open late hours, and G., caught unawares by the bright lights, is spotted skulking down toward the sub-basement. By a drunken Santa Claus, whom the manager has sent back to his locker. G. kills the Santa Claus, but Santa's cries have been heard. This gives M. his chance for a wild mob scene inside the department store that drives G. out of hiding—much as the townspeople drive Frankenstein's monster through the castle before their civil wrath—only G. upward, toward the roof. There he is forced over the edge by the outraged, frazzled holiday crowd and falls twelve stories to the plaza below. But that's not all, in the uncut version. M.: "I still wanted that stake through the heart." The final frames are deliberately phantasmagoric, but there is no doubt how the monster finally lies impaled. Light zings and loops from ropes of tinsel, pine boughs rock under the great, sprawled weight, and G.'s dying fish eye is last seen reflected in the close-up curvature of a jiggling ornament. All I can say is that the Rockefeller Center Christmas tree has not looked all that festive to me since.

From my notes: "Studio objected that ending was too final. Left no margin for revival of G. in case of sequel." Fantastic to realize that hopes for the picture originally ran that high. They cut it drastically, of course, right after it opened. Left G. falling from roof, no Xmas tree bulb, eliminated most of the city violence, butchered the film even to the point of confusing the story line at times. But there was really no way to sanitize the Ghoulgantuan horror. What few audiences saw G. before it was completely withdrawn understood perfectly and fled. The plain truth is that, in 1937, you just couldn't molest the likes of Shirley Temple or demonize Christmas. Moro had gone too far, in real ignorance of American prejudices, I feel, and after this debacle, most critics feel he sinks immediately and uncompromisingly into studio commercialism.

To an extent, that's true. After all, how else was he going to survive? But trite as the Gila Man pictures seem now, were even then, it's a mistake not to recognize M.'s considerable artistry in creating the slithery being that did finally make him big box office in America. Gila Man is no Ghoulgantua—"about as terrifying as my son's pet newt," one reviewer wrote, though wrong-headedly, I feel—but he still far outdistances Lon Chaney, Jr.'s Wolfman or Spencer Tracy's Dr. Jekyll/Mr. Hyde, to mention two other mutants that have been much, and I happen to think, overly, praised. I suppose you really have to see several Gila Man pictures together to gain the full impact of M.'s reptilianism. Last June, I happened to catch *Gila Man* and *Gila Man Returns* on a double bill, and then *The House of Gila Man* at another theater, all in one afternoon on Forty-second Street. Over and over again, the thin, almost Eliotesque bank teller yielded to the pull of the planet Pluto upon him, dropping helplessly onto all fours, then belly-down against the cold marble floor. The delicate skin of his face rippled over itself into imbricated coarseness—some use of dissolves, but mostly M.'s personal make-up job, applied in stop-motion sequence—the long tongue began to flick, then the hiss, and finally the crawl, the scuttle, up and out through the narrow space beneath the teller's window bars. Human evolution run backward through the camera. Absolutely eerie. The plots, of course, were nothing. Comic strips. But there are still individual scenes. The opening of *House*, for example, where Gila Man is discovered lying out on the desert flats, covered with sand, his eyes seemingly cataracted, completely lifeless. Ingeniously, M. revives Gila Man in the very way Nature herself might have chosen: by simply shedding his entire skin.

Then there are all the Nazis he played during the war. Either the bad Nazi who dies horribly, justly, or the good Nazi who turns against Hitler and dies bravely, sacrificially.

"The bad Nazis I didn't mind," M. says here in my notes. "I could do them as an objective reality, Brechtian, if not as a real character. Build up a loathing in the audience that was healthy. But the good Nazis. They were migraines, maybe eight different pills I had to take to sleep at night. Such lies. The studio was trying to bank some sympathy for me, for after the war, that was the idea. My de-Nazification. But all I wanted to do was see that the public *didn't* forget." I mentioned I'd seen *Hitler's Camps* as a kid, and remembered him as being quite convincing as the commandant who suddenly walked out and began cutting open his own barbed wire. But he shook his head. "The only good Nazi is a dead Argentinian."

He did, in fact, do very few pictures after the war. Perhaps the drug thing, though that never stopped Bela Lugosi. In any case, he left the studio and began working hit and miss, mostly miss. He returned to Germany briefly to produce, direct, and act in a film (which he also apparently wrote) that is, for some reason having to do with the Bonn government, unobtainable. Nor will he talk about it, even the title. "Didn't have a title. Never got that far. It was a conscience picture. What really happened inside the cabinet of Dr. Caligari." Asked Miss Clio to track it down, since she supposedly knows German, but all she could come up with was: "Prints are under court seal in Frankfurt. Certain officials threatened action for defamation, but there'd been no public release. Moro signed an agreement to do no more movies in Germany, and returned to U.S. Some rumors that financing was East Berlin deal, but unable to verify." There are several cameo appearances, including one for Mike Todd, though most people miss his bit in *Around the World in Eighty Days*—some very funny business with a Pernod glass on top of a barrelhouse piano—because the main gag is Frank Sinatra is playing. Then in a musical, *Slippers and Shoes*, where he sang for the first time. "Like a cracked

Jew's harp," he says himself. And he was hired to do the voice of Toad for Disney's *Wind in the Willows*, but apparently became "indisposed" and had to be replaced. "I flubbed the dub," he told me. His puns in English can sometimes be woefully Teutonic.

Most of this, unhappily, was self-parody. Not even imitation. An important distinction to draw, since M. is actually quite a wonderful mimic. He has, for example, a superb imitation he does of the people who go around imitating Simon Moro. He does the overly nasal rasp, the overly squeaky sibilants, the glut of gutturals exactly the way cocktail-party hams have been doing them, so badly, ever since this craze began. The catch is that he gives his own fake Simon Moro a cultural twist. Recites Goethe in German, or Roosevelt's speeches in English. The effect is incredibly schizoid. For instance, he can deliver the line "The only thing we have to fear is fear itself" so that it absolutely breaks you up, but at the same time, leaves you feeling distinctly anxious.

That, however, is a private performance. The public self-parody has never been that subtle, despite what Terry implies about a sudden coarsening of M.'s behavior lately. He's only gotten coarser, almost savage, who knows what? (The crux of the matter, the problem at hand.) There's some excuse: he has to play himself broadly to fit the crudities of these inhospitable "guest appearances," which have been his only gainful employment for a long time. The Raven is actually the first solid part he's had in eight years. Before that, his last decent film was *The Shoplifter*, 1960, a low-budget, on-the-city-streets gem, expanded from an old Philco Playhouse script. M. went a lot farther with the character than Rod Steiger was ever able to go on TV, emphasizing the sexual pathos of the nervous, crypto-transvestite thief in "booster bloomers." But, typical Moro luck, he turned in a low-key, almost Chekhovian interpretation a year after the Paddy-Chayefsky thing was as dead as *Marty*.

Low point, the real nadir of this self-parody, from a film I happened to catch on the *Late Late Show* one night: his chase scene with Lou Costello. Awful. The studio had loaned him out, against his wishes, and he was forced to play a rickrack version of Ghoulgantua. He looked like a medical school joke, and worse, Lou was shown trying to run away from him in drag. Girlish squeals, lace sleeves, and Mary Janes. A mockery of all the great shock moments he'd created in *Z.* and *G.*

I had a brief conversation with him about this in his dressing-room trailer one lunchtime. He was sitting with the skirts of his black caftan—"Ravenswear," he calls it—tucked up under him, gobbling Ry-Krisps out of this big, black calfskin purse, drawstrings yet, that Mike Todd sent him five thousand untaxable dollars in, under a layer of black excelsior and licorice jellybeans. Try checking that, Miss Clio.

"It was your great theme."

"Still is."

"Even after what they did to it?"

"Remember. I left the studio."

"Over that?"

"Not totally. But right after that."

"Will you ever go back?"

"To the studio?"

"To the theme."

He grinned. "How old do you think Lenore is in this film?"

"Scoff."

"Really?"

"Hazel Rio?"

"She's ageless."

"Look. Simon."

"Yes."

"Is it personal with you?"

"Is what personal?"

"Little girls."

"You expect me to answer that?"

"Why not?"

He grinned again. "Actually, it's very American. Your Edgar Allan Poe. What did he say was the most poetic idea? Sadness at the death and destruction of a beautiful woman."

"He said 'woman.' Not 'little girl.' "

"But what was his idea of a woman? His thirteen-year-old cousin."

"Your victims are never over eight."

"But I *think* of them as older."

"You're trying to put me on."

"And you're trying to push me around."

"You started this in Germany. During a very decadent time."

"*Ja,* you think so?"

"Everybody loves children. The whole world. The Italians. The French. The Russians are supposed to, especially. Even you Germans. Here we've got a child-centered culture."

"You have children?"

"Four."

"Boy? Girl?"

"All girls."

"Wonderful."

He thought he had me stopped, but I kept after him. "*You* have any children?"

"Alas," he said, with a big sigh, full of fatherly feeling all right, but it didn't really come out yes or no.

"Do you *like* children?"

He nodded. "As you say, the whole world. Yes. *Ja. Oui. Si.*"

"So how could you pick the one thing that everybody, *everybody* agrees is heinous—I mean, shocking and disgusting and revolting, or whatever—and make that your whole career?"

Said more than I meant to. Or maybe I didn't say it quite that strong. ("No, I don't use a tape recorder," I told them at Breadloaf, "but I'm accurate in the main.") Anyhow, I know I'm accurate, dead right on what he answered, with that goddamn amphibian little smirk of his.

"Why not aim high?"

THE DAY BEFORE I flew out to the coast, I managed to track down a man here in New York who'd known Moro during his old Vienna days. Dr. Horst Yost. I suppose Miss Clio really deserves the credit for Dr. Yost. She'd somehow unearthed a reference to M. in one of Yost's early books, among the acknowledgments—". . . and especially to the actor Simon Moro, the earliest of my auxiliary egos . . ."—and passed it along to me, adding a note that Yost met with a group in the city every Tuesday night at an upper Broadway address. I gather she follows the analytic scene fairly closely. Half expected to see her up there, delving into her own depression, but Yost is really too much bombast for anybody with her delicately poised analities. His is the theatrical approach. "For God's sake let us sit upon the ground/And tell sad tales of the dearth of selves. . . ."

I was a little late for the performance, i.e., therapy, coming in just after he'd begun to warm up the crowd, i.e., initiate ego involvement. What made everything seem even more showbiz was the hall. It was really a run-down dance studio. An exercise bar, a dark shimmer of speckled mirrors, and two large standing neon lamps. Pink and yellow. Though maybe he'd brought those with him. They certainly added. At least to my own impression of him. To wit: there is a portrait you often find in books on the Surrealists by a sixteenth-century Italian, Arcimboldo, of a man composed entirely of garden produce. A pear for a nose, grapes for hair, pea pods for eyelids, leeks for mustachios, and a melon for a chest. Under that garish light, almost like a bakeshop window, Dr. Yost could have been done the same way in Viennese pastry. A blintz for a nose, sugar cookies for lips, meringue for hair, macaroons for cheeks, bon-bons for eyes, marzipan for teeth, cinnamon for beard stubble, and, for those overly rich chest tones of his, a huge pot of chocolate, thick enough to stand a spoon.

In other words, an overbearingly sweet man, who was working his sugary way through the crowd, seeking out the gullible, the delectable. And I'd have to admit he was good at his trade. He pushed two bobbed-and-bullish types several giggles beyond any pretense they were just working-girl "roomies," then got a jawless homosexual, male, to say he wanted to be a therapist himself, dwelling long on the poor man's insistence on a "non-directional" approach. He even picked on me, of a sudden, an unfamiliar face, and wormed out how much of my novel still lay unfinished before me, something I don't usually admit to in public.

But these were just the try-outs. He was after the evening's big act, and finally lined up a cast of two, a husband and wife, in their late thirties, from Bronxville. They were both unattractive enough to dishearten each other thoroughly, and stood up in front of us, side by side, blankly troubled. The first thing Yost did was have them turn and face each other squarely, really *look* at each other. "As opposites," he told them. This disconcerted them, him even more than her. "After all these years, my dear," he said to her, "is he still so shy with you?" She smiled quickly, really to cover her embarrassment, but Yost immediately snapped at him, "Does she consider it such a joke?"

"It's no joke," the man let out. He was saying it vaguely—to himself, if anyone—but he was facing her, squarely, so the quarrel was on.

"Who said it was a joke?" she demanded.

"You don't have to say."

"I'm not allowed to speak?"

"You want to say, say."

Then they both stopped, not really wanting to say anything, either of them, not even wanting to be there. Until the little heat they'd worked up began to kindle another snappy, inconclusive argument to keep them momentarily warm and safe: whose big idea was it to come here at all, in the first place, anyhow?

"Yours."

"Mine? You."

"Never."

"You, you, you."

Yost broke in again. "I'm sure you wanted to come, my dear. Didn't you? You've always wanted to come, but . . . somehow . . . difficulties arise. . . ."

It was so saccharine with innuendo that it set my teeth on edge. Hers too, and naturally she knew whom to blame for opening her up to such insults. It was still silent blame at this stage, all in her squinty glare, but he reacted numbly, stymied somewhere back in their cozy quarreling.

"I'm not the one who made you come."

Titters from the, I guess, audience. Quick cattiness from the wife now. "No indeed." Mumbles from the husband. But, after some loud prompting from Yost, he picked up his lines again.

"You want to let everybody know all about it?" he challenged her.

"Let her know all about it," Yost sharply directed.

"Want me to tell them how—?"

"Tell her how."

"—you ride me all the time?" From what I could see, it was Yost who was riding him, but he let fly at her and meant every word he was saying. "Ride, ride, ride!"

"So ride her! That's what she wants." Not from Yost. From the audience this time: a catcall. But when the heckler stood up, a tall, black-jawed brute of a guy, it was obvious he was part of the act. He got over behind the husband in about four long strides and leaned into his ear, taking a lot of pink light on his coal jaw. "Saddle up, fella."

I realized I'd seen him before. On *Gunsmoke* or one of the others. The lesser coyote, the one who's always hanging back behind a gallery post outside the saloon, never brave enough to come shouldering through the swinging doors. Always the first to get gunned down in the big shoot-out, usually off the roof where he's tried to take a dirty advantage. That grizzle along his jaw, a deliberate, almost kempt growth, was how he quickly, rawly indicated deep lack of character. A powerful-enough-looking guy, bulging everywhere, big, brawny hams out the double vents of his suit jacket. But those grubby whiskers, the seedy way he scruffed and scratched them, won out.

"Don't let her throw you now. She looks mean, but they don't last long, them mean little ones with the short legs. You see how short she is there in the leg? A damn stool's got longer, and a damn stool needs three. How's she gonna stand up to you on just two?"

He even gave the husband a brisk, friendly pat on the butt, which jolted him, made him nearly forget he was a coward with women.

"You ride me," he snapped at her, "and it's not even me. It's some idea you got of me."

"Some idea. Some idea I got of you," she lamented, "lemme tell you."

The heavy actually bent down, cupped his hands into a stirrup, and made exaggerated lifting motions with his arms and shoulders. "Come on, fella. Get up there on her."

"You never had a *decent* idea. Of anything or anybody." Still pretty weak, but he was beginning to eye her up and down now, kind of like a wrangler. Then, all of a sudden, he lit into her. "And not only short legs, but you got a short neck. You got short ankles. You got a short waist. You got a short forehead. And I don't like your hair short either."

"Attaway!" muttered the heavy. Then he abruptly turned and stretched over toward the wife, hiding his mouth behind the back of his hand but booming everything so it could clearly be heard. "Anywhere he's maybe lacking a little, ma'am?"

She took that harder than anything her husband had said
to her, but even so, she didn't hesitate to use it. "Not all that
lengthy some places yourself, poopsie."

"Switch!" Yost commanded.

They both stared at Yost, frozen, but the heavy grabbed
them by the elbows and yanked them across each other to
opposite sides. This left the heavy talking close into the
wife's ear now, but he pretended, still rough-glowering into
the pink glow, that there'd been no exchange.

"What's she mean? She wants you to drop your pants
right here, prove something? You're not gonna do that. You
don't have to do that, fella."

She just kind of gawked at him, very stubbornly.

He practically snarled. "Fella, for once in your life, tell
her where to get off!" Then he pointed hard, forcing her
gawk straight down his arm to the husband.

"Tell her. Yes. Tell her," Yost intoned, by contrast soft
and fulsome as a topping of whipped cream.

It was hard to believe. Her moves were slow, maybe even
involuntary, but she actually hitched up on the belt of her
wrap-around skirt with the insides of her wrists, and rolled
her shoulders into a big, swaggering shrug.

"I can get plenty of women," she drawled at her mate. "I
git plenty of women. And no complaints. It's only tight
asses like you give me any trouble."

It was a gross parody: if hardly of him, then of what she
probably thought he might want to be, or if not that, maybe
what she really hoped he'd be. Hard to say, hard to say.

"Attaboy," the heavy applauded her.

The husband went back on his heels, shuffling nervously
in the yellow light. Then he rose up on his toes, stiff-legged,
almost high-heeled, and began speaking in little, qualmish
spurts.

"Can I afford to care? Can I even stop to care? When
you're never home anyhow. Never content when you *are*

home. Gloom, gloom, gloom."

The heavy sidled across to the husband now, taking a much more gentlemanly approach, showing he knew how to treat a lady like a lady. "Now, ma'am . . . he only needs to be made to understand."

"I've got the whole house, all the laundry, the children," the husband kept on, "more than I can do already. You can't even keep up with the yard. What do I need with another adolescent, hanging around the house, growing gray?"

The wife fired back, almost rowdy. "None of that. They're just as much my children as yours."

"But the way he treats them . . ." the heavy whispered.

The husband winced a little at that insinuation against himself, but picked it up, twisted it to his use. "Oh yes, and you're so kind and gentle to them." Real female sarcasm. "Never known you to raise a hand against them."

"I love my children!" she boomed back at him, like a Victorian father.

"Switch!" Yost ordered.

This time they crossed over without help, nearly bumping into each other.

"No you don't love them!" shouted the wife, picking up her own last line as a cue. "You despise them! You call it discipline, and it's nothing but loathing!"

"It just so happens . . . I adore my children!" He put a lot of feeling into it. Still, you couldn't help but compare. She'd said it far better for him, in his place, than he had on his own, and he knew it. He tried to recoup. "Everything I do shows how much I really . . ." Couldn't, went into a funk. The heavy moved behind him, talking cow-punch to him again. "She's gonna use them against you. She'll use anything, that woman."

"Let's keep the children out of this," he tried to compromise.

"When were they ever in it for you? When?"

"Switch!"

She gave Yost a withering look. Didn't want to switch, now that she really had hubby on the run. But the husband, that slyboots, eased around her into the yellow light, took right up for her, very heatedly, against himself.

"You come home, you never play with them. You don't come home, they never ask for you. All they have is each other, and what little I can do to make things up to them, so that I'm with them all the time, day in, day out. Do you know what it's like, day in, day out, *never ever* having any adult companionship?" Very clever of him: played out her legitimate complaint until it got to sound like nothing but silly female whining.

She saw what he was doing, tried not to respond, then gave up with an unwilling, male-exasperated sigh. "That's why I can always count on that big welcome home. Everybody rushing to the door, *so* glad to see me, you've all been *so* lonely."

"Half the time it's the middle of the night!" he said, forced to give her very good excuse.

"So now I'm breaking and entering?"

Small joke: real sorrow. But for whom? Couldn't really tell. Their identities were beginning to muddle together, turn almost syrupy. They weren't exactly people any more. They were conditions: what it was like to be *her* husband, *his* wife, as either of them saw it. The only thing that stayed straight was the lighting. Those two naked neon tubes that flickered inconstantly but still never changed hue. The one on the left, yellow, for shrewishness, the one on the right, pink, for, I suppose, impotence.

Still, the dramatic tension mounted. The heavy began to fade into the limited scenery, the way I'd seen him do so often on *Rawhide* whenever real action threatened. Couldn't remember his name for the life of me. Every now and then, though, he got off a good line. "Sure you married her. Man's got to take what's available. That don't mean he don't *know* when he's riding muleback." But they had reached a point, didn't need any auxiliaries. She said it, husbanding every word: "Back off. We'll handle this." Then, obversely, they went at each other, sometimes even anticipating Yost's switches. Their son: maybe not quite that far gone, yet, but still his mother's little elf, irremediably, according to him. Their next-down daughter: too old for her age already, damn near matricidal, according to her. Her money, according to her as him. His mother, according to him as her. The goddamn mangy, hermaphrodite cat: still hadn't been fixed either way, nothing ever seems to get done around here, both to blame, somehow. Then the time he didn't call and didn't call from Chicago. No, he couldn't get through and couldn't get through from Detroit. Was that, or wasn't that the same time? "I never know where you are. A gypsy. What do you do for a living? Steal children? Better steal more, it's not bringing in enough to feed our own." Her lines, but he was playing them, loud and pushy, and she was being stoical, no, stolid in his place. They were at a point. A sheepishness began to creep into the tight, pink-lit, desperate expression she was holding for him. His eyes, narrowed into her low, unforgiving squint, started to brim with her bitter tears in the jaundiced neon glare.

Yost caught the moment. *Au point.* A perfect soufflé of anxieties, and before it fell, he unctuously commanded, "One last time, my dears. Switch." They reached out to help each other cross, then could not let go, hung on. She burst into her own tears. He patted her manfully, kissed her forehead, all for himself. The audience, I hate to say, gave them a quick round of applause, but at least no curtain calls.

Underlying cause of immediate personal depression as audience filtered into the aisle: it was really pretty tame stuff, old-fashioned, almost vaudeville compared to all the other group-grope therapeutic theatricals around nowadays, but it

also just happened to be what we used to call True-to-Life.
Too damn true to life. No deep, roiling emotions, no origi-
nality, nothing, really, underneath. Jane and I. You have to
stick to the surface when the surface is all you've got.
Maybe marriage isn't even good fiction. Maybe it's only
pulp.

Again I think of something Moro said to me during our
long interview out at his home in Portuguese Bend. We
were talking about teratology. Seems to me we were talking
about everything misshapen that day. "You want a monster?
A plain, ordinary, everyday monster?" M. demanded. "The
beast with two backs. Not so bad in a wild state. But domes-
ticated. Kept in captivity. Caged up in the—what do we
say?—the union of husband and wife, to grow shaggy and
neurotic and snarly, and begin to pace, pace, pace. *Mein
Gott.*"

But the rest of the assembled were of much greater cheer.
In a brief epilogue, Yost encouraged further dramatic endeavor, if not here, once everybody got back home. "Use
what you've seen here tonight. Learn to understand yourselves"—taking one of the wife's small, fat fingers in his big,
doughy hand, like a sausage inside a puff pastry—"as this
woman has understood herself as this man." Then sweetly to
the husband, nipping him by the elbow. "And as this man
has glimpsed himself in this woman. If, for only a little
while, we can all be each other, we will soon be much more
ourselves."

That seemed to placate them, or at least caramelize their
distress, though people were milling around, loudly gossip-
ing in factions that violently favored one side of the marriage or the other. There was even a small divorce element,
led by the non-directional queer. Only the heavy seemed a
little out of it, coming forward off the exercise bar to try to
bug the wife a little more. Instant replay. "He put the ugly
on you, but you never put it back on him. You gotta be

more nekkid, get at each other more direct. Or else it's too homelike."

But she was having nothing more to do with him. "We seen you on TV," she said, like she'd caught him crawling through a back window. "Don't worry. We seen you."

Since nobody else would talk to him either, I went up and introduced myself, saying I was from *Esquire*. He cottoned, said he was Lars Syndor, which still didn't mean anything to me.

"Getting anything out of this?" he asked.

"It looks to me," I said, nodding toward Yost, "like a director's medium."

"Yup," he smiled. "He's the man."

"Tell me something. You enjoy this?"

"Been through it." He shrugged, lots of beefy, beaten shoulder. "Bad days at Black Rock, baby."

It occurred to me that the seediness might not be all an act. Maybe he was right down to living the part, and just a touch manic.

"It's work. You get tired of recording for the blind. Pays about the same." He drew himself up tall, stretching his nerve more than his body, I felt, trying for a brave front. "I'm going back out soon. Shake this town." Then he rubbed his chin, almost vainly. "Got a shaving commercial first. Need a week to grow it back, then I'm gone." He took a whistle at "Cal-i-forn-ya, Here I Come," went flat on the first six notes, and bone-dry on the last.

Lars Syndor. It was beginning to register with me, but from somewhere else altogether, and a long time ago. "Hell yes, Gillette." I could see he was waiting for me to catch on, but wasn't going to be that happy when I did. "Back when it was Blue Blades. You were with the Rams. Corner back?"

"Defensive half, same thing."

"You were . . . good."

"Some folks say."

"Then you had some trouble."

"The knees," he said quickly. "They go first. Once those ends start getting behind you . . ."

That wasn't the trouble I had in mind, but I let it pass, being dim on the details anyhow. Subsequent research: the girl's name was Fanny Lou Mayberry, the usual business about being "under contract" to Miss Rheingold Enterprises, and she claimed he'd taken her out to some local high school football stadium, told her there was going to be a party for one of his former coaches. One of the great *Daily News* bits was their report that Miss Mayberry had suffered "minor contusions, bruises, and skin blemishes from lime." The lime "appeared to be customarily used in marking off yardage on the field of play."

He began shaking his head, very hard, like he was trying to get some obscure buzz out of the exact middle of it. "Don't look back, baby. You'll trip or get tackled." He stopped. "Used to have me in front of my locker, cleanshaven, with the shoulder pads? Ten, eleven years ago. Now it's just the hair on my left cheek. They keep coming in closer."

"It's money."

"Yup. And nothing else."

"When did you turn actor?"

"What d'you mean?"

"When . . . I mean, you were a Ram."

"I always been an actor." He was suddenly almost standing up for himself, a little hot-eyed. "Had to find that out."

"Sure."

"Found that out here. It wasn't easy, but I hacked it. Listen." He had hold of my arm. "He's a genius."

"I don't doubt."

"Those two." He cocked his buzzing head at the couple. "They weren't trying. My fault. I went at them too lighthearted."

"I thought you were fine."

"No. Listen. He kept me alive."

"I don't doubt."

"Come on. You gotta meet him."

"My pleasure."

"Wait a minute." He tightened his grip on my arm, like maybe he was going to switch me. "My first wife. As far as I'm concerned, she walked out on me when she walked out on him. That's how I feel. That how you feel?"

"I'm open-minded."

He kneaded my arm, not really satisfied, but yanked me along anyhow, through the folding chairs to where Yost was having last little crumbly chats with his votaries.

"Dr. Yost, Bill Warner."

"Warner Williams," I smiled. It's always happening to me.

We shook hands, and I swear his felt slightly granulated.

"You are joining us?" he asked.

"Not exactly."

"Wants to do an article," Lars boomed.

Yost looked me up and down with those bon-bon eyes of his, a very minty stare. "These sessions are private."

"I understand entirely, Dr. Yost." I plied away at him. "I don't want to interfere in any way. This is really about somebody who used to work with you."

He seemed a tad disappointed. Naturally. But he opened up a little more. "I go a long way back." He mentioned knowing Adler, that name first, deliberately, then brought up his acquaintance with Freud more casually. "I was usually at the Wednesday meetings, but I preferred to see him elsewhere." Where he didn't say, and pattered on down through the lesser names, Rank, Abraham, Eitington, Ferenczi, making the most out of Ferenczi, who was "closer to me than he realized." He also had a long, oven-warm sigh for "poor little Otto, who so needed an auxiliary ego." He'd even gone to see him once in Philadelphia, after they'd both immigrated. "Hopeless." None of it quite jibed, at least with what I could remember from reading the Ernest Jones biography a long time ago. But it was probably meant more for the faithful than for me. I let on I was impressed, even a little ignorant. "I don't know quite when this was. You mentioned him in one of your books. About all I know about it. Simon Moro."

Yost was surprised. "Rudi?"

"Yes."

And more than a little disturbed that I knew that other name too. "You've seen him lately?"

"I'm about to."

"Rudi Eckmann." He pursed the name slily between his lips, like the last of an old gumdrop, then turned to Lars. "He had your duties, functions. He was the first one. In some ways, the best."

Lars frowned, began shaking that mid-point buzz out of his head again.

"At the time, Lars, at the time. In other ways, the worst." But he'd checked himself. He rose, said his savory good-byes to the few who remained, including the Bronxville couple, now avidly converted. Then he asked Lars to please turn out the two neon lights when he left. "Switch them around for next week." I thought I'd lost him, but then he said, elaborately, "Perhaps you might still have time for a small bite to eat?"

We went around the corner to what you might say was his stage delicatessen. At least he had his own napkin there, richly food-stained. He tucked himself behind it and feasted upon flanks of smoked salmon, about a firkin of cream cheese. I stretched out a cup of coffee in silence while he ate.

"Lars," he finally said. "Quick on the attack, but very slow to reach any depth. Too slow. Not like Rudi. Rudi plunged. He could be more yourself than you." He tidied his mouth. "We are talking now only for your own information?"

"Fine by me."

"Good. You know how I started out?"

"No."

"Working with prostitutes." He seemed especially pleased to tell me this. "Professional women. Not opera-goers." Then he added rather primly, "While I was still in medical school."

"A clinic?"

"In a way. Research, independent studies." He fixed me with his first definite, unconfected expression, a kind of nostalgic leer. "Do you know Vienna?"

"I've been there."

"When?"

"Nineteen fifty-six."

He shook his head. "You don't know Vienna. All that stucco was once very real."

"Plenty of it around when I was there. Pale yellow."

He still shook his head. "I want to tell you something you probably won't approve. It is supposed to be such a scandal. But I am very glad they never renamed Berggasse after him. There should be no Freudgasse. If there is to be a street like that in Vienna, it should be Schnitzlergasse." I was having trouble finding his point, though apparently he was coming to one. "Schnitzler understood. All that sex was also once very real."

Could've said there was plenty of that around too when I was there, but I didn't. Dirty white.

"That's why I went into the streets. Not into a lot of silly *Hausfrau* dreams. They had to be paid, they were always paid to come, but never that much, not enough to lie. Rudi helped there. He kept them down to pfennigs."

"Moro got them for you?"

"He had them already."

I cocked one eye at him over the lip of my coffee cup.

"Yes, yes," he insisted.

I began taking notes. "How many?"

"A string of them. Ten, twelve, as I remember. I used eight."

"The same eight?"

"Always. I required that."

It seemed just possible enough, just nutty enough, if he really had details to offer. "What did he look like then?"

"Much the same. Tall, thin. All neck and nose. Hungrier. He had a straw hat, a Panama. Inside, on the hat band, he kept all the names and such. With a little red pencil. He used to bite the end of it to sharpen it. You had the feeling he was living out of that hat, maybe saving a meal a day, feeding off his pencil."

"Was he acting anywhere?"

"Don't I make it clear what he was doing? They were very young, the ones he brought me. No real depth of experience, but the truth was closer to the surface. I could get at it. Much harder with people like those two we had tonight. You strip them naked, and they have hides, not skins."

"But he wasn't an actor then?" I kept after my query.

"A great one. For my purposes." He got off on his own kick. "You've seen my method. Re-enactment. Documentary drama. Not dreams. I would have each of them repeat the previous night. No fantasies. What really happened. The strolling, the bickering, bargains, prices, undressing, false breathing, fake orgasm, kinks, the fatigue. Not everything, naturally, we had to condense, but the pace of things."

"Jesus." It just slipped out. "How far did you take it?"

"That depended on Rudi."

From here on, I had trouble keeping up with my notes because Yost got headlong excited.

"Let me tell you something about Rudi. Sometimes a girl,

he would be up on her, telling her what a strudel she was, what a miserable dry screw she really offered a man. *In coito*, you understand, never missing a stroke. And I would be encouraging the girl to speak her own thoughts, how much she hated the terrible, battering sex act, wanted to be a child again. She would begin to curse Rudi—but not Rudi really—he was always the brutal man from the night before —call him the filthiest cock-wilting names. Show him how she was faking, jam her toes into his ears, spit at him even. And then Rudi would make some little tweak, maybe turn and kiss her ankle, or slide his own foot up under her neck, fondle her with his toes—he could do the most incredible tricks with that bony body of his—and she couldn't help herself. She'd try to stop. I'd shout at her to stop. But she would climb right to it, still cursing until the moans started, *inamorata*. He was that good with them."

"With *all* of them?"

"At first. Then I saw I was wasting him that way. So I divided them up, had half of them play the men. There was that between most of them anyhow. That left Rudi free . . . well, just to chat. I had a feeling that might work even better, and it did. He wasn't cunt-trapped. If you are screwing, even if you are Rudi, you can't really concentrate all your effort outside yourself. This way he could work with one of the girls, aggravate and titillate her, while I did the same with the other. You can understand what was beginning to evolve." He looked hard at me to be sure I did, only going on after I gave him a knowledgeable nod. "I took it the next step when I saw he was just so much more adept at it, more prurient than I could ever be. I realized my own limitations, not enough therapists do. I let him work on both girls, turn them into furies, lather them into weeping sweats, while I kept outside, at a clinical distance, and controlled the vignette. Essentially the same arrangement as you saw to-night. Only Lars will never be any Rudi."

"Was it—I mean, two at a time all the time, or more sometimes, or everybody all at once ever, or how . . . ?" And I remember thinking: phrase all questions clearly, even salacious ones.

"Again," he yielded, "I left all of that to Rudi. We were after realism, so it was usually only two. Lonely, furtive. What you could find down any Vienna street, done every which way, sometimes right there on the cobbles. But if three girls did get themselves into some beastliness with a man, we repeated it all the next day with four of them. Rudi took great care with the fourth, made her feel like a man, virile, even without the anatomy, which he said was all rubbish anyhow. He was amazing, you must realize. Even after you say it was his livelihood, he still had a miracle touch. And they always had good words to say for him. Even when he beat them."

Before I could raise an eyebrow, he was sniffing back at me.

"Yes, yes. It all came out, it always does. You saw how this evening. We got onto the subject one day, I forget how, and *they* suggested that one of them play Rudi, beat the others. If you care to know, I'm convinced the idea came up out of respect for Rudi. Because there was never trouble about any one or the other of them being beaten, but always a lot of back and forth about who was going to be Rudi. They were finicky about that. It was an honor." He pondered. "Perhaps something they wouldn't have felt later on, but they were still, remember, all very young."

"Did you ever write any of this up?"

"Only in the abstract." He shook his head. "You couldn't tell this was the source."

"Shy about it?"

Maybe I put too much edge on that. He gave me quite a look: bitter almond. "My research was never completed."

"How come?"

"Rudi, one day, just didn't show up with them."

"Like that?"

"Like that. Though I think I know why."

"You know. I don't."

"I was beginning to help them."

A little bit of the *pâtissier* crept back into his manner now. Once again, the sweets of life.

"Fine for me, and them, but he was in a bind. If he kept bringing them to see me, he would lose them. One girl—he called her Esmeralda—when she first arrived, she was tightly oral. So I had her play a man going after normal sex with another girl playing a normal girl. There were many tears, Rudi was very hard on her, had to be. But when she was at her most distraught, I suddenly had her switch, play the normal girl. The sheer relief was enough to do it. A very touching thing. But not so good for Rudi. Even if he wasn't losing his girls yet, the girls were losing their specialties. Once the fixations go . . ."

"Fascinating." All I could think to say.

"You can hardly blame him, but of course—since it was also a question of *my* livelihood—I do blame him. As understanding as he was with those girls, spiritual even—and you can say that they weren't going to know any better life, his protection was at least some protection—still, he was a corrupter. An evil, really. It never surprised me that he was so menacing in the films. I wonder sometimes. Suppose he'd known he wouldn't be a starving pimp forever, that money and fame were coming. *Then* would he have let me continue, bring help to those girls? And I have to say—" He was folding up his napkin, tucking under the food stains so that a fairly clean white square lay before him on the table. "—I have to say, I doubt it."

That's the gist of what Yost had to tell me about M. We talked on a bit more, about how much the work he'd done in Vienna was still in advance of what any of the kooks were doing out in California. He half apologized for the poor show I'd seen that evening, not really up to the bold sexual standards he admitted were "the real spice of therapy." But I don't really think it would have been any better as a nudie. His real problem was simply being sixty-seven years old. "What I can ask now is limited. Nobody trusts the coaxing of a dirty old man." I felt some sympathy for him, trying to cover his eld with a lot of flour and sugar. That is, until I happened to bring up his name to Moro. In actual fact, I had to bring up his name three times before M. made the connection.

"I don't know any Dr. Yost."

"He knows you."

"What kind of a doctor?"

"Sort of a shrink."

"You have me."

"Knew you in Vienna. And eight of your girls."

M.'s eyes popped. "You don't mean *Horst* Yost?"

"Right."

"It was the *Herr Doktor* that threw me off."

"He's not a doctor?"

M. smiled, his Viennese smile: the *gemütlich* death's-head. "In Vienna, always grant a man a little bigger title than he really deserves. But *Herr Doktor* is stretching things. Horst was a nurse."

"Kid me not."

"Not for a living, I don't think. For kicks. He was a medic at the Somme, picked up a taste for the macabre—to add to his other tastes. I found out about him through the medical school."

"You've lost me."

"Those days in Vienna I was very broke. All I had to cover my head was an old Panama, kept it together with shop twine, and I got an infected ear. So I went around to the clinic there. This overweight male nurse signed me in, then hastily started examining me. I remember the pad of his thumb was almost as soft as my ear lobe. An interne came along and shooed him away. 'That's our Horst,' he told me. 'Did he diagnose you?' I said no, and he probed into my ear, a little roughly, I thought. 'Too bad. He could have told you there really is no pain.' When I finally said ouch, he smiled, gave me all the dirty gossip about Horst. This Yost fellow was not only vaguely aberrant, but a definite pest. Even tried to break in on those Wednesday nights that Freud used to chair. He sneaked in as a case, through Rank, apparently, but then did nothing except denounce everybody else there. He sounded right for us, so when my ear got better—thanks to the clinic, where I stole a nice warm scarf—we went after him."

"Who's we?"

"Me and those eight girls. *Les Huit Chats.*"

"You were making them out to be French?"

"Rumanian."

"Rumanian."

"Perversion always comes from the east."

"I follow."

"Just one more little touch to help protect us, give us an excuse. We were decadent, therefore people would tolerate what we said."

"Said?"

"Politically."

"How did politics get into it?"

"That's all it was, at bottom."

I scratched my head. "Start over."

"That's what we were doing. Political cabaret. We still didn't go over very well. My all-too-gentle Viennese. But we tried. In Berlin, we would have succeeded." He smiled again, realizing he had me badly caught out. "You don't know about this early career of mine? You should. *Les Huit Chats* was a revue I created. A little Marx, a lot more ass."

"I don't know if we're talking about the same things or not."

"We are. You'll see. *Les Huit Chats* was the kind of satire you'd know from George Grosz. The big come-on was the girls wearing nothing but big, furry tails wired straight up the buttocks crease. Each of them was supposed to be the pet of some European leader. Lap cats, I guess you would say. I did the imitations while they rubbed all around me. I had a wonderful Ludendorff, could do him for you right now. Except you weren't even born then, wouldn't have any meaning for you. I did an even better Hindenburg, no helmet, only a big spike coming out the top of my head. The French were harder. Pétain I had down all right, by making him very Prussian, but his cat very svelte, very piquant. But my Poincaré was bad. Finally had to show him down on his hands and knees, lapping milk out of the same saucer as his cat, Marianne. Too bald. And she was a fat, tabby-looking Municher, not French enough. I think I did the English best, after my Germans. I had a young Churchill that I made sound a lot like the later Churchill—just chance—I was thinking of him as a warmonger then. One of the girls did a very nice Clementine, purred very, very pukka. My finale was Lloyd George. Did him with a Welsh accent and a Bible, had the piano tinkle 'Rule Britannia,' all the cats rush him at once, pile on, tails quivering. For a curtain call, I gave each girl a kittenish bundle to hold, and they sang, '*Lloyd George ist mein Vater, Vater ist Lloyd George!*' Then, meeooowww, and a terrible, screechy alley-cat cry that, if you listened closely, came out '*Verrr-ssaaiillees!*' " He was off chortling over these W-W-One gross canards, down humpy old memory lane, but I wasn't going to be led astray.

"Did Horst know about your act?"

"I doubt it. Horst was different, something we did privately. To keep the act going, understand, for the money. But, then again, not *all* that different . . ."

"Let me ask you something straight."

"You want their ages again."

"No."

"The youngest was thirteen. She was Hindenburg's Siamese. The joke was he couldn't surrender to her because of his oath to the Kaiser."

"Were these girls whores?"

"Such a question."

"Why?"

"Doesn't really have an answer."

"Were you pimping?"

M. glowered. "What kind of a story is that, even from Horst?"

"Horst says you even beat them."

M. thought a moment. "I think maybe we *did* put on something like that for him once."

"No. For real."

He laughed very hard, even at me, I suspect. "What is this 'for real'? Nothing was for real."

"His research."

"Be serious."

"I am. He does have some standing."

"Impossible." But he started to do a little more explaining. "These girls weren't whores, exactly. They were performers, *artistes*. They screwed mostly for their own convenience. Whom they liked, when they liked, for whatever they wanted to get out of it. Me, for instance. I admit it helped them to stay in the act, but I never heard any complaints from them either. We all knew each other very, very well. We wanted to stay together if we could. Succeed."

"How would *you* describe what went on with Horst?"

"Horst may have had his own ideas, but it was an act. *Our* act. That simple."

"Same as the cabaret?"

"With variations, almost. We did it for him five, maybe

six times. We went pretty far sometimes, but this was private. Maybe, in subtle ways, he influenced us, turned us more macabre. We would've dropped him if our real act had ever caught on, but that never happened."

"He told me you brought him a string of hookers. Your string. On the cheap."

"Let him tell it any way he wants, but he paid through the nose."

"He claims you paid them in pfennigs."

"In front of him, yes. He loved that. Part of their humiliation. Understand, he had quirky tastes, even for a voyeur."

"Jesus."

"You must realize what you are up against in Horst. He is complete that way, if no other way. You know why he broke off with us?"

"One day you didn't show. He says."

"Why should I do that? We stayed open a month on his money. We cherished him. I was doing every kinky trick I knew to keep him entranced. So were the girls. But one of them slipped up. Esmeralda. I had her playing a fluffy Angora for my Woodrow Wilson. She really was very hairy. Tyrolean-Italian, or gypsy maybe. Horst was fascinated with her. She misunderstood, or just didn't think, or maybe she was a little hot for Horst herself. She rolled out from under one of our ensembles, all-girls-together it was, and saw Horst standing there, panting and blushing, with this weepy, almost honey stare of his. She reaches out for him. 'Why don't you ever join us, *Schwanzmeister?*' *Mein Gott, Schwanzmeister!* To Horst, who doesn't want himself to know he's there. He ran into a corner and froze. His back to us, like the little bad boy sent to stare at the wall. I went over to him, tried to coax him away. He dropped to his knees, wedged his head into the corner, and began to grind it against the plaster. Wouldn't stop. Tearing out his hair but keeping his hands to himself, if you understand. All we could do was leave him in peace. That's the only time I really did feel like beating one of them, the stupid slut."

"But," I felt I had to say, "he's got a following. He's published. His is now considered a legitimate approach."

M. shrugged. "We put on a good show. That's all I can tell you. Used to block things out ahead of time, work up improvisations for him. Essentially, of course, it was mime. Just as hard to do, too. But he wanted us to talk dirty as well, so we did. Mostly me. Maybe that's what he wrote up. . . ." Then he got a shade more curious. "Horst seems to have become much more sly. Tell me again, how is he getting away with it these days?"

I went over the same ground more fully, trying to explain how far removed Yost seemed now from any such raw and lubricious scene, how tame and proper, how sweet, how innocuous, how dull. M. puzzled over this, picking at his hooked nose so long that I thought he'd gotten distracted. But that's how M. gets at his thoughts sometimes, through either nostril. Not a pleasant habit. Best delete.

"No. Horst is still up to his same old tricks."

"How could he be?"

"You must realize how extreme a voyeur Horst really is. He is still getting people to do their act for him, isn't he?"

"Come on. A man and woman bitching at each other with all their clothes on? Can't be very many jollies in that for him."

"Not many," M. smirked, "but still some."

I have been trying to reconcile these two discrete versions. If you take Yost for a clever fraud, which I'm perfectly willing to do, they can be made to coincide at most important points, but for an exact fit, you have to include a few of M.'s own personal quirks. One, his attitude toward cats. He has great feeling for most animals—he's almost Elizabeth-Taylorish about them—but for some reason, not cats.

"Cats," he once told me, "are really fur-covered snakes. They do not curl up in your lap. They coil. And they do not purr. If you will listen carefully, you will find they rattle." Significant, I suggest, that M. set these girls up as *Les Huit Chats*. Can't have really had all that much respect for them as women.

The other point is this business of voyeurism. M., frankly, tends to see voyeurs everywhere. I suppose it comes from being in showbiz for so long, but even then, he carries it to extremes sometimes. M. disapproves, for instance, of things like microscopes, practices like bird-watching, or one-way glass, especially in nursery schools. "If you have to watch something, at least watch something that knows it's being watched." This may very well have colored his view of Yost's experimentation. I suggested as much, circumspectly. "Let me tell you something," he snapped back at me. "I never lost a staring contest in my life. Because I always catch the other guy *looking* at me . . . Blue-eyes."

N OW ABOUT Quincy Adams. Yes, and how about Quincy Adams? Just when you'd think his career had finally collapsed, all that ham, all that very thin, pink, damn near transparent *prosciutto* turned trichinoid, he comes through in a low-budget blockbuster like *The Flea Man* (1966). The gross, according to *Variety*, was absurd enough, but the net, and this I have only from Quincy, was "fiscally obscene." He wouldn't tell me if he had a percentage, probably didn't, but I know from Terry they had to give him a small piece of *Raven*, while M. was working—one more reason why these two were never really going to get along—for a flat fee. What Quincy mostly wanted to tell me, re: *Flea Man*, was all about his Portrayal. Silly word. "I derived my portrayal" —possible caption for Quincy: *The actor as a derivative*— "from one of Blake's visions. Do you know he once drew the ghost of a flea? Marvelous thick-set, muscle-bound, very Blakean chap." I've seen a print since. Looks like Charles Atlas with an overshot bite. In no way does it look like Quincy Adams in *The Flea Man*. "For its size, a flea has great strength. Immense. At my height and build he becomes almost Superman." Quincy is about five foot seven, when his pompadour is at crest, a hundred-and-eight-some pounds, and has very long, very pronounced wrists. "We worked everything out proportionally. Those titanic leaps, the hopping over walls. All well within my extrapolated capabilities. And, of course, appetitious. Supernally appetitious." You'll find *The Flea Man* listed sometimes as a vampire picture, but with the gamma-ray bit, the accident-in-the-lab gambit, I put it as Mad Scientist, or sci-fi horror. M.'s opinion: "Yes, I went to see it when I heard they wanted me for this part. I was shocked. To ask a man to play a flea when he is so obviously only a midge . . ."

Quincy claims he is the one who got M. hired for *Raven*. Professes great reverence for the early Moro. "I've never gotten over seeing him in my early youth. Gave me the wil-

lies then, still does now." He did "the willies" for me, about
a three-second spasm of free-form *frissons*. As for his "early
youth," if he wants to believe he first went to see Moro in
knee pants at half price, who am I to say he had to be at least
twenty-nine years old at the time? Maybe he scrunched
down in front of the ticket window, the same way the rest
of us Saturday-matinee sneaks used to.

Shouldn't make him out to be all that much of a fraud. He
was forthright enough, crack-off-the-bat about getting some
things straight. I think about the first words he said to me
when I met him, out at La Guardia for our flight to L.A.,
were: "Now tell me, Mr. Warner, are you a family man?"

That unctuous tone of concerned citizenship. I looked at
him, too directly, right dead into that languid, rippling gaze,
entirely backed with red flocking.

Did I ever answer for a family man.

"I see," he sighed, commiseratively. "But I must say
you're fortunate in having only daughters. I think it's very
hard to know quite what to do with a boy these days."

He was about to pat me on the near knee, to show the
matter was, gentle squeeze, settled, but I stood up too fast
for him. He even passed that off. "Are we ready to board?"

We weren't, but I made him stand for ten minutes.

"I'd as soon stand as sit in an air terminal," he went on
suavely. "I'm certain those plastic seats cause piles." Then he
got off on the subject of his decorating business, which, the
reason he'd come East, he was hoping to sell. Big. To Sears,
no less. The idea was to computerize several interiors he'd
done out in Hollywood for the stars, Tuesday Weld, Mrs.
Jack Benny, then feed in any Sears customer's room dimen-
sions, choice of color, furniture requirements, et cetera,
whether they wanted "Mod" or "Period." Quincy is the
master of both epochs. "Period is more or less what used to
be called Traditional, but people tend to want Period now as
something they feel is even a little out front of Mod." Any-

how, in a matter of micro-seconds, out would come your living room, done by Quincy Adams Associates, Hollywood, Calif., right down to the last curtain rod. "I don't know if it will really work. They say they can construct a mathematical model of my taste. To tell the truth, I never thought it really added up to anything specific. Far too eclectic. But now I gather certain do-dads will always turn up with certain other geegaws, even if I do over a pagoda. I'm still not totally convinced. You have to be a bit of a psychologist to do up a room to a woman's real satisfaction. Even a bit of a proctologist."

But he'd gotten pretty far along in his negotiations with Sears, was going back out to think things over, do the picture, then decide. "We're so *lucky* to be working. I hope Simon realizes that. It may not be art, but it's jolly well not a few blue movies I've done in a dim light in my time. I've been through so many lives out there. I don't mind saying I'm grateful for horror. I even like horror. I enjoyed being scared as a little boy. I suppose I really miss being frightened. Of course, I'm scared to death of flying, aren't you? Partly why I adore air travel."

We were told to board then. One of the stewardesses recognized Quincy, but didn't flame up about him much. "Nice to have you aboard, Mr. Adams" was the total ego-boost he got from her. Later I overheard her talking to the others, back in the rear of the plane. "Josie told me she went to see him in that flea picture? Just for laughs? She didn't laugh once."

"Now we'll wait around for an hour. You'll see," Quincy brooded. "Just like getting stuck in the Lexington Avenue. Here, you wanted to read the script. I'll read your *Esquire*. I've lacked lately for Mr. Wilfrid Sheed's assured disapproval."

Correctness of Quincy's simile: after maybe ten minutes on the ground, air traffic completely stacked up, the Boeing

707 did begin to feel like a stalled subway car. Everybody was irritably waiting for power to be restored. Two seats ahead of me, a busy executive had an old *Holiday* open to a piece of mine about the Jersey Shore. I could tell he was speed-reading it, and when he got to the "Continued"-line, he didn't, the son of a bitch, obviously thought he already had the gist of the thing. Then again, I must confess I never read the whole script of *Raven*, adapted from Edgar Allan Poe's Original Poem, by Beau Fletcher. Nervous waiting, easier to skim, because, sure, it was awful, dreary, midnight-dreary, but also, just like that *Holiday* reader, I quickly got the gist, could see the drift, only needed the feel of Fletcher's damnable scribblings.

In fact, I much prefer, even admire, the five-page treatment that got Beau Fletcher his original fifteen thou up front against seventy-five for the completed script. It will serve here as an action memo against which to judge the havoc—no, consider: the art that Moro eventually wreaked upon the film. Clear enough that the picture, as originally conceived, was supposed to be a lot more Quincy's than Moro's, a fact that Quincy wanted to drum into me, I found once we were airborne and I couldn't escape. Anyhow, for comparison:

RAVEN
Adapted from Edgar Allan Poe's "The Raven"
by
Beau Fletcher

Fletcher thought "the simpler title" would have more horror impact, though Terry worries a lot about the loss of the definite article. "Sure, it frees you a little more from the original," he says, "but a straight Poe title really helps that Family rating."

Baron Scaperelli, bereaving his lost wife, Lenore, in a gloomy castle, high up in the Transylvanian hills, is visited by the Raven. In reality, the Raven is a vampire, one of Dracula's seed, but the Baron construes the bird as a friendly harbinger, come on darkling wings to lead Scaperelli to Lenore's unknown resting place. They travel through the long and stormy night, to an icy cave deep in a glacial fault. The Raven cannot enter—until the Baron invites him to follow—and there within, a vast crystal crypt is revealed. Lenore lies on a bier of snow, seemingly lifeless, but perfectly preserved. The Baron takes her from this strange place, rushes out through the opening just as the ice cave crumbles into the start of a freak avalanche, passing just to the side of him.

Re: M.'s initial objection that vampires are bats, not ravens. "If we show a bat, the audience *knows* we're going to show a vampire," Terry argued. "They're hip now. But if we show a raven—which the audience tends to think is more a friendly than an unfriendly—then we got them peeing when we show a vampire. I consider it a big advance." One other small question, from me: what kind of a name is Lenore Scaperelli?

The Baron returns to his castle with Lenore, lays her sacredly in a rich coffin, surrounded by tapers, while he searches through incunabula for potions to revive her. The coffin is kept under heavy guard in the Great Hall, but the guards grow nervous in the hovering shadow of the Raven's wings. Suddenly the shadow elongates, turns into the gaunt figure of a man not quite a man, yet more. Horrible screams. The Baron rushes into the hall to find all the guards hideously mutilated, Lenore vanished. Only one man is alive. "Raven," he utters, then dies.

Ravenus, the vampire, has abducted the lifeless Lenore. He has only befriended the Baron in order to get at his victim, who was protected by the ice which contained some frozen holy water. He carries her down, down into the secret dungeon deeps of the Scaperelli Castle. There he secretes her in a cobwebbed boudoir,

"With the Phantom of the Opera's old, out-of-tune organ, right?" I put it to Quincy, but he came right back at me. "No, I'm afraid not. Ruined . . . all that sewer damp. . . ."

and begins an unseemly, almost erotic ritual that ends with him bending over her full, pulsing throat. But the Baron has come in pursuit, armed with a silver-tipped, hawthorn-shafted arrow, notched into a crossbow. He surprises Ravenus, who instantly transmogrifies back into the Raven and tries to escape. But in mid-flight, the Baron's arrow plunges into his heart.

As Quincy explained to me, somewhere over Ohio, full of iron determination: "That will have to be changed. The crossbow is a graceless weapon. It should be simple bow and arrow, not even a quiver. Did you know that I played with Errol Flynn in *Robin Hood?* A bit part. One of his numerous band of, if you'll pardon the expression, merry men. But I saw what Flynn could *do* just by pulling a bow string taut across his clear, white cheek." And in this, and in such things as being robed in lawn and pancaked fair, not swarthy, Quincy did get his way.

Then the Baron turns, runs back to Lenore. To his astonishment, he finds her standing before him, beautiful and statuesque. Whatever the curse was, it has apparently lifted. They return to the Raven, who has corrupted back into Ravenus on the dungeon steps. In horror, the Baron recognizes the vampire as his own prodigal brother, who years ago fell into occult ways.

With mixed feelings, torn by sorrow and revulsion, the Baron prepares to bury his brother at the crossroads. It is almost too much for him, and Lenore, a little eerily, insists on helping. It is she who closes down the coffin lid. Then, as the procession winds down from the castle, a close-up reveals that Lenore, her hands hidden in her medieval sleeves, is breaking to bits and pieces the extracted shaft of Scaperelli's arrow.

A plague settles strangely over the area, and Lenore wanders through castle, town, and countryside in a disconsolate reverie. People shun her, hurl accusations of witchcraft, but the Baron, despite crumblings within his castle, the sudden insanity of his game keeper, still cleaves to her.

Late one night, Lenore lies sleeping in her canopied chamber, far too deeply. The wind outside seems to call her name, trailing off into a rustle of wings. The Baron enters with a chalice of wine for her, but sets it aside, bends down lovingly over her breast. He catches sight of some sort of amulet tucked into her bosom. He pulls it forth. It is the silver arrowhead. In dismay, he sweeps back a long ringlet of hair from her throat and finds the two tiny punctures cicatricing the blue vein.

All is turmoil now, the time being almost midnight. The Baron runs to his armory, seizes a jousting lance, and leaps on his horse. He rides through the howling night, as the church bells toll. To make it to the crossroads in time, he must cut across a graveyard. The dead seem to seep up from the misty ground, entwining him in their fearsome miasma. At the crossroads, the earth begins to tremble, stir, rise up. The hooves of the Baron's horse are heard. A skeletal hand reaches up out of the earth, as if pushing back a heavy door. Or lid. Then, just as the earth begins to crack open altogether, at exactly the last stroke of midnight, the Baron's lance, also hawthorn, strikes home. It breaks off halfway up. The earth quakes, heaves, then subsides.

"Up to this point," Quincy explained, heatedly analyzing the script for me, somewhere over Utah, "it could almost be a love story. But now we give them the kind of picture they paid their money to see."

The Baron returns, full of apprehension, to his castle. Hungering, unearthly cries echo in the great hall. His own retainers, blood-mad, try to set upon him, but he turns them away by raising the hilt of his sword, cruciform. They cringe back, set upon each other. He rushes up the stairway, into Lenore's chamber. The curtains on her canopied bed have been drawn. He throws them back. In the bed lies only a skeleton in sere bedclothes, the arrowhead amulet actually hanging down into its rib cage. The Baron covers his eyes and falls back in grief, terror. "Nevermore," he moans, over and over.

The Baron's cries of "Nevermore" whirl into the sounds of the storm, once again howling over the crossroads. Dead souls keen and moan. Thunder answers them, raging. Then lightning strikes deep into the earth at the exact right spot. The grave at the crossroads is torn open. Ravenus is revealed, with the Baron's lance sunk deep in his bleeding breast, but grinning, grinning, grinning. . . .

"But pray, at whom?" Quincy asked me, coming down into the brown bathtub ring of smog around L.A. "And with what? Relief? Pain? Glee? Why leave any ambiguity? I realize we have the famous Moro grin to get in here somewhere. We must have it, I quite agree. But why not earlier? So that we can end where we logically should. I don't want you to misunderstand—I realize I might appear to be serving my own interests—but we really ought to end on my last cry of 'Nevermore!' Don't you think? You can at least see that by ending that way—which, after all, is Poe's way—we avoid the charge of straying too far from the original."

"But 'Nevermore!' " I blurted out, "is the Raven's line."

He shot me a low, enervating glance of real fag hate. Easy to see how it must have sounded to him, like the final, flippant betrayal: I was trying to give his one good line to Moro. He'd been getting more and more edgy, defensive the whole trip, inflating the Baron's role, sniping away at M. through his effusive admiration for "mature talent." "Simon has not stood still. So many people try to say that he simply annealed to a particular style in the Thirties. Mr. Sheed, for one. I can't go along with that. I've never worked with Simon before, of course, but I couldn't think of any living actor that way. He is *always* my contemporary." When he saw I wasn't prepared to join in this sly bitchery, that I was already partisan, he got unutterably prickly. Though I guess that really started way back at La Guardia, after about twenty minutes of quivering on the ground, when he gave up on *Esquire* and tried another approach to me.

"You work for an excellent magazine. Don't see it as often as I should." He filed it down the seat crack between us. "Now, tell me if I'm correct." That same gaze, only with a harsher sheen on the red flocking. "You consider yourself more a writer than a journalist."

"In a way." I didn't like him hovering that near.

"I can sympathize."

"Can, can you?"

"Yes. I've always considered myself more an actor than
a . . ."

He dropped away into an epicene, begging smile, without
saying a what. Various possibilities: Than an afternoon TV
celebrity? You rarely see Quincy on any nighttime show.
Than a Rodeo Boulevard interior decorator? Than a spot
endorsement for a Javanese men's cologne? Than an
Adams? Which, indeed, he is, if only a tiny sprig, or small
fungoid knarl, on that blasted genealogical oak. Than a three-
dimensional wax monster? See *Hall of Howls*, with special
glasses (1957). Than Mr. Viper, Your Host of Horrors? A
TV series he briefly announced, or rather his head alone did,
superimposed on the hood of a coiled king cobra. Than an
insect? Than a fainéant, a flâneur, a farceur? He is, has been,
or will be all these things, far more than he'll ever come near
being an actor. Oh yes, always the choked inward cry of a
strangled talent, but try to think of one role, no matter how
far-fetched or deviant, that Quincy could really master: Sa-
lome? Goneril, Regan? The Sphinx opposite Oedipus?
Cunegonde? Marguerite? Richard I? Edward II? Hadrian
VII? Pope Joan? They all lie within his propensities, but
hopelessly beyond his range. That was demarcated very
early on, check date with Miss Clio, at the Princeton Tri-
angle Club Show, ca. 1928. Quincy played the lead flapper in
a chorus of truly wistful-kneed beauties, and there is still
something petite, cloche-hatted, rope-beaded, even small-
breasted about him. Only it don't make much whoopee any
more.

Ah, but you see, mustn't, mustn't. Not allowed such
thoughts under the venal, creepy exchange of counterfeit
confidences Quincy was offering me prior to take-off. In
sum, if I would be willing to consider him more an actor
than a . . . what shall we settle for? Than a flit, he would,
in turn, be happy to regard me more as a writer than a hack.

Mutual admiration plus elevation. We would understand that both our lights were hidden under a bushel, and how cozy. Blame faulty fate. "I never change," Quincy trilled, "except in my afflictions."

Missing, later found mutilated: one more epigram from Oscar Wilde. Quincy loves this sort of dastardly deed. A little sadistic twist, and somebody else's old, worn-out witticism is newly yours. Quincy, curiously, seems to attack only other dandies for these cleverisms, e.g., Noel Coward. One day, on set, he'd had enough of Hazel Rio. "Some women should be struck regularly," he hissed, "like tents." Not bad, not bad. But at this particular moment, while he was trying to reach his hand up my mind, I had one for him: The poove is in the pudding. If I'd been lucky enough to become a goddamn queer, I would've *done* something with my life.

The envy bit, typical me: homosexuals are the only ones in our society who have the freedom to pursue the highest arts. They don't have wives, well, maybe, sort of, but not families, mortgages, insurance, school bills, responsibilities, et cetera. Okay, we are all ambivalent. But, therefore, why should I be penalized because I'm a heterosexual? Buggery should be legalized, certainly. But taxed. On a progressive scale. Old men working the Pennsylvania Station Men's Room pay least, are exempt after sixty-five. Russian ballet dancers pay most. And this would work no hardship because the money is already going down the drain in blackmail.

Usually, I'm pretty good at covering up this anti-Socratic bias of mine, but I assume I said something to Quincy, must have. Can't think what, maybe some quiff-pro-quo remark about M.'s cat show in Vienna that tipped him off, or a weak crack about my being a reporter in order to remain a provider. But anyhow, he caught me out, an anti-queer, another William F. Buckley, Jr., and handled my latent feelings with consummate poove tact.

He pulled forth a red-leather wallet, exquisitely Florentine, with a Medici crest like a gold thumbprint. "I'd like to show you something, dear boy, if I may."

A rather direct remark, and he had that gaze again, much deepened, diabolically mauve, velvet drapes now drawn, tassels hanging from the eyelashes. He opened the wallet to its picture window, in a flourish that came all the way from his elbow. I was sure it would be some Polaroid shocker, maybe himself going down on Roddy McDowall, but the photo was really a bigger surprise than that. Two or three blond ringlets, tiny, fat, little legs, standing up in her stroller, trundling along on baby shoes and two-inch wheels.

"How old?" I asked.

"A toddler two."

"Granddaughter?"

"Daughter."

And damned if she didn't have his thin chin, that same juicy mouth like a bubble in a blueberry pie.

"She looks a lot more like my wife than she does me," he lied. "My wife's French, as I suppose you know."

He knew I didn't know.

"I'm a bit old to be starting a family perhaps," he glowed, "but isn't she darling? My wife is devoted to her, and a man should, if he can, live a whole life. Don't you think?"

"Do you want more?"

Our 707 was rolling out onto the runway now, at last, and Quincy began adjusting his seat belt, like a silk sash. "Depends upon my wife, really. She's much younger than I am, of course, many things still ahead of her. But I don't really think she wants to go back to acting. What with me, and now Alma, though, much as I hate to be away, I'm not home that often. Don't you think Alma Adams is a lovely name?"

"Yes."

"Yes." He smiled. "I really should tell you what Basil Rathbone wired me when he heard." The motors on the 707 went into their gunning whine, a sound that Quincy distastefully waited to shush. Then we rumbled toward the sky. "Just three little words. 'YOU OLD DOG.' "

B Y WAY of contrast, the point about M., a simple enough point, but the real point: he is just such a dominating performer on set. I don't mean on film. That's another point, already made; *ne plus ultra*, q.e.d., some of his movies are classics. But there's a larger . . . what to call it? . . . *spill* performance—over the edges, more than creative: procreative, and work, work, work—that never reaches the screen. And I don't mean, left on the cutting room floor, bad directing, purblind editing, any of that elegiac, Peter-Bogdanovich crap. What he does can't be got on film. Too extraordinary, too elsewhere. Or if it gets on film at all, only through its blink-blink impact on other actors. What you don't see, what you'll never see, except maybe in reaction shots, aren't intended to see is the self-immolation, the way he allows himself to be . . . no other way to put it: gradually annihilated by a part that it was My Unique Privilege to witness, et cetera, et cetera, horseshit, the week I was out there watching them shoot *Raven*. In a way, a paradox: in order to get things exactly right, he overacts. (Overlives?) Doesn't come up to a performance, drops down into one.

One immediate example: Friday morning, the arrow scene. Terry, moving along prestissimo, neck and neck with the budget, was up to where Quincy—right profile: index, middle, and fourth fingers evenly curved around drawn bow string, jaw tensed to remove unsightly hollow from cheek— wonks the Raven right smack through the breastbone, pinning bird to convenient oak timber above landing on steep, wet dungeon staircase. Wild, back-lighted, feathery terror, and unearthly ululations. Then, slowly, the blackness of the bird "transmogrifies" into Moro's black-caftaned corpse, which drops to the landing, head hung grotesquely down over first stone step. Most of this was a lab job. All Terry needed was this quick shot of M., flaked out and corrupting, arrow-up, on the stones. Had a first thought to do it as an aerial shot, with zoom, plus spin; effect of throwing the horror right into the viewer's eye, splat, but turned out it would take too much time, i.e., money, to set up. Terry's sometime esthetic salvation: his economic censor.

M., on the other hand, wanted to do a dead fall down the dungeon staircase, but by now Terry was trying to cut him back. He nixed the idea, too much Moro. "We'll let you rest on this one, Simon." So M. lay down in the fresh seepage, pretended to be tired, mumbled away, willing himself to Beelzebub, over-incanting, you might say, until Terry, who was really pissed at him, yelled, "Knock it off, Simon. Die." M. went instantly into a tremor—a long and, I'd have to say, lifelike . . . death-rattle—then froze so dead that there was almost a jinxy sense of odor on set. Terry was using the dolly, up along the rising steps, quick into M.'s face, then twist, and out. Nothing complicated, nothing costly, rush, rush, so what M. evoked doesn't amount to much more than a moment, a one-two beat of shock, maybe half a second of underlying pathos, on film.

But when the take was over, he didn't get up. That's what has to be understood. It wasn't that he *wouldn't* get up. He just plain *didn't*. It felt that straight, that ghastly awful, even though we all knew it was an act, deliberate as hell. In a way, of course, it was okay: Ravenus's corpse was supposed to be somewhere in the next scene. But not really: M. wasn't supposed to *stay* a corpse, not take a break, worry a lot of people. Terry didn't say anything for a while. He has this sly move; he puts the toe of one sneaker against the instep of the other and squeaks. Irritating enough to grate people into doing what they ought to be doing. Earwiggy. But it wasn't getting to M., and nobody else was moving much either. So Terry had to give an order. To the grips. "Let's get set up. Chop, chop."

Immediate activity. One of the grips hustled up the dungeon steps, hesitated at what lay in his way, looked back at Terry for guidance. Terry said nothing, only pinched another squeak out of his sneakers. The grip shrugged, stooped, took gingery hold of M.'s stiff, bare feet, started to lift them aside. Instead, all of M. came up like a plank, resting on the crown of his head. I mean, right on the crown, against the edge of that step, even if it was only wood, not really stone. The grip was so surprised he dropped M. again, and M. hit the wooden stones, flat slap, without a hint of vital signs.

Terry couldn't see straight. "Goddammit, Simon, get the fuck up, or I'll throw a drag chain on you!" Then: "No. Hell. You. And you. Stand him up." Two more grips got up there, got hold of his shoulders, got him up, more or less butted on his feet. Not that new, this rigor mortis stunt—the Living Theater makes a whole big scene out of it—but the way M. was pulling it off, he had his eyes rolled up, pure whites, and somehow he'd drained his face, mummy blank. Even his lips had disappeared, sucked up under his gums. He didn't look just dead. He looked morbific, rotted. The grips had him pretty well balanced, teetering back and forth, but they really didn't like touching him. "Now. Back off," Terry ordered. "Chop, chop."

They'd had their underhanded go-rounds before this, Terry and M., but this was the first time it was right out in the open. The set went quiet as a take. M. tottered a little but didn't fall when the grips let him go, and I thought maybe Terry had him, but then I caught on. M. was tottering just enough to get himself faced directly around toward Terry, so he could stare at him with the up-turned whites of his eyes, if that's possible. Still paralytic, with that grotesque twist in his neck from the step. Twitchings in the face, mesmeric; who knows how he does it, but somehow he was forcing his own toothy skull to show through the sagging flesh. Terry still wasn't budging. "Forget it, Simon. We don't need it."

But M. had already begun his next moves. Corpse shivers,

pulling him up taller, nearer danger. Then a kind of cadaverous rocking that teased him forward, threatened any moment to take him that long dead fall right down the staircase. *Ars pro artis:* M. was still going to do the scene his way, by damn.

Terry did scramble up then, took a few springy steps to the bottom dungeon riser, set himself. "I said no before. I didn't want you to hurt yourself. I still don't." M. twitched several dirt-blackened toes blindly over the edge of the landing, claw-like, but too far out to hook and hold. "But now I'm not going to stop you. You'll bust yourself up like old chicken-bones. But you want to try it, go ahead. We'll have the funeral on set. We'll have lilies. Big, fat, wax ones. Promise." Terry put both fists on his very low, serpentine hips. Hardly crooked his elbows. "Only go if you're going. You're fucking up my schedule."

Terry sounded pretty confident, for Terry. M. slacked his jaw, did some eerie, unhinged chattering with his back teeth, but didn't make any other move. "Yeah." Terry smirked at him, thinking he'd won. "Yeah, yeah, yeah."

And M. came down. He could have buckled a little, legitimately, the way he was playing it, but then he couldn't have reached Terry. So he went straight out and dead down, nothing to save him, falling right off his own bones. Hazel screamed at the top of her lungs. Maybe that's what really puckered Terry. Anyhow, he went for it, plunged up the steps, got his shoulder under M. just in time, half an embrace, half a tackle. "You bastard," he snarled. "You know I need you." M. went totally limp. He could have been nothing but feathers, from the easy way Terry hefted him down the steps. In fact, what he looked like—his long neck hung head-bobbing over Terry's back, his fluttery arms lost in his billowy black sleeves, his feet curled up, even more pitifully claw-like now—what he looked like was a big, damn, dead raven.

Control: that's what these risks got him. For example,
over the very next scene. M. knew, foresight, how Terry
was hoping to shoot Hazel's reaction to his rotting corpse on
the wet dungeon step. Terry wanted a coldly indifferent
Lenore, still withdrawn into high, demonic trance-hauteur.
It was going to be Quincy's scene, his impassioned discovery
of the long-lost, occult brother. But M. had fixed that, irrep-
arably. Hazel may have her troubles getting hold of an
emotion, but once she's got a grip on one, whether it's the
right one or the wrong one, stranglehold! Try to shake her
loose, she only squeezes tighter. And she was *horrified* by
what she'd seen M. just go through, even more *horrified* to
see him lying there, on the step, a crumple of flesh and bones
and, goodness gracious, maybe lice. Quincy never had a
chance. She was relating to M. like a Pietà.

Terry tried to work her out of it, naturally.

"Think bad birdie. Nasty sparrow. Ugly buzzard. Sick
canary. Dead robin."

"I dig, I dig. Dig, diggity-do," she chirruped, but her face
remained set in unbroken horror.

Terry stared down at his sneakers, then piped out, "Say
'Blue jay!' "

"Blue jay!"

"Say 'Jaybird!' "

"Jaybird!"

"It's a loud, big-mouth jaybird. You hate it. You're glad
it's dead, but now that it's dead, what you're thinking is,
when will somebody come and pick it up and put it in the
trash?"

Hazel suddenly looked like she was going to cry. Horror
and grief.

"Hazel," Stanislavski sighed, "what's a bird you really
don't like?"

"Crow."

"Okay. It's a crow. A lousy crow. The farmer shot it."

That gave him a devilish idea. "Kick it to see if it's alive."

Instead she drew back in utter, straightforward horror again. "Couldn't touch him, sweetie-poo. Crows are too . . . horrible!"

It was no use, and to stay on schedule—M. always knew he had the budget on his side—Terry had to shoot it, probably her strongest close-up in the whole picture. Her chill-pointed, shocked blue eyes and that trembling, buttery lower lip: a sensual thriving of the Raven's menace in Lenore's mad-luminous brain, hence, that much more a Moro picture. "Dear God," I remember Quincy pouting during the rushes, "she looks worse than Leda after the swan."

Control. Underground artistic control. That's what M. wanted, and he turned himself inside out, upside down to wheedle it away from Terry. "You must watch what they do to you in a picture like this. A straight commercial picture is never straight. Always a crooked artistic vision in it somewhere. I know. I've made them that way. You hide it. Let me tell you about Gila Man. I was on about five different pills then. How many did I say before?"

I found "eight" back in my notes. "But that was when you were a Nazi."

"Correct. Five to be a lizard, three more to turn Nazi. I can find out what they were later, if you're interested. But the point is, they were beginning to be me, and on screen, I was secretly saying, 'This is what I'm really like, inside. I crawl. I inhabit slime. I leave a wet trail that never breaks off.' Not so secret either. Don't think the audience didn't know what they were seeing. They paid to watch me go down on my belly, instead of going down on their own."

Speculation: another ride on his favorite hobbyhorse, voyeurism?

"Not this time, though. I get my own back this picture. I'm serious. I've seen how this little rat works. This town needs rat guards. Would you like to know what his little rat

vision is? All of us rotting in our graves, and him gnawing
through to us. I'm very serious. Read the script. What are
you left with in the end? My blood reek, Lenore's stenches.
You can smell them through Quincy's little perfumes.
Terry wants to show the grown-up world as dead and
buried, but with its grave broken open. The flesh of adults
visibly corrupting. That's Terry—that's *youth* for you. I
won't have it. Quincy he can do with what he wants.
Quincy's nothing but a special effect. But not me. I have
my own hidden vision. You watch. In this picture, the dirty,
old Raven is going to get the sweet, young thing."

He was too old to stunt much, try to get his own that
way, as per example above. That was rare. Mostly he
worked on the mind, any mind, like a sapper. He went after
Quincy early on, very cleverly. He'd begun working up a
voice for Ravenus that was different from his past horror
voices, a strange, twittery, disembodied falsetto. Not so
much undead as unreal, sometimes barely intelligible. Took
me a while to figure out its source: Pol the parrot. He was
speaking in the mock voice of a bird that has been trained to
talk. Quick, rote bursts of cackle and caw, resembling human utterance, but, of course, meaningless to the bird itself.
In other words, throughout, M. favored the Raven over
Ravenus, to quite startling effect on film, especially when he
slips into pure ravenese in his passion for Lenore. On set,
however, the one who was most startled by that voice was
Quincy. M. had little enough to say to him, but whatever he
did say, he trilled at Quincy in this bird-like gurgle. Excuse:
working up his role, but I noticed he didn't "rehearse" that
voice with anybody else except Quincy. And I could tell it
gave Quincy the real "willies" this time, infuriated him, but
also left him cowed. Because what none of us knew immediately—only M. had it spotted: Quincy is an ornithophobe,
just plain shit scared of birds.

With Hazel, he was—true significance to be gone into,

below—kind of the Raven of the Lord. Victorian father figure. Crazy. Full of little preachments, vicarish and finicky.
"Tuck up your skirt a little more. Under you. That's the
girl," he'd cluck at her while she was lying, déshabillé, in
her coffin, under swirls of gangrenous green candlelight.
This was the abduction scene, from the Great Hall. Her
"skirt," of course, was the lower windings of a dimity
shroud. And what does he do after she tries to make herself
modest, settles demurely into chaste corpsehood, ready for
take? He lunges into the coffin, rips at her grave clothes, his
digits like scythes, lofts her out of there with one long boob
flying, naked as a goat's udder. But high enough: angled just
right, so that the boob whips past camera, the same dead-
green lighting, with the nipple just over the other side of the
rise, so to speak. You know it's there, but can't actually see
it. Just like in *King Kong,* so Terry still has his family picture. On that same swing round, M. also grabbed a taper.
Terrific lighting effect, blue-blue, but also a complete surprise to Hazel, keeps her gaze fixed as M. rushes her out of
the hall, down the dungeon steps. "Gracefully now, gracefully," he whispered to her. Still that boob. It's going like a
churn. M. has that action hidden from camera, but she can't
be sure, and she's concentrating on the candle, on trying to
stay decent, keep pectoral control, gives her this perfect
tranced-out expression. Young too, virginal even, because
M. is muttering at her like a prelate. "The body is the soul's
raiment. Let us wear it righteously that it may show the
humility of the inner spirit." I don't mean she believed a
word he was saying, but it kept her wide-eyed, hence, inno-
cent-seeming. Terry was furious. "Simon," he yelled, since,
again for economy, there was no audio, "shut your goddamn
dirty mouth!" But M. had still another touch to add. As he
came around the last turning into his dungeon boudoir, he
lowered Hazel's head, swept her face past camera, and she
looked zong, wow, beatific: agony and ecstasy and eros, a

vision of Lenore loveliness. Until, right at the cut, she began yelling absolute bloody murder.

That taper: M. had dripped wax on her, one plash smack on the nipple. He was too honest to pretend it hadn't been deliberate. Instead, he hurried to help her peel the dripping free before it hardened. Regrets: "I'm sorry, my dear, afraid it may leave a blister." She was howling tears, everybody else was glowering at him, Terry swearing blue fumes, but, real truth: all in awe of him. He had them that wrung-out already, and it was only Wednesday.

They'd been through Monday's shooting, of course, which helped. A boon day, that one, for M., nothing he could have counted on, just happened, fortuitous. Worth going into in some detail, since it was the poor showing by the real ravens, not their fault, that put M. back in the film. Up to that point, Terry wanted the genuine bird, with M.'s voice-over, as much as possible, among other reasons, I'm certain, so he could keep M. contained. M. didn't object, biding his time. Besides he was fascinated with the ravens, huddled with them, studied them, imitated them, told them funny stories, one about a fag bald eagle, in their own dialect. There were two ravens. Rupert, who did the trick stuff, and a stand-in, nameless, for the rough stuff. This was the first "Nevermore!" scene, where the Raven flies into Scaperelli Castle, has words with the Baron. Quincy in a long, silver-on-black brocade tunic, just a tuck or two short of complete Helena-Rubinstein drag.

The ravenkeeper was a guy named Tarkas, a funny, little, fuzzy, whispering Greek with dirty nails and a big lick of glossy black hair. The two ravens would sit, each on a shoulder, and shine their beaks in his tarry curls. Beautiful birds. Dark, iridescent feathers, coal turning to diamond, and round, wigwag eyes, blinky-red, railroad signals. And size, real size. Also an angular, dignified bearing to the head and neck, sacerdotal. Easy to see how they get into legend, liter-

ature: strong minor roles. Cf., Dickens: the wandering Bar-
naby Rudge with a raven on his shoulder, his only companion in his haunted loneliness. Cf., the Tower of London:
ravens perched in the crumbling Norman stonework, three
shillings' keep per day, and if they ever leave, the Tower,
the Empire, night will fall. Night birds. Machiavels. Power,
policy, menace. Sleek lines. High, tapered heads, with those
great thrust beaks. Not just *aves*. Aircraft.

Part of the trouble, Monday. The first quick take Terry
wanted was a shot of the Raven landing on the bust, straight
E. A. Poe, nothing interpretive. It was a pretty standard
Caesar-looking bust, bald, a little flatter above the laurels
than most of the imperial line, cf. Suetonius, but still not
much of a landing strip. Tarkas brought Rupert in as low as
he could, tried to put him down right between the ears, but
every time, Rupert would either overshoot or stall out.
"He's gotta have room," Tarkas finally admitted. "He's not
a robin." So Terry said okay, the hell with it, fuck him, just
let him perch. Tarkas set Rupert up there—that name is all
wrong, from some cutesy TV commercial for birdseed,
where the parakeet is Pauline, and the canary is Casanova—
walked him right off his elbow onto the cranium, stroked
his feathers, cooed him down all calm. The shot looked
good. But Rupert couldn't hold it the nine or ten seconds
that M. was taking, maybe deliberately, to deliver his
line. Can't remember the exact words: shtick, shtick, shtick,
". . . never . . ." then several seconds of pregnant silence,
"mmmm . . ." M. never got to ". . . ooore!" Not Rupert's
fault, just couldn't keep his footing on that badly sloped Ro-
man forehead. He finally worked it out his own way—very
clever birds, ravens—hooked one talon over Caesar's nose,
the other around his ear. But Terry wasn't having it. "He
looks like an eyepatch. We'll take it from where he goes to
Quincy's sleeve."

That's when we found out how bad Quincy is about

birds. He kept a stiff, caked smile as Rupert came skimming over the chairtops toward him, but the minute those fine talons hooked into the brocade, tweaked at Quincy's flesh, the beads of sweat started. Rupert cocked a smart eye at him, stayed put until the first one damply fell. Zoom, right into camera—Terry used a clip of that as part of the arrow scene—and back home to Tarkas. Tarkas sent him winging back to Quincy, but Rupert took a very wide circle round, buzzed over Quincy's shoulder, down his sleeve, and home again to Tarkas. "He's wise to you," Tarkas whispered. "He's wise to you." Quincy, by now, was fighting total Alfred Hitchcock breakdown.

Elapsed time going nowhere: an invaluable hour, so Terry decided, spur of the one remaining moment, to have the stand-in raven tied to Quincy's wrist, so that there'd be a real raven at least somewhere in the picture. Tarkas got above a whisper, warned Terry. But the prop girl turned up six feet of packing twine, and Terry rashly ordered the bird and Quincy manacled together, like Tony Curtis and Sidney Poitier. And it was just as bad as Tarkas said it would be. The stand-in had an even more immediate nativist response to Quincy's clammy smile. He flapped off, squawking like a crow, snap to the end of the twine. A vicious yank. Then into a mad, trapped, tumbling gyre, zooming around Quincy like a one-cylinder model airplane. "Keep him off the ground!" Tarkas pleaded. "Off the ground!" Maybe that was just what Quincy wanted to hear. In any case, he raised his arm, hiked the roaring bird way up, whoop, over his head, and then hauled straight down, bash. Looked damned diabolical to me. Quincy Adams, bird-murderer. Only a couple of feathers, actually, luckily, but when a raven breaks a live feather, it bleeds like the bejeezus.

"Break," Terry made himself say. "We'll break." He had to, but how he hated to. Some first-aid folk came in to attend the injured bird, cut Quincy loose, and everybody started making stupid suggestions about rewrites. M. seemed the only unflappable one, off behind a stack of leaning flats, sitting bird-like in a busted wingback chair, chatting to Rupert. Terry was all over the set, pacing that vast, jerry-built expanse of initial expense. Out to the styrofoam crystal crypt, back to the Great Hall with its balsam timbers, down to slats-and-canvas dungeon walls. He prowled in agony, trying to think of some way to use precious studio time: dust settling on his clipboard, money turning to chaff in this empty, useless Hollywood barn. It is maybe the only time I could say I've ever seen him suffer.

He stopped himself in the dungeon boudoir. "Cobwebs!" he shouted, just to get something moving, I'm sure. "People are supposed to be dead in here. More cobwebs."

Silly: the place was already thick with them, but an old grip, looked like Charles Coburn, hurried forward with the cobweb-maker, looked like a hand-mixer with a big motor-boat propeller on it. Terry jostling him over to the sagging, canopied bed, back under the dungeon's low vault. "Do those pillows." They already looked tented, but so what? "Do them again." The propeller turned over, whirred to a zinging pitch, and spewed out these great flumes of gossamer, getting on Terry he was standing so close. He kept nudging the grip along, pushing him where he wanted the torrent of cobweb to fall. Like a spider with all its spinnets gone berserk, burying coign and crevice in a riot of dirty, silken dribblings. Disturbing: noisome. He kept bumping the grip, shoving him around, until I guess it's what they call a freak industrial accident.

The grip staggered back, that old Coburn hang-dog look still heavy in his face. The cobweb-maker was grinding around on the dungeon floor, taking crazy kicks, splinters, throwing more web, but reddened web. The grip had his hand up in front of his face, almost like he was trying to count on it.

"First aid!" Terry shouted. "Over here! Chop, chop!"

The emergency folk came hustling through, their second call. Terry was trying to get something, his neck scarf, over the grip's hand, and the grip had this terrible look of curiosity, kept asking, "Where is it? Look, will you? Where is it? You gotta find it for me."

That was the awful thing. Didn't seem to be around anywhere. People started searching, hard, but that was the nutty thing: not high enough. It was up in the webbing. Way up, caught. I didn't see it. Nobody else spotted it either, except Rupert. They're meat-eaters, ravens.

Just nobody noticed. Tarkas was still so busy with the stand-in, cooing him down, trying to keep him from having a heart attack—another problem with ravens—that even he must've forgotten about Rupert. Then all that confusion: rushing the grip off the set, to the hospital, yank the plug on the cobweb-maker, laying a fünf-hundred down on its side to light the floor, still trying to find it in the blaze . . . another grip even swept under the bed for it once or twice. So right over our heads: flew in, picked it out of the webbing, got shooed off. I'm sure somebody said, "Get that goddamn crow out of here!" But did anybody really look? Not me. I still wouldn't know, except I happened to peek over at M., always keeping tabs, and saw *he* had his eye on Rupert.

That's when I really started keeping tabs, on that zoo scene M. played back there behind those flats, away from the confusion. The Return to the Aviary: Rupert came hovering in, this thing in his beak, still with strings of webbing on it, and perched. M. tucked himself deeper into the wingback, blinked up at Rupert, warbled. The raven birdlegged across the bow of the wingback, I moved closer, M. blinked and warbled. That's what I mean by a performance. M. had his eyes going, blink-red, blink-red, and his head bobbing . . . no, not bobbing: nicking up and down, bird-style, and his bird-boned body, under that caftan, preening for

Rupert. Then he let his head drop back, way far back, so that he was only staring up out of one eye. A real con eye, a single fleck of bird-intelligence flicking on and off, on and off, like a ticking sliver of broken reflector glass. Then, very quietly, M. said something. Way back in his throat, a little bead of grackle sound, deep, like a seed crumbling in his gizzard.

The raven cocked his head to meet M.'s con eye. Then he dipped down with his beak, and dropped that damn finger right into M.'s lap. It was the little finger. M. instantly popped it into his Mike-Todd purse, cried something low in ravenese, and as far as I can find out, didn't let a soul know he had the damn thing until he went on the *Tonight Show*.

S o FAR, so good, but suspect I'm too fiction-minded. Things just don't happen that artful, climactic, *Lights-Out!* way. Am living to regret more and more all the yammer I spooned out at Breadloaf, like potted cheese: "Yes, I use fictional techniques sometimes. In order to revivify dead facts." Looking back over carbon of article on M., am appalled at how far beyond (or how short of?) the facts I reached to Delineate My Central Character, a figmentary creature-hero dubbed, in the zippy words of my tentative title, "Moro Man!" Lord, lord. And besides, what exactly did I mean, up there at the lectern, by a dead fact brought back to life? Some kind of necromancy? There's a thought. Develop further: pray, what is journalism, sirrah, but tampering daily with the Unknown? Argal, beware thy immortal flame. Let the facts speak for themselves, aye, but Do Not Dig Them Up. To traffick in information that lies buried in closed files, sealed letters, locked hearts, faulty memories, the *Congressional Record*, other mortuaria is to risk unhallowed commerce with the Newsworthy One himself. . . . Anyhow, nowhere in the article does that finger appear, even though I had that bit way ahead of TV. Admission: too ghoulish to fit my preconceptions, therefore withheld; Harold has me cold. But even in the above reconstruction of events, utterly honest-Injun, am I trying now to make too much of the incident, too telling, too garish a scene? Who is going to believe that Simon Moro is Dr. Dolittle? Do even I? The raven dropped meat in his lap, period. From here on out, only what's down in my notebooks. (Even apropos H.R.? Any notes there?) Immediately hereafter, the remaining facts, and opinions—"The fact of somebody else's opinion is still a fact," as I told them at Breadloaf, "whether the opinion has merit or not."—gathered during long afternoon interview at Portuguese Bend, California. M. on M.

First, the locale: far down along the coast, another slide area, affluent cliffs slipping from time to time sumptuously into the Pacific Ocean. But M.'s house still well back, safely tucked among citrus and cypress, a Tuscan hacienda. Dark Spanish interior to fit somebody's idea of early California, sparkling palazzo exterior to suit somebody's memory of sunny Italy: now a rental. "He was a banker," M. explained. "Milanese, not Sicilian." Until the Crash, Signore loaned large sums to the studios, and after, still kept some penurious ties by letting out bits and pieces of the property for location shots. Old Europe: Iberia inside, Italia outside. And more. Up that cliff ran the earliest rickety version of the Thirty-nine Steps. You want the foggy John-Buchan English seacoast, we got the foggy John-Buchan English seacoast. And out along its verges rolled the downs that lay beyond both Wuthering Heights and Manderley, their windswept, heathery sod long since gone slump into the sea. And back in the formal French garden, now brown of yew, blasted of bloom, some Napoleon or other nearly brushed shoulders with a figure not unlike the Scarlet Pimpernel. M. took me over all the points of interest—*Home and Gardens* plus *Photoplay*—then out along the cliff's marge to where a few thin Ionian columns lay on their fluted sides, a half cord of marble stacked and left to rot. I asked him what movie they were from.

"No movie. He was planning a gazebo out here for himself. A little Greek temple. But he never got it put up. So, you understand, instant archaeology. The glory that was Greece, the grandeur that was RKO. Your Mr. Poe again. I very much like this spot. Sounion, only purer. These pillars never stood. Therefore they never fell. They lie here in a pristine state of ruin."

That was his mood. He sat down on the butt end of a column, brooded out to sea, like a lank old man on a log, whittling something down to a fine point: maybe failure.

"I suppose we all fizzled, my—what shall I call us?—my generation of monsters. Even those who were never too serious. Lugosi, for one. He had the best role. Something very priestly, eucharistic about a straight, out-and-out vampire. Bela had the mannerisms, the Transylvanian suavity, the cape work, all that, but I don't think he ever really felt the urges. I worked with him once. *Gila Man Meets Dracula.* You won't have seen it. Even you. Never released. That bad. Bela never did know much English, always learned his lines phonetically. Gave him the right voice, like an echo in a crypt, and that queer emphasis, but I knew somewhere in the back of his drugged Hungarian brain, he was always asking, 'Vot does in hell dis mean?' In the eighth reel, we have this terrific fight. My venom, his canines. But it was really two losers losing. The Opium-Eater versus the Pill-Head. You know what he did, really, when he went for my throat? Kissed me. Something very maternal about Bela. At heart he was more a witch than a vampire. I always thought the part for him was Medea, carving up the kiddies, weeping away, dropping tears and little toes into the wine-dark sea.

"Oh, we frightened people, my generation, but it was only a scare and a giggle, nothing lasting. Terry knows that, wants that pop-top horror. Maybe I should too. I know it works, but that is not enough for me now. If it ever was. You understand what I mean by the bus effect?"

Sure I did: Val Lewton, *The Cat People* (1942). Simone Simon is maybe a black panther stalking Jane Randolph through Central Park. Suddenly this loud screech-hiss, terrifyingly animalistic, but it's only the bus pulling up to the curb, springing open its doors to offer public refuge. Wow, wow: famous bit of film-editing by Mark Robson.

"Sure I do."

"No you don't. You just think you do," M. snapped. "Not Lewton. Exactly what I don't mean. That was empty trickery. This is years before. Before even the real silents. A Frenchman, back in the Nineties. George Méliès, his name was. Look him up sometime. He was shooting a crowd scene, the traffic in front of the Paris Opera. Horse-drawn, but bad even then. What they once called an omnibus goes by. Full of people. His camera jams for a few seconds. Starts up again, more horse-drawn traffic. Nothing, a slight interruption, but when he screens his film, he is astonished to see the bus go by, and then, jerk, suddenly turn into a hearse. That's what *I* mean by the bus effect. The shock is not a relief, a sleazy bit of business for the audience's nervous sake. The shock is a shock. Even a moral, always the greatest shock. That they don't do any more. But it is still there to be done. Even in this film. Or don't you see what's really wrong with this film yet?"

"Terry's rat work, you said."

"It's more than that."

"You tell me."

"His direction is amoral."

"So?"

"There's a rule you better learn. Perversion abhors a moral vacuum."

"So, still?"

"That's how Quincy's able to move in. He's turning the picture queer."

"I don't see that at all."

"Wait a while. These things are very subtle, and very long drawn out. It's all in how he plays to Hazel. He's trying to turn her into an ice sculpture. And the script's helping there. All that arctic-fartic business. I'd like to meet this Beau Fletcher sometime. If Quincy can freeze her out, he can suck himself in. Then the whole film comes out a fag vision of society's mad, inquisitional persecution of male purity. Homo-medievalism. Remember, he ends up lancing *me.*"

"Simon, this is supposed to be a family picture."

"That's what *I'm* trying to make it. Hazel's the key. She's got to be pulled in erotically. Give her a snowy exterior, all right, but internally she's got to boil with real witch passion. She can't just be back and forth, a cunt on the shuttle. Underneath she's got to be ready to roll over in the fires of hell for me."

Actually I was impressed, one better than *Rosemary's Baby*, but I only said, "Hazel Rio?"

"You are not kind to that poor girl."

"Viveca Lindfors, maybe. A younger Judith Anderson, okay. But Hazel Rio?"

M. sniffed, off to sea. "At least you see how it could be played."

"If she had everything, including your grin."

Then he digressed into a long, involved explanation of the psycho-mechanics of his famous Ghoulgantuan grin: wasn't the denture alone, depended upon the surrounding facial composition, adapted in part from Edvard Munch's *The Shriek* (1895), trenchant acting also needed to make grin "a visual sound," but only possible to "hear it" in black-and-white, inaudible in Technicolor. Can't reconstruct the whole argument—this wasn't Truffaut talking to Alf Hitchcock—but it gave me an opening for a moot question. What did *he* really think was truly horrible?

"I've said, I've said. You should know if you don't already how much thought I gave to that when I first came here," he answered slyly, resourcefully. "After all, this was America, not Nazi Germany. At the time. A different horror. I studied all that was being done in Hollywood. I concluded that the most terrifying was the giant rodent."

"Giant what?"

"Mickey. And his evil dam, Minerva. I know, I know. You probably think, ha ha, not so frightening, but how would you really like to confront a living, five-foot-eight-or-nine-inch mouse, with every normal human drive?"

The hell with it, I told myself, let him ramble.

"You can say that Walt Disney's creatures were very

primitive. Like cave drawings. But then what about the Chase and Sanborn talking boy sarcophagus?"

"The what?"

"Mostly on radio, Sunday evenings, but it also made some movies. You must have seen it. A small wooden coffin, crudely shaped like a little man with a monocle, nothing inside, hollow. A Swedish sorcerer named Edvard Bergen put the sarcophagus on his knee, made it talk. It had a succubus inside."

I suggested to him I was serious.

"So am I. Finally what I concluded, that the most horrible of all was the three-hundred-pound flesh-and-blood female werewolf."

I refused to ask.

"In broad daylight, at high noon every day, she would begin to bay across the land. 'When the Mooonnn Comes Over the Mountain . . .' Her human name was Kate Smith."

There was more of this deliberate malarkey—*pensées* toward Ghoulgantua, M. claimed—none of which I included in the article, settled instead for his one serious answer. "All right. Once again I go along with your Mr. Poe. What's the most horrible thing, at least for an American, is premature burial. Think yourself what it would be like, up there under the green hillside, to wake up smelling moist earth, or your own lead seal. Terrifying. But for you Americans, the fear is not just below ground. It is also above ground. 'Let me out, please, oh please, I can hear your footsteps across my heart, please let me out!' Your Mr. Poe does not exaggerate. Everybody goes around afraid that somebody near and dear wants secretly to inter him alive. Every split-level in the country is as cracked as the House of Usher." Only used part of that quote, dropped everything after ". . . your own lead seal. Terrifying." Restore it altogether? Maybe, if I also include, as balanced reporting, what M. had to say about the Viennese, to scotch any charge of anti-American bias, i.e., so as not to be caught out, buried too soon myself by somebody—Harold?—"corpsed," as St. Samuel à Beckett would say.

How did we get onto the "Mayerling drama"? I guess because M. mentioned there had once been talk of some studio's turning his hacienda into Crown Prince Rudolf's little hunting lodge out in the Wienerwald. But it would be hard to Biedermier that place. Anyhow, M. on the Crown Prince's shooting of his seventeen-year-old mistress, Mary Vetsera, then himself: "Ponder this tragedy. Think of yourself as *echt*-Viennese, as the Emperor Franz Josef himself. What do you privately wonder in the depths of your Hapsburgian soul? I will tell you. You wonder, as does all *Wien*, did he screw her before, during, or after he shot her? And that is what I mean by a baroque question."

Other "baroque questions" M. and I pondered that afternoon, and later over dinner: were the Invisible Man's excreta—Claude Rains, 1933—also invisible? I said yes, but M. argued for opalescence, rainbow hues. Or, what is the exact degree of a man's guilt who has a *fiasco* during an assay at incest with a consenting daughter?

"That may have happened to me once," M. said, very seriously.

"*May* have?"

"My paternity was highly questionable."

"Oh."

"Largely her mother's claim. Or delusion. I have my doubts."

"I asked you before if you had any children."

"Please. Entirely a private matter."

"But this . . ."

"This only happened once."

"Isn't once enough?"

He grinned. "Perhaps you misconstrue me. The fiasco

only happened once. Our relationship has since flourished."

"What relationship? Who?"

But he was off on another baroque foray, this one a consideration of Bert Brecht's parable for his own political quandary: if you have only one dose of penicillin for two people horribly afflicted with V.D., one an old lecher (the West), the other a pregnant prostitute (East Germany), to whom do you give the shot? "Brecht felt he had to dose Walter Ulbricht's pregnant prostitute, in hopes of the child, you see. What he didn't realize then was how allergic she was to penicillin. But don't think he chose that easily either. He liked a little lechery himself. Peter and I—Peter Lorre— a shame he isn't still alive to talk to you about Brecht—we almost had to push B.B. to go one way or the other. Brecht went down to Washington to testify, told them 'No, no, no, no, no, never!' had he tried to join the Party, came right back to New York, told us he would have to flee, but would go by boat. Escaping with all his manuscripts on microfilm, but still there is time for a European cruise! We put him on a plane for Paris that night. That is really what the Committee had against me. If you like baroque questions, theirs were rococo. Was I now, or had I ever been, involved in black-market operations with Bertolt Brecht, smuggling penicillin into East Berlin?"

Must confess I'm fascinated by baroque questions, especially this one, which M. put to me over Cognac later that evening: what would be the proper Christian attitude to take toward a Bible bound in human skin?

"I used one in that picture I did in Germany," he went on.

"After the war?"

"Yes."

"Will you talk about that film?"

"I'll say this much. It had a religious dimension."

"Did it?"

"My atrocities paralleled the sufferings of the saints. That Bible was a tribute to St. Bartholomew."

"Go on."

"I think that's enough for you."

Tantalizing. Sufficient to indicate a turn of mind, yet reveal no inner thoughts. Mind admittedly not quite that of my forthright, fad-famous "Moro Man," but still integral, seized of the macabre as a value system: a clue to integrity. "We judge the weird by the normal—normally—yes, I am twisting that word—because I want us, instead, to judge weirdly. That is really why I play monsters. I believe we can only tell if we are 'normal,' that is, actually human, by whether we are really any *better* than monsters. My armless strangler-clown, my robot, my poor Hans, my Ghoulgantua —my favorites, I admit—they were all of them soundings of this proposition. Reified. Take Gonfried, my robot. What did we do in its fabrication? Gave it artificial hungers without any biological function. So what happens? Very quickly my tin manhood becomes uncontrollable. A sex-crazed, flesh-tearing, bloody marauder. All that stops me is a chance jolt that loosens my thirst screw. I sluice down gallons of water, but gag, rust out inside. Flake apart, crumple. While still ravaged by these purposeless appetites. Horrible, but now, understand, are you and I—in these prophylactic times—are we really in any better shape? Or are we Gonfried? That is the point. I remember when the decency people began attacking horror films for causing public paranoia. I used to tell reporters, 'You think we have Frankenstein, Dracula, Wolfman for our nightmares, delusions? You are wrong. It is *they* who have *us*.' "

Made me wish I could see *Manmade Man*, but by now that film, fallen down some dark studio crevice, has surely turned into a jelly of silver nitrate.

M., another variation on this theme: "I am sorry to keep harping on your Mr. Poe, but he understood so well how the weird underpins the normal. Do you know his story 'Berenice'? The madman who falls in love with his mistress's teeth, rips them all out of her corpse's mouth to keep in a small box on his desk? A ludicrous situation—think how . . . who is that man?—Terry Southern—would treat it, ruin it. But your Mr. Poe has written a masterpiece. He knows he is dealing with a true passion. He endows his madman with reason, knowledge of his circumstances, sorrow, but nothing can save him. I have always wanted to play that madman. Because it is truly, horribly, a love story. Love is never normal. It is always aberrant. In our hearts, we do not embrace. We mutilate. We fall in love with a pair of pretty eyes, or sparkling teeth, or twinkling toes, or perhaps a delicate little finger. . . ."

It hung there a moment, that phantom hint, secretly crooking at me for more attention. Should I have made my own baroque inquiries then? Failed to. Because—or at least I say now—M. rushed off into far more distracting observations.

"That, as I say, is what I must work up with Hazel. The Raven's love for Lenore has to be romantic as well as horrific. And she must respond. Or what is it but a bite in the neck?"

"Been pretty . . . indelicate so far."

"You think so?"

"Pedophilia bordering on religious mania, with a little sadism—that trick with the candle—thrown in."

"That has all gone to assist Hazel."

"Of course."

"She is a dear, sweet girl, but there are, as you hint, difficulties. For one thing, she is almost forty."

"Kid me not."

"She is also a thoroughly experienced, even jaded sexual being. Quincy just makes her laugh. To keep from laughing, she turns cold. And that helps Quincy all the more. I have to bring her youth back."

"How do you do that?"

"Not even her youth. Almost her childhood."

"What do you know about her childhood?"

But he would say no more then, except "an old family friend, hope we will be working together as much in the future as we have in the past" crap.

Earlier, I had tried to ask him about somebody else's childhood, with even less success. Rudolph Eckmann's.

He'd run his right thumb down a few feet of fluted column groove, picking up the rotted-out marble dust, like lime. "You know about Rudi, do you?"

"No great secret."

"From Horst?"

"From old cast lists."

"*Ah so.*" He brushed his thumb once across each cheek, chalking blotches that hollowed out his beaky face even more. "I hardly remember Rudi myself. Except as hungry." And he did look a startlingly sallow famine figure. "I suppose he was once a child."

"Where?"

"Shall we say Vienna?"

"That would fit," I nudged him along.

"I seem to remember him . . ."—all very Maeterlinck-y and *Bluebird*-ish now—"to remember him spitting."

"At what?"

"A gas lamp. High above his head. Lighting a yellow corner of Sievering. He must spit straight up, and through a narrow opening in the rim. He jumps to give himself more power, a closer target. After a peak effort, the flame sizzles. Smacks out. Dark."

"Rudi sounds very determined."

"His father is the lamplighter."

"Of course."

"But Rudi keeps his mother's street always dark."

"He loves his mother?"

"As much as he loves anyone. She is a waitress at Demel's. It must have all been very nice, once. Every Sunday she marched to mass at St. Stephen's with the other waitresses, in her high black boots. Rudi remembers when she tucked him in at night, there was always a little sugar in the bed afterwards."

"Then what was the problem?"

"Rudi did not, I think, care to be a *piccolo*. Rudi could not see himself working up from breadsticks to a white napkin over his sleeve."

This Rudi business was getting silly. "Okay, but what made him want to be an actor?"

"I'm not sure Rudi ever did. That was more Simon. Though Rudi may have had a small part, one time, in a local Oberammergau."

"King Herod?"

"That would suit him."

"Then what? The eight pussycats?"

"No. Before that, I think Rudi would have gone off to war. He was wounded perhaps, by his own grenade, suffered partial loss of memory. Or perhaps at Verdun, seeing the French troops march into the German machine-gun fire, deliberately bleating like lambs, he deserted. Best not to say which way it was. Either way, he came back Simon Moro." In article, used grenade version: hedging?

"You were still calling yourself Eckmann from time to time."

"I have no such memory."

"Gonfried the Robot was played by Rudolph Eckmann. Nineteen twenty-seven."

"You make an understandable mistake. The American credits are confused. Perhaps you can now clear them up. Only Simon Moro, of course, could have played Gonfried."

Saw his point, but still insisted, "Horst knew you as Rudi."

M. winked. "A name I probably gave him. You don't think I wanted him to know who I really was? I can only regret he ever found out."

I could have brought up his HUAC listing—"Rudolph Eckmann, alias 'Simon Moro'"—but by now, the charade has its own momentum. "So you have buried Rudi that deep?"

"He is very dim in my mind. A little street urchin in dirty *Lederhosen* . . . suddenly huddling in a German trench. Perhaps the shrapnel."

"Perhaps."

"Rudi has utterly disappeared. I much prefer my old studio biography."

"I don't need that from you."

"But I need it for myself. You're not interested in the Moro genealogy?"

"Come off it."

"We go way back."

"As far back as some Hollywood hack could take you."

"I gave the facts to Robert Benchley, and he—"

"You're wasting my time, and yours."

"Actually, we Moros come of an ancient line of cemetery-keepers."

"So you knew death from birth, right?" Maybe a little disdain, I figured, would turn him off.

"I was the one who grazed the sheep."

"What sheep?"

"The ones that kept the grass down on the graves."

"Moro ingenuity."

"Though my mother objected, said it was like letting them eat the dead. She used to go through the cemetery herself with a scythe. Clanging against the tombstones. Injuring the sheep. She was a little mad."

None of this, nor any of what follows—what sly, familial comic was M. trying to imitate, Jean Shepherd?—did I include in the article. Obviously. But I think it's informative to see how M.'s tale-spinning builds on itself here, culminating in an emotional coda that does, I suspect, express certain psychological truths. A useful fantasy, a self-mocking memory print.

"And Simon's father?" I asked superciliously.

A longish, saddish face. "Simon's father was born a deaf-mute."

"It happens."

"So, in fact, was his younger brother. Also, very nearly a dwarf. Simon learned much of his art very early by having to act out whatever he wanted to say to the two of them. All the mother would do is yell louder. She favored his older brother, in any case."

"Who was born normal?"

"But money-mad. Even when he was a tyke, he was out after his own corpses to embalm. Down in the storm cellar."

"And how was it that Simon Moro managed to escape this deadening existence?"

"Let's see." Imaginatively stymied, or pretending to struggle to remember? "Simon's father died when he was fifteen, his mother a little over a year later. They lie side by side in the cemetery. His older brother took over the family. His cruelty brought Simon and his younger brother closer together. The younger brother's name—curiously enough—was Rudy."

"Better keep your stories straight."

"I am. This Rudy was with a 'y.' The other Rudi is Rudi with an 'i.'"

"Crapola."

"Rudy was the only one Simon felt he would really be leaving behind. Recruiters for a sort of circus came through town. During Oktoberfest."

"Oktoberfest."

"Every year. For this one, Simon taught his brother to play a simple patriotic *Vaterland* tune on the piano. Their father used to play the piano despite his handicaps, and Simon's mother used to sing and dance under the pines around all the wrong notes. Simon did the same for Rudy, stomping out the martial beat, drowning out the discords. The recruiters for the circus heard them, and made an approach to the older brother. He put it up to Rudy and Simon. There wasn't enough in the cemetery, he said, to support them all. So either Rudy went as a freak, or Simon went as a clown. I couldn't let that happen to my little brother. So I went. Simon Moro was first seen in public as a clown, dancing among firecrackers, and snapping off long strings of his own."

"What circus?"

"It played all of Europe from 1914 until 1918."

Very clever. Very, very clever.

"So everything dovetails," I said.

He nodded. "But lately I feel a great desire to return home."

"To Vienna?"

But he wasn't going to be caught out. "To my roots. Vampires show a certain wisdom, carrying a little of their own earth with them wherever they go. We all need that."

"Of course."

"I'm sixty-eight. I guess you know. As old as the century." He snickered. "My companion for life, sure to outlive me. I'm losing my powers."

"Nonsense."

"No. It's the sad truth. I should have no trouble twisting this schlock picture to my own uses. But I find the twists come very hard. I need a rest, a trip home."

"What would you do?"

He sighed, greatly, off to sea. "I'd go see Rudy. If he's still alive. . . ." Uncanny schizoid memory ties. "He never considered himself strange. No speech, no hearing, but that was like our father. All that ever really worried him was being shorter than other people. He hoped he would someday grow. I want to go back, look him slowly up and down, and then say, as straight as I can, how much he has grown in the last fifty years. Really grown. Even if he has shrunk some."

Simple insight: M. was talking about himself. In a very complicated way. Rudi who'd created Simon who'd re-created Rudy. Who was the decrepit little unhappy monster-child soul still skulking down there inside him somewhere. Stunted, deformed, locked both ways into silence, its feet forever unable to reach the pedals. Un-Moro-Man. Must talk more about him when I revise article. Personal mythology is psychic truth, even when facts lie elsewhere, and M. unwilling, as he said, "even to mention the hemisphere" from which the Moros originally come.

For as he also said, "You can then . . ." hesitating a sad smile, dropping his eyes, as if much in the face of the Humble Truth, ". . . believe what I say?"

And as I said, "I believe you. Absolutely." Making, of course, as per above, allowances.

MAYBE M. hadn't searched out all his twists yet, but during the next day's rushes, I saw scenes that were pretty damn contortionistic. Takes from the dungeon-boudoir seduction sequence, that "unseemly, almost erotic ritual that ends with his bending over her full, pulsing throat." Doubt if Beau Fletcher ever had his words made quite such searing flesh before. No, wait; not words made flesh; words made carrion. That's how M. played it. Erotic-horrific, but butcher-block and funky. Ambiguous whether he is biting into a live Lenore or a dead Lenore. Long time before he bit into her at all. First he twitted at her in raven-ese. Obscenely this time, I'm certain, has that lubricious *timbre*, though no intelligible utterance passes his charred lips. Fantastic make-up for this scene: total blackface, even his tongue, the snaggled teeth like burnt stumps in a mouthful of wet soot. Then he edges—struts, really—along her curd-white body, blinking a redder and redder eye, that single bird eye again, until it fixes on her columnar—but cold or warm?—throat. M. goes for the obsession here. Clear enough from the rushes, still half-clear even after Terry's hack editing—or rather his producer's—that Ravenus has fallen stark in love with Lenore's throat. Cf. above, M. on Romantic Aberrancy. But still the Raven has all the horror action. A shock twist because Lugosi, Christopher Lee *et al.* always do a Valentino on the vampire kiss: bloody, but never really gory, only gooey. Not M. He hovers over that throat, fixated, then, in a quick, gawky shock move, pecks at it. Viciously. His black tongue comes away stiff, flecked with a gout of blood. He pecks again, harder, jarring Lenore's head violently aside. More blood on the tongue. A taste in the sooty mouth. Two, three more vicious pecks, and then M. rips at the throat, not like Cary Grant, but like a real raven, tearing out a feast.

Left intact, it would have been a real shocker. Even Hazel, sitting next to me in the tiny, wooden balcony, stopped giggling at herself on screen. She'd been relief-giggling—that insipid reaction Terry always plays for—but this dried up with M.'s first peck, became a tremble I could feel through the loose arm rest.

"What's he trying to do to me?"

"We'll fix," Terry assured her, from two rows back.

"Sure, sweetie-poo, you fix-fix. But what's he trying to do to me?"

"Your friend. Not mine."

"I'm all throat."

"We'll take out the wrinkles."

Touché: her age did show in her throat, badly, signs of an incipient wattle. Odd because nothing else had slackened. (As I well know?) Her body youthful, bloomful, if a trifle ripely overstrained from surgical salvage. She reached one hand behind her neck, pinched the skin tight, began massaging her stretched gorge with an open palm.

"He was supposed to *hide* my throat."

"Worry not. Look at yourself next."

The rushes had gone on ahead, telescoping the story, into the last bed-chamber scene. On screen, Quincy bustled across to the canopied bed, whipped aside the double curtains—far too evenly for the tension of the moment—and stared down . . . no, *pas avec angoisse, mais* at least with avid curiosity. Cut to standard medical-school skeleton, lying on rumpled bed. A few yards of old mosquito netting girdled around pelvis and femurs, and a little facial putty for femininity on the frontal skull. The effect was very stale *Psycho,* without even that bare bulb winking the hollow eyesockets. Terry's trite camera then zoomed down into the rib cage to pick up the pendant silver arrowhead, hanging, right from Woolworth's, where Lenore's heart had once thumpily pumped. We could all go back to giggling again.

"Just imagine being that old," Hazel said in wonderment.

"No wrinkles."

"No fuckles either." She stopped strumming her neck. "I'm really very angry with Simon, Terry."

"So solly to hear."

"A girl's bristol is one thing, but her throat is another."

"Tell the press."

A little bit of the old Talloolah: that's what she was trying to pull off here. But pretty hard to do Tallooolah on Penny Singleton's brain power. That's who she really reminded me of: a bitchy Blondie, divorced long ago from Dagwood, whom she'd probably married when she was fourteen. "Only woman I ever knew," Quincy got off another good one about her, "who baby-talks dirty."

"You haven't interviewed me yet," she accused me.

"No."

"When?"

"And in depth," Terry winked.

"I want you to know," she said, absolutely flat, "I love Simon."

"Let me get that down."

"A dear, sweet man."

"Anything else?"

She thought. "It's work-work to keep up with him. He can be very driving sometimes, but also very feeling. He's been like a father to me."

"Helps take years off your age."

Terry laughed knowingly, and she cooed at me, without the slightest change in tone, "Prick."

"Sorry."

"Don't give it another thought." She waved her fingers in a coy fan: bye-bye. "Must run-run. He's expecting me."

"To do what?" said Terry.

"Outside the studio, my life is my own. Prick." She called him that as indifferently, as sweetly as she had me.

"Well, give him our best. While doing yours."

"As ever-ever."

Instead of going out on her own side, she crawled across me. Before I could get up, she whispered, "Hands off my bod."

I tried to give her room, but she stayed teasingly straddled there.

"You're on *my* bod," I insisted.

"Sorry, prick." She smiled, and slipped away in the dark. It was like an endearment.

"Loverly talk," I mumbled.

"Loverly," Terry laughed.

"Anything between them?"

"Hard to say. I thought I introduced them."

"Not so?"

"Simon was down in my office on Sunset. Hazel barges in about something, I forget what, maybe just because she knew Simon was there."

"She call him prick too?"

"Doesn't say a word, just hangs. Nor does Simon. Funny vibes. So I start to introduce them. Simon gets up, stiff, all Austrian, gentleman of the old school."

"Like he treats her on set."

"Exactly. Takes her hand, starts to bend down over it. Only halfway there, he lunges and bites her right in the tit."

"*Charmant.*"

"Well, in a way, it was. He didn't bite her that hard. Play-ful."

"What did she do?"

"Wriggled."

"Away?"

"No. Just wriggled." Terry considered. "Like she wanted to please."

"What did Simon do?"

"Showed distaste." Terry considered again. "But *familiar* distaste. Like, how many times had he told her not to do that? Tell you. I know she blows. She does indeed love to blow."

"I see."

"But in this case, him three times a night or only his nose for him when it's runny, I honestly couldn't tell you."

"No way to find out."

"Ask."

"Sure."

Terry shouted a few instructions back to the projection room, mainly cuts to mark in M.'s performance, got the lights turned up. He looked tired, cranky, like a kid who'd been kept indoors all afternoon.

"Still too damn nude."

"Really?"

"Horror's not that far along yet. I ask you. You seen any *Danish* horror films?"

"Can't say I have."

"My point. Someday maybe we let the vampire go right for the old snatch, but that is not where we're at now."

"Simon is."

"Spare me Simon."

"And leave you Quincy?"

"The real trouble is fifteen days is too long."

"You're on schedule."

"Too much time for everybody to screw around, try to act. Especially Simon."

"You don't want acting?"

"I want action."

"I see."

"There's a real difference. One stops you dead. The other keeps you humping along. And the American family audience wants to hump along." He squeaked his sneaker. "Ten days would've been better."

"But not five."

He nodded at me, appreciatively. "No. My five-day days

are over." Made it sound like he'd lost his wind, or had a bad stitch in his side. "You ever see *Sea Beast?*"

1962. Giant sponge ravages Malibu coast. Old skindiver (Tab Hunter?), turned coward after "a revery of the deep," regains courage, kills beast with underwater acetylene torch, finds treasure, rescues admiral's daughter (?).

"Can't remember who the girl was," I said.

"Hazel Rio."

"Of course."

"We were out on location only two days. Mostly underwater, so no lighting problems. Another day in the studio. One more day in the lab, shooting the sponge. Make it four. Four days, sixty thousand dollars, everything right there in the can." One thing to be said for Terry: even though he may not be right up there with the more talked-about cinéastes, but cf. Clouzot's recent tribute in *Cahiers du Cinéma*, he still has most of the back-lot dollar records, certainly one kind of *cinéma vérité*. In, to date, some sixty-odd films, he has never gone a penny over budget, never run a day behind schedule, never been an alpha wave off on any audience profile. Judith Crist can carp that his pictures "go in one eye and right out the other," but there is at least some argument that while you're waiting around for Stanley Kubrick to finish *2001*, somebody's got to keep the drive-ins open. That is what was worrying, even infuriating Terry about M., that M. was going to go and do something memorable that couldn't be repaired, ruin "what little there is left of what we used to call Hollywood."

I sound sympathetic.

"So why did you sign him?" I asked.

"You get bigger out here, you take people as-big. On my way up, his way down, we hit."

Just damned, dirty, Heraclitean luck.

"You getting any kind of a story?" he muttered.

"Some kind."

"Tell you. There *is* a hell of a story to be done about Moro. Only you couldn't print it."

At Breadloaf, I referred to this kind of statement as "the prelude to disclosure," and listed various motivations: vengeance, envy, insideritis, p.r. guilt, an appetite for large bites of back, et cetera. But with Terry, while it was certainly all these to some degree, it was basically still promotion. More build-up for the villain in his picture, even at this lowest level of scurrilous whisper. However, I'm the one who asked, "How come?"

"Too incriminating."

"How so?"

"That film he did right after the war? In East Germany?"

"West Berlin."

"Who knows? But it's about the Nazi medical experiments in concentration camps."

"He won't say what it was about."

"This isn't from him. I got it on excellent authority that it's about stuff like how long it takes to freeze a man to death. In a control tank. All that William-F.-Shirer-*Third-Reich* nasty shit."

"All right."

"Not all right. The point is, he's for it."

"What d'you mean, for it?"

"Pro, not con. He plays the chief Nazi vivisectionist. The fucking hero."

"Crapola."

"True."

"How can anybody say for sure? He never finished the film, and he's intensely anti-Nazi."

"You ever seen Simon play for anything but the hero? That's what it is with his monster bit."

Had a point there.

"It's a complicated plot. My opinion, too complicated. This Nazi doctor is really a Red. He sees a chance—since

everybody thinks he's a foul Hitlerite—a big chance to do
all the doggy work on the New Soviet Man. He sacrifices
himself—becomes a pariah in the scientific community—in
order to pursue the necessary vivisectionist research. Also
throws shit on the German reputation at the same time. But
he gets caught sneaking out his secret data to the Russians—"

"Those experiments were worthless!"

"Don't tell me, tell Simon. He gets caught, and the Nazis
put him in line for vivisecting too. The last bit is, he's being
laid open by this other doctor—ribs, lungs, just about bleeding to death—his tongue already cut out, so he can't scream
—when the doctor leans down and whispers to him. 'Do not
worry, comrade. The work goes on.' A real double switch-
eroo."

"So he dies happy."

"I'm told. And I got good sources. Face it. When Simon
did that film, he was a convinced Stalinist."

"Blacklist crap."

"Don't look at me, I didn't put his name down. Think
about history. Think of all the pain and shit Stalin put the
Russians through. Simon was trying to justify him. But it
was n. g. My sources say Ulbricht didn't dig it."

"The film was locked up by the *West* Germans."

"Think they'd dig it any better? If he wasn't naming
names, he was showing some pretty familiar faces. It was
part documentary. Tell you. Doesn't sound too right to me
for *any* German audience."

"Or Russian. Maybe that was the point."

Terry scowled. "Maybe it was. And if it was, that's
Simon's whole trouble. Like I'm having with him now."

"Or genius."

"That's no excuse." Could see the very thought of genius
bugged him. "You don't go and hang your audience. Whatever you have happen in a picture, *they* didn't do it. Also.

Must have been one hell of an m.-s. party, that film. Remember that. My opinion, he's a little over the edge."

Re-evaluation: is that what I've missed all along, the maybe simple fact that M.'s taste for monstrosity is not an esthetic, or a social norm, but a few crossed wires? Add things up. The baroque questions, the morbid fantasies about variously mad or deformed Moros, the Heidi hang-up, the lost—or jettisoned—childhood, the possible mental deterioration after all those years of pill-popping . . . and then, really: is a vote for weird a vote for normal? Why on earth, concretely (except for fissures?), would a sane man want to go around with a severed finger tucked away in his handbag? *Handbag?*

"The picture needs a little of that," Terry went on. "But only a little. He's right for the Raven. I never said any different. He was my choice in the first place."

"Thought he was Quincy's."

"Quincy's *idea*, my *choice*. What I'm trying to make clear is, this is not going to be a bird picture."

"You mean, not a Moro picture."

A couple of sneaker squeaks: contemplative. "I don't want to take anything away from Simon. Since what this could be is his last picture. He's lucky the one before wasn't."

"Come on. He was great in *The Shoplifter*."

"You know, and I know. Who else saw it?"

"It's still around on TV."

"Sure. The Late Late Show. Like all his movies. Never Early, never Late, always Late Late. Face it. Simon's got a revival on with the insomniacs. The ghost walks for the sleepless."

"He's never played a ghost." A fact: occurred to me just then.

"Too keen an artist, right? I know how you feel about him—all that cine-shit—but I'm telling you, he's a crazy old man. He's more of a coot than Adolphe Menjou."

I never did get a real chance to reply to that last slander.

"He's used up," Terry kept plugging, "or almost. And I got to think about use. That's how everything goes together here. So much out of Quincy, so much out of Hazel, so much out of Simon. And no more. I don't need more. I'm fighting a bad surplus in one place already. You think Simon's giving me problems, let me show you."

He could've told me, but he had to show me. So out of the screening room, down the wooden fire escape, across the empty studio street—an abandoned Paramount back lot, where one lonely retainer, shuffle-sad-funny, was still sweeping away at his custodial post (Eddie Rochester, Jr.?), even the bristles on his broom growing gray—and back into the barn again. This was way late in the afternoon, the set long since closed down, except for a few grips mugging coffee around the crossroads grave: an intricacy of traps, hydraulic engines, effigy, topsoil, et cetera, more to come, cf. below. This was what Terry had to show me. The actual, physical, material enormity of an illusion occupying too much real estate.

"This son-of-a-bitch cost forty-seven thousand. And it's another fifty-five hundred a week to stay here."

This son-of-a-bitch loomed, a horrendous overhead: the stale Scaperelli apartments, unoccupied *oubliettes*, unused kitchens, dungeons; the barren Transylvanian mountain fastnesses; untrafficked byways, cemetery paths; or have I written all this before? The plan was tight, clever, space-saving, hideaway, and at the same time, it offered long optical reaches, angles, trackings, openness. But still: "I never put that much into a set before. Never get it all out again. Unless . . ." A man who's overspent on raising the Sunken Cathedral just can't *afford* to let it sink again. "Unless we can do another picture." Here. Now.

If I ever have to work out an *auteur* theory for Terry, it

will run something like this: "Every Terence Cowan picture contains elaborative, sometimes exiguous pictorial echoes from his immediately previous filmwork. There is, invariably, a striking scenic continuity. Locales do not change so much as they become exhausted. A shift in style for Cowan is, therefore, primarily a matter of changed art direction, and may indeed occur abruptly midway through a picture. *Hang Ten Cylinders* (1960), for example, moved suddenly from inside the Speed Shop he had made famous from every conceivable camera angle during his automotive cycle, to the stretch of Malibu beach where he actually now makes his home. Exhaust and sea spume. A strange filmic salad. But Cowan still kept to this mixed cinematic metaphor in *Drag Surf* (1960), eking out the last of his stock-car footage in order not to draw too heavily on his still-meager bank of surfing shots. He then stayed with the Malibu beach for the next eleven months and five more pictures, up through *Surf Monster* (1961), the film that convinced him to go under- water for *Sea Beast* (1962). *Sea Beast* can be considered the germ of his present horror cycle, though it was still some time before Cowan really brought his camera to the surface again. Many have charged that economy alone has dictated this stylistic seamless-web effect in the director's work, but much nearer the grain would be an analysis that cuts both ways, allowing the fast-paced Cowan, so oddly static and almost home-movie-ish in his choice of locale, his talent for finding, in Christopher Marlowe's words, 'Infinite riches in a little room.' "

"You dig?" he said, waving at the burden that surrounded him.

"I dig."

But he still seemed to have more on his mind.

"Something I've been wanting to ask you."

"What?"

"I need a quick script."

Skip went my heart.

"I can get Beau Fletcher to work this weekend." Unskip again. "But he needs something to start him off." He moved close to my elbow. "Know any good Poe stories?"

He said it almost like "Know any good Polack stories?" I swear.

"Let me think," I said.

"I mean, a *really* good one." Not like *The Pit and the Pendulum* or *The Tell-Tale Heart*. Everybody's heard those. A dozen times. One we haven't heard before, so to speak. With a really socko punch line. Could I come up with one? Wasn't I in the lit. line? Admit I am.

"You want one that could go with this set."

"Right."

"And these same actors?"

"That'd help."

"Well then," I said slyly, "do you know the one about Berenice?"

"No. Tell it to me."

So I told him the one about Berenice. My own way, except for the punch line, which I'd looked up since talking to M. ". . . so then this servant comes into the library in the morning. The little box is on the desk. The servant points to the spade, still full of mud, leaning against the window seat. Then to the little box. Our hero shrieks, grabs the box, spills it. A few dental instruments. But then what does he see? 'Thirty-two small, white and ivory-looking substances that were scattered to and fro about the floor.' "

Terry's eyes already had that wide-angle-lens look. "Or we could pick them all up even better with a fish-eye."

Confession: I thought I was casting M. But the next day, the last day's shooting, I notice Terry, on the quiet, arguing with Quincy while we're waiting for them to set up M.'s gravebreak. "Five days. That's all it is out of your life. I got the lab. I got this set. We repaint the crypt. Red. Make the whole cavern like a big mouth. You got all the billing. You can co-produce. . . ."

Quincy gave a slight but apocalyptic gasp. "You want me to play . . ." Yet you knew he would. You knew he'd love to. ". . . a monster of such vicious orality?"

S KIP TO that last day, the final shooting: M.'s gravebreak. Lots of frosty Hazel-Quincy footage before that, but nothing to my purposes, only proved M.'s point. Q. saving himself for horseback, to become highly hippodramatic, if a wee bit side-saddle-ish, as lustful lancer, sticking it to Ravenus. But he did at least replicate a passion for Hazel in one scene. Got off his "Nevermore!" line very, very sweetly, though as I caught the subtext: "(Thank God!)" Terry also stuck in a flashback, Beau Fletcher rewrite, dissolve to traumatic childhood of orphaned Scaperelli brothers as wards of the Inquisition. Q.'s voice-over. It shows what a wings-off-flies, blood-guzzling little shit Ravenus was from the age of six on, counters that rapport M. had built up with Hazel as iced corpse in dungeon. But only somewhat. M.'s pernicious artistic influence still prevailed over Q.'s effort to creep ahead of him on a frame-by-frame basis. Especially on that final day. Terry, since he wanted that grin, was forced, unwittingly, into further ravenizing of the film, even if he botched . . . no, worse, deliberately tried to destroy what M. offered him in the way of a denouement. Terry succeeded, through underhanded lab work, in partially obscuring M.'s true-great intent, but despite fog, filter, and phantasmagoria, much is comprehensible, if you have the least clue what you're really seeing.

Terry took a long time to set up that day, however, and until the shattering moment, I suddenly had Q. back on my hands. Waylaid me into conversation for the first time since we'd come in on that NYC/LA flight. Full of himself, thought he'd finished off M. for good, wanted, naturally, to tell me about his Upcoming Role: the tooth freak I'd already overheard him agree to play for five-day Terry. Who was suddenly "my co-producer," much as I was suddenly somehow supposedly his secret ally. "We'd like to find something here for Simon," he said magnanimously, "but it's a small cast, a very tight schedule, and Simon can be expensive." Eight thousand they were paying him for *Raven*. Not even peanuts. Peanut shells. "Of course you'll keep this quiet." Because the deal was still a little if-ish, a touch shoe-stringy; in fact, the way I read it, they were planning to embezzle the set. Quincy's own company, Quinco, was going to lend (worthless?) paper to Terry's Maliproductions for credit to purchase the set outright—Terry was on the tab to his present producers for it—the said set then to be resold to Quincy Adams Associates, Hollywood, Calif., on a lease-back, so that Quincy could have the tax loss when the set was scrapped, plus all the furniture, curtains, carpets, other curios and bibelots for his decorating business. "Some wonderful paintings. Very Trad. I'm sure Sears will back the loan, maybe put up a bit and a piece for—"

I'd have stopped dead in mid-sentence too, if I'd been talking. Eye-blitz: M. walked on set, straight from make-up, having done most of it himself, three and a half hours, had on his Ghoulgantuan grin. "Had on" is not right. The brutal denture seemed grafted into his face, flesh-welded, and M. had chipped off one of the tusk-like canines, leaving only a nerve-raw, bloodstained root. I mean, convincing: a really nasty mouth injury. Couldn't talk, of course. Waved at us, a flutter of sleeve. His "Ravenswear" had been soaked down in some wet-look red reek, but I remember noticing particularly how lumpy the caftan was. However, my only thought then: he was affecting some new broken-bodied-ness.

Terry ecstatic. Led M. over to crossroads, helped him into the grave, supervised fitting of hawthorn stake into his ribs. "I want only one take, Simon." Excited. "Just keep straight to camera." The shot was complicated technically, an aerial zoom with spin, plus long-angle lens, Terry's old favorite, but had to be timed just right to the popping open of the coffin lid, done with an Air Force hydraulic braking mechanism. The coffin-popping was to be immediately preceded by lightning leaping to hawthorn spear-stake, wired, above ground, as a positive electrode. So, in the right order, the shot sequence was (1) lightning strikes, (2) grave breaks open, and (3) Ravenus grins. "You'll have to be down there fifteen, maybe twenty minutes before we're ready to shoot," Terry explained. M. nodded. Should say something about that little nod, slight as it was: most actors in that much mask don't animate the mask, especially when they're not playing. But not M. Correct to say, Ravenus nodded, and they lowered the coffin lid down over *his* grin.

"Can you get comfortable?" Terry shouted, nervously.

A nasty scratching came from under the lid, like expletives.

"Trouble? You want out again?"

More scratching, but this time, don't know how he managed it, the scratching clearly said, shut up and get on with it.

"Okay," Terry ordered. "Throw on the dirt."

Two grips set to. But with trowels, not spades, and very delicately. The coffin was only to be buried about four inches down, the long-angle lens adding the depth. The grips smoothed and patted, while M. seemed to do a lot of tossing around inside the coffin. "Keep it still if you can, Simon," Terry shouted down to him. "You're disturbing the earth."

Quincy was still pulling at my elbow.

"This'll take a while," he said. "Let's get ourselves a cup of coffee."

I figured I'd better find out what skulduggery he was really up to. So we headed for the mobile cafeteria across the set.

"Don't think I'm not aware how helpful you've been," he gushed immediately. "Plots aren't that easy to come by."

So that was it.

"I think you can count on Beau. Feverishly as he'll have to work, he'll do right by you."

By me. By my story idea. After all, if it was really Poe's, he should have come forward with it himself.

"Personally I think you should stay out here another week with us. Serve as literary consultant. Maybe look into some publicity matters. . . ."

Another question I was asked at Breadloaf: *Are you ever offered money to write something about somebody?* "You mean, bribed? Indirectly, yes. But it isn't worth it. Bribes pay about the same as the New York *Times Magazine*, and usually only on publication."

Since he saw he wasn't sucking me in, Q. quickly slipped into a diversionary Parke-Bernet-high-rollers-pre-auction routine. The set he would soon, through his subsidiary, own. I was asked to admire a quattrocento refectory table— "Italian oak, top and bottom"—a travertine tazza, and a Titian-blue-*école* landscape of a lute festival on Parnassus. I'd say they were all circa 1949. The canopied beds weren't bad as Heritage reproductions. But Q.'s real prize was a small, dark, diabolic painting that was hanging in Lenore's bed chamber. "Shame it doesn't show up on film. If it's not a Bosch, it's very near."

Maybe: a swinger, in any case, a Norman O. Brownie candid. The surface was filthy from long storage, but underneath there was at least a Hieronymus *borscht* scene that stopped you, no question. It was An Entrance Into Hell, a long march of scratch-limbed damned souls, padding one after another up the devil's puckered, hairy, and flaming anus.

The trouble with pederasts like Q., they never give up. "It needs cleaning badly," he said, "but the composition is excellent." Then, honest to God, he licked an index finger and started spit-shining a patch of the anus, precious-art-fancier style, to reveal hidden *brio*. "Perfectly balanced focal point. I'm determined to keep it for myself." He looked tassels at me again. "Sure you wouldn't like to stay and help me hang it?"

Never give up, never give up, never give up. So why was I still bothering to be polite?

"Don't really care for it much, personally," I countered. "Like you, I've got my own Madonna at home."

He really smirked me down. "How all evasions do inform against us, dear boy."

Which stands as yet further proof that the Shakespeare of the Sonnets was queer as an Avon sheep dog.

We maneuvered each other toward the cafeteria; sealed sandwiches, coffee from a spigot, and one formica-topped table. It so happened Hazel was already sitting there, and I made us join her. She was out of costume, in shades, hip-huggers, and tit-hangers. Some bod, all right-right, but a feeling, any minute now, it's all going to go Shelley-Winters on her.

"Here for the burial, sweets?" Quincy asked her coldly.

"How far along are they?"

"He's all but interred."

She gulped at her coffee.

"Still time," he slowed her down. "Let the dead bury the dead."

I bought the coffee for Quincy and myself, then sat down between them.

"Quince poo," she said ickily across me, "was that clever-clever you?"

"Was what?"

"What you just said."

"Why do you ask?"

"I'm hoping it wasn't."

"Why so hopeful?"

"Because I liked it."

"You're safe," I said. "It's a cliché."

"Didn't ask you, prick."

It turned out I seemed to be the solid distance they

wanted to keep apart.

"Don't abuse the lad, sweets."

"Does it hurt your feelings when I do?"

"He's only trying to set your jumbled mind to rights."

"He's a love."

"Yes, isn't he a dear?"

And the damnedest thing: they both, underneath the table, had a hand on each of my knees, roving independently. I thought about letting them slowly, inevitably meet, but decided I preferred to choose for myself. So I interlaced with the delicate one, then shoved my cup of coffee under the table and spilled on the horny one. For a ridiculous moment, I felt maybe I'd confused them. But then Quincy got up, surreptitiously wiping his scalded knuckles on his pants crease.

"Careful where you pour your libations, lad," he snarled, and went off.

Hazel pulled both our hands up on top of the formica.

"So you're not one of the boys?"

"Guess not."

"Funny. Never known the Quince to be wrong."

"His word against mine."

"Need more proof than that."

We were heading somewhere, if I wasn't careful.

"You were going to tell me about Simon," I shifted matters.

She pouted exuberantly. "Does he have to be the only man in my life?"

I said nothing, and she giggled, began coyly hand wrestling with me. I pinned her quickly to the formica.

"I surrender," she said languidly. "The Quince and I do this sometimes."

"Do you?"

"Helps build strong wrists."

I disengaged.

She giggled again. "Sure he isn't right about you?"

"I have only myself to go by."

"You just won't *say*."

"Look, Miss Rio. . . ."

"Hazel."

"This isn't telling me anything about Simon."

She grabbed my hand again. "Let's have another go."

I kept my hand stubbornly lax.

"No?"

"Now. About Simon."

"Why Mistah Willyums. . . ." All sympathy and sudden, sweet discernment, fondling my limp hand. "Maybe you don't do it at *all*."

"Try me sometime."

Out it slipped. Or is that quite the way to put it? No, if I'm talking that way: she reached in and *pulled* it out.

"Really?" she beamed. "Tonight. Eight o'clock. At Dino's. Drinks and din-din, and . . . come what may." A bitchy wink. "Or come what can."

"Afraid not."

"You still haven't talked to me about Simon."

"Go ahead about Simon."

She gulped the last of her coffee. "No time now. Tell you all about him tonight."

"I've lost interest."

"Come off it, prick. You can be had."

That simple. Also turns out to be possibly true.

"Let's go. Don't want to miss Simon."

"He's not going anywhere."

"Just *mustn't* miss Simon."

So. So, so, so. At least that much is now down on paper. To Be Continued. Meanwhile, *in medias res*, Hazel and I rushed back to graveside, where there was about to be some action.

A certain broad-daylight eeriness, different from shots of Q. riding up and lancing coffin: everybody, even that Charles Coburn grip with his trussed-up hand, was standing around in a wide semi-circle beside the grave, back out of range of camera, made me think of awed mourners afraid to draw too near. The camera itself hung close over the maybe half-inch-high mound, like a big, black buzzard. Terry was up on the crane with the buzzard, and some intricate adjustments were being made in the buzzard's mean red eye. I was reminded of Terry's earlier threat to hold a funeral for M. right there on set, and in a mock—or mocking?—way, this seemed to be it. No lilies, but a hush that seemed deeper than the ordinary quiet for take. The only cue: the Last Trump.

"You ready, Simon?" Terry called down.

Another scratch: affirmative.

"Okay. Chop, chop. Let's go with the lightning."

A bright, pink-blue-colorless zap of sizeable voltage pitched itself across the gap from the crane and touched the hawthorn shank sulphurously. A tart whiff of ozone. Only a big spark, really, but it would, did, does look mighty and puissant on screen.

Then that hydraulic brake snapped, threw its pressure against the coffin lid, and dirt, pieces of spear, rot, decay, odor of death flung up at the buzzard camera. Worked wildly, smoothly enough to put *Raven* in line for an Academy Award nomination for special effects, though I doubt film will win any Oscars. Comes at you on screen a bit like an up-draft avalanche, until most of it falls back into coffin, close-up view now of Ravenus, a swerve-spin-swirl down, down, down into that fine and private place where none, I fear, do there em—

Brace yourselves, horror fans, take a good, close look at this shot sequence in *Raven,* and you will find, as we all did then and there, though admittedly without having to penetrate Terry's additive mists and movie murk: M. is not alone.

At first I thought it was alive, even attacking him. The bone-white patina of the skull flashed at us, a lunge. But that was really M. pulling it closer to him, nuzzling into its upper vertebrae, then biting, lovingly, into its scapula with his great Ghoulgantuan teeth. Next I guess I realized how it was positioned: mounted on him, femurs extended at straddle, patellae squeezed to his sides, tibiae under his back. Final, great cinematic touch: Lenore's necklace, with the silver arrowhead glinting right into camera, wrapped around *both* their necks—or rather, *his* neck, *its* upper spinal column—for stark-shock visual image that leaves no question whom M.'s got in there with him between the winding sheets.

Why Terry didn't yell cut immediately, I still don't know. Too aghast, I guess, or too fascinated, maybe a little of both, like the rest of us. The hush on set was absolutely sucked away. Sharp, gusty intakes of breath all around. Then a kind of desperate, knowing tension. Same with the audience, or at least the few who caught on, at the screening I saw. No giggles, and underneath, a funky feeling of moral turpitude: shouldn't be watching, somehow. And M. doesn't let up, not for a minute. He fondled the breastless, slatted ribs, pulled grubbily at the mosquito-net skirting, and, slowly turning in the debris-filled coffin, started to push himself on top of the skeleton. The skull's ecstatic grin rose up over his hunched shoulder. Almost the same grin as his, G.'s own. Around me, even shallower breathing, a deeper aversion, but still nobody stopped watching. I saw Q. across from me, wide-eyed, no "willies" this time, frozen, as M. began a sleek, iniquitous body movement that shook the coffin. Focal point: the anklebones. They were crossed over each other, high up his back, as if gripping him hard, seemed to pick up the rattling, bone-slapping rhythm almost on their own. In fact, M. made it look as if he had to catch up, to plunge after some wild, grisly lust that was already way ahead of him, burning in the whited pelvis that ground its flanges fleshlessly against him.

It was Hazel who stopped it, with a simple, clear-cut astonishment: "He's balling *my* bones!"

And Quincy hissed. Tried to sneer, but hissed like a skinned viper.

"Cut, cut, cut!" Terry shouted. "Simon, you *ghoul!*"

M. rose up from the grave. Lenore's skeleton stayed wrapped around him—tied, we could see now; must've sneaked it into the coffin under his caftan: that lumpishness. It clung to him, as if obscenely unsatisfied.

"Get that thing off of him!" Terry yelled at the grips.

But M. broke loose a few bits of string, and the skeleton flopped to the floor. With its femurs still spread wide, hideous to say. That finally did bring a titter, which blew Terry completely. He swore unstintingly at M. for a whole minute. "And quit your goddamn, shit-faced grinning!"

Probably what M. was playing for. He had the denture loose, and out of his mouth, in a trice. His emptied mouth looked raw and sore, almost violated.

Terry realized his mistake. "Wait. Put it back. We're not through."

"We are finished."

"It's a retake."

"It was perfect." He had a towel, was already wiping the raven blacking off his face, working gingerly around his mouth.

"Put it back, and get in that coffin again," Terry threatened, "or I'll wipe you out of this film."

M. smiled, even though it hurt. "You can't now."

Terry didn't say he could: a breaking point.

M. then made as much of a speech as his throbbing gums

would allow. "You wanted my grin. I gave you my grin. I gave you something a little more. I gave you a horror. So far, the only one. An inescapable horror. Now you go and make a horror picture."

A direct challenge, and for once, with everything coming at him so fast, Terry looked just a little scared. "You goddamn good and well *know*," he shouted, trying to keep control, "you *know* we can't have her in that coffin with you!"

"Why not?"

"The nabes, the drive-ins, the P.T.A.'s, the—"

"Why not?"

"*How?* How would she ever get in there?" Part of what was frightening him: sudden lack of story continuity, a real abyss. "How, how?"

"She came to me. Fled from Quincy, begged, pleaded with me to open my grave to her. Take her in."

"Where do we have that on film? *Where?*"

"It's implicit." M. ogled Hazel, with raven glance. She smiled back. "In her every look."

"That's blue! You're trying to make me make blue horror!"

M. nodded. "Exactly."

"You can't!" Terry yelled for the script girl, tore through the pages. "We already shot it. She is back there dead in her own bed where Quincy finds her!" He found the right page, shook it at M. "Right here! Dead in bed!"

"You cut that."

Terry blanched. "Who's directing this film?"

"You cut that." It was M.'s moment, Terry, Q., Beau Fletcher, even E. A. Poe be damned. "Shoot her bed empty, and everything works." The blackest of black directorial arts: recutting a leaden drive-in B flick into a Golden-Age art-house horror classic. If only they'd done it M.'s way, all the way: *Quelle différence!* "Go back to where Quincy finds out Hazel is wearing the arrowhead necklace. Outrage, not just fag surprise. Real sexual fury. He rides off into the night, same shots, beset by your foggy specters. Only they're not a flit show, but his own terrifying jealousies."

"You're being very extreme," Q. sniggered, but to no effect.

"He thunders down on my grave—with a murderous passion now, understand, no giggles—drives his vengeful spear into my buried guts—a little mad, you see—then thunders home again. But what does he find? An empty bed. That's the only new shot. Lenore gone, vanished. Then Quincy's 'Nevermore!' makes sense. Or much more sense, if we can get him to say it right, dub it back in. He has really lost her, will nevermore know how, where, why, anything. Excruciating. But then we show the audience what is the horrible, ironic truth." M. had worked himself up to quite a personal pitch. Foamy rave cream. "Quincy has really caught us in our secret trysting place. Worse. Horror of horrors, he has driven his cruel shaft not only through my heart, but through his beloved Lenore's! Pinning us together, fatefully. So that even in the reeky tomb, in hellish death, her body almost corrupted away, we go right on—"

"Sick," Quincy broke and wheezed. "Sick, sick, sick."

Terry could hardly speak. "You get your ass back inside that coffin. You give me five seconds of that shit-eating grin, *straight*, no shit, then you get off this set so goddamn fast—"

But M. was already walking off the set. And Hazel along with him. Dutifully? Yes, how about: like an obedient paramour?

"Simon!"

Only Hazel turned. "Do like he says, prick." She spoke with an odd trill of erotic authority. "Simon says make a horror film. Do what Simon says."

THAT'S WHAT Terry never forgave her, I'm sure, though
he ignored her, shouted again after M. "I'll scrap the
whole picture, Simon! I'll scrap and sue!"

All M. did was chirrup back at him in pure ravenese. The
only inflection I caught was one of feathery glee.

Later, when I had a chance—Our Last Conversation Together—asked M. about this highly original ending. He
quoted me sources: "Your Mr. William Shakespeare. I think
he sets some thoughts going, does he not, when he lets Hamlet jump into the grave after Ophelia? And don't forget
your M. Victor Hugo. Take a look at the conclusion of *The
Hunchback of Notre Dame.* How do Quasimodo and Esmeralda really end their days?"

Correct enough, as far as it goes, but, of course, Shakespeare—or even Hugo in that final charnelhouse embrace of
skeletons—never went quite so far as M. tried to go here.
Just not possible, even in our permissive cine-society. What
Terry, his producers eventually did was to compromise. Lenore's skeleton remains in her own bed, story-wise, but also
flits, figures in and around climactic grin sequence. Kept for
effect, not plot: bits of Lenore, bony bits, barely distinguishable. Oh they're there, despite cuts and distortions and
the tight-in focus. They're there all right. I know. Terry
knows. Hazel knows. M. knows. The grips know. Some
people I know very, very well now know, and a few dinner-
party guests I've let myself astonish. Yes, we savants know.
Question is, as I sit here, broke, the ten-cents-a-line truth-
giver, shall the General Reader know too?

I began interviewing Hazel in earnest halfway through
my pepper steak at Dino's.

No, first, since I'm being holistic about the truth: my telephone call from the Hollywood Hills Hotel to Jane before
going out that evening. Partial explanation of my . . . de-

termination . . . stick-to-it-ivity? . . . later that night. Sometimes wonder: should I maybe just show her this manuscript, pull a kind of Lev Tolstoi? "Here is my most intimate diary, dearest Anya Jane-ova. I want you to know what kind of a heart-sick, wretched man it is you have married." Try to force the issue between us that way? Predictable reaction: sincere, stern, unforgiving. "I don't know what to tell you, Warner. It's . . . well, it's always better if I wait to read your things after they're in print."

Anyhow, the gist of our long-distance conversation, across the Rockies, the Great Plains, the Wide Missouri, et cetera, et Shenandoah.

"Be home tomorrow night."

"Didn't know you had a home, Warner."

"I fly out of here at one o'clock, my time."

"Sure you don't want to stay where your time is your time?"

"Jane . . ."

"I'm beginning to like my time being my time."

"How are the kids?"

"Just fine."

"How are *you?*"

"Just dandy."

"Everything all right?"

"Fine and dandy."

"Fine."

Couldn't think what to ask next.

"Any phone calls for me?"

"No phone calls for you. And very few *from* you."

"Any mail?"

"There are several letters here addressed to 'Occupant.' Would that still be you?"

"Jane . . ."

"I wish you'd let your more important correspondents know where you've moved to."

"I'll be home eight, nine o'clock. Your time."

Nothing.

"Been a pretty hard push out here, honey. It really has."

"Has it?"

"I want to begin writing Monday."

"Good."

"Not going to be an easy piece to write."

"Unlike the last one, or the one before that, or—"

"Jane . . ."

"Tarzan . . ."

"I'm still interviewing."

"That why you're not flying home tonight? Like you said you would?"

Careful. "I have to take the director out to dinner."

"Have a ball."

"I wish you could understand. It isn't really fun."

"Of course not. Pure pain."

"Sometimes, almost."

"What would you ever do, Warner, without pain for an excuse?"

"I don't want to argue."

"Must write to Edmund Wilson about you sometime."

"Look. Tomorrow. I'll get a taxi home from Newark Airport."

"All wound, and no bow."

Very bad interview. She hung up, and the Nation once more hung between us. Yawned, stretched, gaped. I was conjugally smarting, a condition, I find, that leads to loss of appetite at home, though an intense sharpening of hunger when I'm away. I took on that pepper steak. First.

"You eat like Simon," Hazel told me.

"How does Simon eat?"

She thought. "I guess all men eat the same."

"Had one, had them all, right?"

A pretty unsubtle nasty, not at all like me, really. The

martinis. Expected much nastier back from her, but she'd begun to grow too cozy for snarls. More happily, less bitchily infantile. Had, in fact, stopped calling me prick altogether. Much too formal a term, I guess, now that we were getting to know each other better.

"Tell me something, Hazel," I urged her on toward greater confidences. "Did you know Simon was going to pull that freak stunt with the skeleton?"

"I knew he was up to something."

"But were you surprised what?"

"I was surprised that he really did it, but what he did . . . I can remember . . . to tell the truth. . . ."

Getting somewhere, getting somewhere. "Yes?"

"He once made love to me that way." She giggled. "So there."

"In a coffin?"

"No. In the woods. But with all his scary stuff on."

"You're serious?"

"Remember it very well now. It was on my birthday."

"I see."

"Simon always remembers."

"Most girls just get spanked. Not very hard either."

She giggled again, but not quite at my feeble joke. "You don't understand. It was my birthday wish."

"Your birthday wi— . . . you *wanted* him to?"

"As I recall, I asked him to, yes."

"Why?"

She fidgeted. "Better ask him."

"I'm asking you."

"I don't think I can tell you." Definitely nervous about all this, for some reason. "You better ask Simon."

"Wait, just a minute. To start with, which 'scary stuff'?"

"What he had on this afternoon."

"Exactly?"

"Well, naturally, less clothes. No clothes. But those teeth.

And he made his skin all horrid."

"Ghoulgantua then."

"Who?"

"Ghoulgantua."

Didn't mean a thing to her, honest to God.

"You don't know Ghoulgantua?"

"I've got a terrible memory, especially for names."
Dawned on me that is maybe why she calls so many men
just prick.

"Don't you know his movies?"

"I haven't seen them all."

"You haven't?"

"To tell the truth, I don't go to the movies that much."

I shook my head. "Rather do other things?"

"The way I look at it"—very *grande vedette*—"you're
either a person who *goes* to the movies, or you're a person
who's *in* the movies."

"But how could you want him to . . . I mean, if you
hadn't seen . . . ? How clear are you about this incident?"

"A lot of it came back to me today. Don't get me wrong-
wrong. Wasn't that big a thing in my life. I mean, underneath, it was still just Simon."

"Okay, okay." Tried to think: next question. Blunt. "Still
just Simon. But just what is Simon?"

"How do you mean?"

"To you."

She shrugged. "Important."

"Do you live with him?"

A big laugh. "I don't live with Simon. I *stay* with Simon
sometimes. I've *been* with Simon. Off and on. That's only
natural."

"Natural?"

"Even my mother agrees."

Getting nowhere, getting nowhere. "Put it this way.
How long have you known Simon?"

"One way or another?"

"Yes."

"Ages."

"Beginning when?"

"Hard to say. Most of my life, it seems like."

It really was like talking to an amnesiac Baby Snooks.

"Hazel, what I'm trying to pin down, if you don't mind my asking, is *when* did he make love to you in his scary stuff?"

"Must've been a long time ago."

"*How* long ago?"

"You'll have to ask Simon."

Decided to play it her way. "You mean . . . it was *that* long ago."

"Has to be. If I still thought I could really have a birthday wish."

"Which birthday?"

"Don't remember."

"But you were maybe . . . just a kid."

"Older. Must've been. It was a pretty grown-up wish."

"Unless Simon put it there."

"What do you mean?"

What *did* I mean, at that point? Was homing in on a parlous thought-wave, sifting Hazel's loose words for solid evidence of a certifiable M. kink, long suspected, but found my own self a bit muddled. Undertipped on the exorbitant bill, overtipped the hat-check girl, dropped all my change for the car hop. Largely due to demon drink: gin horns, Burgundy hooves, and a brandy tail. Drink alone, however, wouldn't have done it without the week's fatigue suddenly coming down on me—a tired snap—plus inner rankling of repartee with wife Jane. But what was worse, total disorientation. Didn't know where I was, in our conversation, or anywhere else. She was driving, a green VW with a fumey temper all its own, ripping around Sunset Strip landmarks.

Circus Maximus behind Dino's. She used to work there. Brutal. Ben Franklin's. She used to hang out there. Funky. The hospital, like a gun turret. She used to have herself redone there. Painful. It all added up to no past in a place that is no place. But then, to me, that's L.A. I find it, especially at night, a low-lying, depressed area of total uncertainty. The sneaky back way into some other, more *real* city. Like Port Said, or Trenton, N.J.

So I WAS a little drunk, or maybe more than a little drunk. Anyhow, drunk without guidelines. Hazel finally got us headed out toward Beverly Hills, while I talked to her "in depth," a lot about her career. From what I gather I gathered: not so *grande* a *vedette*. She'd been in so many movies, too many, from such an early age on, bit parts, nothing roles, couldn't remember them all, claimed she'd never seen many of them. "My mother's the one to ask about them."

"Who's she?"

"An alcoholic."

"Rough."

"Drank up all my juvenile earnings."

"Did she?"

"You ask her."

She said the first picture she could remember doing with M. was *Hitler's Camps*. Might've been in another one with him before that, but I'd have to ask him, she couldn't recall. "I remember *Camps* because I had this near-naked torture scene. Nineteen-Forties near-naked. Rip-rip all around the tittyboos. Simon was this terrible Nazi. Cut people up alive to see how they worked."

"Wait."

"That's what he did."

"I saw *Hitler's Camps*."

"How was it?"

"Don't remember you in it."

"Small part. One of the girls he was breeding to Hitler Youth."

"He didn't cut people up."

"He did."

"You're confusing *Camps* with that film he did in West Berlin."

"Am I?"

"Did you, by any chance, ever see that picture?"

"No."

"He's told you about it."

"Never heard word boo about it before."

Christ. "Look. Somebody's put it into your head."

"I don't know." She tried to think while passing once in the middle lane and twice in the inside lane. "I get mixed up about plots. Is this the one where he escapes a lot in an elevator?"

"That's *Ghoulgantua.*"

"Damn. Damn-damn." Worried her, made her driving even worse. "Maybe I did see that one."

She headed up Coldwater Canyon, managed to find her own driveway. The house was redwood uprights and lashings of thermal glass, not a curtain drawn. She unlocked a section of the utter transparency extending across the front, and walked in. I walked in after her, a little unsteadily, and turned on a light. She turned off that light, and turned on another. I went and turned off that light, and we were in the bedroom.

Partial, somewhat saving explanation: there was, truthfully, nowhere else in that house to go.

It was furnished in functional, adjustable, disposable Danish, the rooms kept right up to good, clean, triple-A motel standards. Check in here anytime, Large Parties Welcome. But not a book, not a magazine or newspaper, not a vase or a picture or a knick-knack, hardly an ashtray, not one personal item anywhere. In Quincy's terms, it was decorated Nil. Not even the fixings for that one more quick drink. Forced to retreat into the bedroom, where the only signs of human habitation still were hidden back in her closet: a few dresses, nighties, bikinis hanging on hangers, and a vinyl suitcase open on the closet floor, full of toiletries, a hairdrier. She hadn't even bothered to take her toothbrush across to the spotless bathroom, ten feet away.

"You just moved in?"

"No." She had her reasons. "I travel a lot, not here that

much. Rent the place out. It's easier if I keep my own things out of the way."

"What things?"

What things, no things. Except a single prize possession. Her bod-bod. That she was now going to let me have a look at, maybe even pick up and handle some . . . sure, here, no, don't mind at all, go ahead, just be careful, go on, *try* it. Not that I was all that against this idea: was undressing just as fast as she was, in the reflected glow that the amber and blue spotlights were spraying on the plantains outside the glass. (Why does that crazy Hollywood lighting always make me think of somebody with one brown eye, one blue, *staring* at me?) But I did have this thought before flesh took over entirely: the emptiness of the house, like her own vacuity, might just be psychologically deliberate. What better way to stay young, eternally youthful than to have no memories, even at thirty-nine—thirty-eight—and only a few belongings? Obliviousness: the sexiest vanishing cream of them all. That's what I have to break through here, I was telling myself, find out a few things. The purely professional reason— how I make my living, support a wife and four children— why I have decided to fuck this dumb broad.

She put a lot of youth into it. And a lot of experience. Also a lot of indifference. I don't think I impressed her very much at first. It was perfectly straightforward, front-and-center coitus: easy access across a broad spread of fatty thigh and just slightly wrinkled buttocks. A lot of buck and bingo there, whatever I mean by that. My thoughts: her taunts. Yes, I've got that kind of real helpful brain, all those sexy stories about M. Tried to hold off, not go bingo myself. But couldn't get over how quiet she was being. Active, physically, but dead still, emotionally, even vacant. So I started worrying, began pushing, humping, perspiring. Bingo. But kept right on pounding, pushing, hard, so hard that I didn't even hear.

"Hey," she stopped me. "It's all right."

"It is?"

"You're done."

"I am?"

"Come on. Get off."

"You sure?"

"I should know."

"Okay. I mean . . ."

What I meant, really, was: how did I miss it?

"Not how much noise you make, y'know."

"Sure. Right."

She gave me a sweet, slothful kiss, kind of like last prize. "You were . . . fine."

Worst part: didn't feel I'd gotten on any more of a familiar footing with her. At all.

"Listen, Hazel."

I got up on one elbow. Made me dizzy: demon drink still. She threw her own elbow across her eyes. I kissed its wrinkled point.

"Rest up," she said.

"Want to ask you something."

Kept her elbow across her eyes. "I'm all ears."

"How come you let him treat you the way he does?"

"Who?"

"Is he that good? Still?"

"*Who?*"

"A sixty-eight-year-old man is not going to . . ."

"Oh."

"It's this hold he has on you. The way he maneuvers you around."

"How?"

"I don't know."

"Think so?"

"Like he had some power, some extraordinary . . ."

She giggled, lifted her elbow, grabbed at the sheet. Pulled

it off me, onto her. "Are you asking me if Simon is that big a dicking?"

"I suppose so."

Seemed very important to know: can't think how I actually planned to include this information in article, but as I said at Breadloaf: "Sometimes you write between the lines. Sometimes you write between the lines even before you write the lines."

Hazel was eying me, heavily, what was there without any sheet over me. Unnerving. She finally spoke up.

"Tell you who you really ought to ask about that."

Jesus.

"I'm asking *you*."

Shook her shaggy blonde head, her big brown nipples. "The best person to talk to about that, really, is Terry."

I fell off my elbow.

"You'd be surprised. Terry knows everything about everybody's sex life around here."

"You're sure?"

"Reason I suggest Terry is nobody knows anything about *his* sex life."

"Hazel . . ."

"He'd be neutral."

"Why should I ask Terry when right now, here, in bed, I can ask you?"

Very solemn she got. "I'd only be giving you my point of view."

"That's what I want!"

She rolled away from me, giggling. I rolled right after her, and she scooted down under the sheet. I felt around for her here and there, through the sheet, and she seemed to get all ticklishly twisted around. Then she hiked up, a bump in the night, and slowly drew the ghostly folds back from her, yessiree, very real, tucked-together, elevated *derrière*. Surprise, surprise. Kept her head wrapped in the sheet, still giggling. *Déjà vu:* looked like the raised nates of that little faun in *Fantasia* (1940), the one whose ass wistfully fades into a Valentine.

No further word. My move. Trouble was, couldn't be sure—how does Norman Mailer phrase it?—whether I was wanted in "the fish house" or "the sewer." Dilemma. Pondered while I hardened, then took an investigatory poke at each portal. Lid tight down on the sewer, thank God, but fish-house door wide open. I slipped in there for—fun images to cover masculine uncertainties—maybe a couple of shrimp, or at most a filet of flounder, but managed to cut myself a great big piece of swordfish steak.

"Better," she sighed.

"You think so?"

"Much better." She got herself turned around again and kissed me with liberal lips. Very liberal. Should have noted that.

"Now," I said.

"Rest up."

"No, I mean, now we get a few things straight."

"Like what?"

"To start with, about my being one of the boys."

She giggled. "I felt you take your sneaky little swipe-swipe at my—"

"That was to check what *you* wanted."

"The man's supposed to—"

"I did choose."

"Okay. I grant. With a little coaxing, you can be headed straight."

"Thanks."

"Just how it is these days."

Decided, by God, it was my turn to castrate. "Understand. I'm only here doing my job."

"Job?" That got to her. "What job? You calling me a job?"

"Pay attention. I'm trying to find out about a man named Rudi Eckmann."

"I don't know any Rudis."

"Maybe you don't. Or maybe you just think you don't. I know enough already about what you think you don't know. I want to know what you *do* know."

"You're confusing me."

"Somebody started long before I did. Put it this way. A few good words in print from me might help further your flat-assed career."

"You think I'm flat back there?"

"I'm offering you a simple exchange. What I can do for you, for what you can tell me about Rudolph Simon Eckmann Moro."

She shook her head, which shook the rest of her.

"You got me all wrong."

"Do I?"

"Simon's somebody I don't . . . you know . . . fuck around about." She seemed to mean that quite literally. "I really have a lot of feeling for Simon."

"What feeling?"

"It's confused."

"I'll bet."

"Told you once, you wouldn't believe me. He's . . . well, sort of daddy."

"You know what they call wanting to sleep with daddy?"

" 'Wanting to go beddy-bye.' "

"Is *that* what he calls it?"

"That's what *I* call it."

"Or, my God, wanting to sleep with dead daddy? On your birthday?"

"Call it what you want. It's how you feel that matters."

"Do you know, Hazel, that you are absolutely crackers?"

"Crackers in bed."

"Kinky."

"Kinkyboo."

"Know what I think? He drove you kinky."

"Who?" Shocked.

"You know who, and I want an answer."

She shook her head again, harshly, some kind of deep denial, then lapsed into an almost unhinged baby-faced smile. "Know what you really want?"

And her hand came spidering up my leg on its tippytip fingernails, skittering around into the dark beneath my scrotum. Like—should have thought of this then—like a black widow sitting on her egg sac.

"Lay off. I want an answer."

"Have to ask Simon."

Dilemma: couldn't very well ignore spider, but didn't dare brush it away. Might get bitten.

"No, not Simon. Or Terry. Not even Quincy. You. Yes or no. Did you get yourself diddled by . . . Cut it out now."

"Feel good?"

Gritted my teeth: wasn't going to give in. "—get yourself diddled by that monster when—"

"Still feel good?"

"—when, goddammit, you weren't maybe even half old enough to be jailbait?"

"Didn't ever think of it that way."

"How did you think of it?"

Virility paradox: want to, maybe it doesn't, don't want to, sure as hell it does. Phallic backlash.

"Oh . . . kind of make-believe, I guess."

"Stop."

"Dress-up, let's-pretend."

"Stop it."

"Really want me to stop?"

"Yes. No." Stop what? Tried to keep my mind on what I was asking, not so much on what she was doing, but the two things were beginning to get mixed up. Made the best of a difficult situation?

"Is that . . . is *this* what you do for Simon? Did, when you were a little—?"

"Depended."

"That's no answer."

"Let me think a minute."

"Haven't got a minute!"

"You don't?" Spider wriggles. "I want to be helpful."

"Then just answer the question."

"What question?"

"I'm asking you. . . ."

But I couldn't phrase it any more. I still knew what it was I had to know, what I desperately, if vaguely, wanted to find out, but couldn't put the simplest query. I was drunk, tongue-tied, erect, and, yes indeed, about to be really bitten. Preciously. She bent down, lipped right over me, peeled me back with all the force and delicacy of her lolling tongue. Even if I'd been able to ask the damn question, how the hell, in those excruciatingly exquisite circumstances . . . I resort here to ripping off a stanza from Rake Rochester.

QUERY AND LOVE'S ANSWER

Then talk not of more inquiry,
  Sharp quips, and questions sly;
If she, with practised ecstasy,
Kept mind on him while mouth round me,
  How could she make reply?

WHEN I BOARDED my flight around noon next day, when I emplaned for New York City with a light head, a *lâche* heart, and a limp cock, specifically, when I crawled through the First-Class seraglio to the cheap, two-dollar stewardesses back in Tourist—going rapidly downhill, ruined by intemperance and a whoreson, Babylonian blow job—when I lifted myself from the lint and filthy scuff of that horrid TWA aisle and struggled into Seat 13C, there was M. Right next to me, in 13B.

Both of us surprised, in fact, downright dislocated by this juxtaposition, proximity, propinquity, et cetera, et cetera. Lit. mind continued to work even if biz. tongue fixed fast by ichor of liquor. M. didn't say much either at first. Always awkward, any accidental meeting of interviewer and subject after exploited personality has yielded up its last tailings of good copy, lies exhausted, played out . . . cuckolded? That's at least my side of what ensued after take-off but before dinner and in-flight movie, *Mary Poppins* (1964), sci-fi psyche-Disnic fam. com. ("Just a cube full of acid makes the musical go down, the musical go down . . ."), over airline's rum ration of two bourbons: Our Last Conversation Together.

M.'s general demeanor: relaxed, elegant, *Viennois*, Old Worldly/Other Worldly. But thoroughly undisplaced person, a preternaturalized American, you might say. Work had done him good. Now travel? Going to see his hallucinatory family?

No, not exactly. "Your Mr. Joseph Papp," M. explained, "has asked me to come to Central Park, to play Caliban."

"Perfect."

"Yes, I think." Obviously delighted. "Central Park, at night . . . you expect Caliban."

"As a mugger."

"My thoughts tend that way."

"Keeping the same ending this time?"

M. smiled low, but said nothing.

"I liked what you managed yesterday."

"Did you? We'll see."

Then he launched into that heady discussion of analogues for his ending, H.let, H.back, cf. above, got very technical when I asked him about lighting, lens length— "I had the cameraman with me" —and how exactly he'd smuggled that skeleton into the coffin. "Wore it around my waist. Like a money belt. Simple enough to pull up my skirts, tuck them back down inside the bones."

"Pretty small bones."

"Skeletons are smaller than you realize."

"Brittle."

"Slight, really."

"Girlish?"

M. ignored that. "Do you know Mr. Papp?"

"No."

"I had in mind suggesting Hazel to him for Miranda." So he could have her near him? Cement their monster-mistress/ parent-child/decrepit December-matronly May relation-ship? What ho: a horror *Tempest?* Not so far-fetched, cf. M-G-M's *Forbidden Planet* (1956), Cyril Hume's rewrite of Prospero's Island as Altair-4 in the year 2200, why not base play on movie?

"Also considered suggesting Quincy for Prospero," he went on.

"Or an aging Ariel," I said.

But generous of M., considering. Too generous, I sensed.

"However," he added, with a slight edge, "I find now that Quincy will be occupied these coming few weeks. Another Poe film." Saluted me with a squeeze of his plastic tumbler, since no way to clink it. "To your first screen credit."

What could I say? "What can I say?"

"You were thinking of me."

"I was."

"Next time, ask first."

"I sure as hell will." I tried to shrug off some of the blame. "But what can you do? It's all in the public domain."

"Avoid taking known vandals there on visits."

We both sipped at our plastic bourbons to ease the strain on a thinning camaraderie. But a jollified M. spoke with even more of an edge.

"Now tell me, how did you enjoy your romp with Hazel?"

"My what?"

"Your romp-romp."

What could I say? "What can I . . ."

"You were thinking of me."

"Matter of fact, I was. Some of the time."

"Next time—"

"Ask first?"

"Won't be a next time."

Discomfiture: felt like saying she was also in the public domain, but kept my peace.

"Please understand," M. went on. "My only real objection is that Hazel gains nothing by it."

"You so sure?"

"She's been had."

I laughed. "Other way around."

"You are not kind to that girl, as I've already said. Trying to trade your tickle for her prattle." That intimate death's-head smile again. "Am I right?"

Didn't like that: at all. "She has some not-so-very-pretty stories to tell, Simon."

"Yes, sad."

"Yes it is sad."

"You're very right. Very sad."

But seemed too sly: had a feeling I might finally have him cornered. "Only backs up what I've suspected all along."

"About what?"

"About you."

"Of course. You have me down as a . . . pedophiliac?"

"Lately, a necro-pedophiliac." Not quite right, but tendency carried out to the nearest psychiatric term, rounded off.

"Frightening."

"She gave me a clear instance."

"Clear? From Hazel?"

I told him, in lavish detail. Spared him nothing. "Yesterday brought it all back to her. You've got a lot to answer for there, Simon."

M. met my hard look with what I thought was an even harder one of his own, devilish even, but it broke up into roaring laughter. He laughed so hard the stewardess came back to check.

"Can I get you something, Mr. Moro?" she asked.

"Yes." He snapped his plastic tumbler at her. "More bourbon. For my necro-pedophilia."

She took mine too, wondered a little at both of us.

"You don't recognize that story?" M. chortled.

"Should I?"

"Thought you were my *meister*-fan."

"I am."

"Seen all my movies."

"All that are available."

"And uncut."

"Yes."

"Well then?"

Then I realized. "Oh my God. The whole incident."

"Exactly."

"She took it from . . . but she couldn't even remember the name!"

"Not surprising. She probably never saw the picture."

"But . . ."

"Her mother never let her see any movie that wasn't recommended by *Parents' Magazine*. Even the ones she was in."

"Ones she was . . . ?" Saw it all. "*She* was the little . . . ?"

So far have not been able to verify this from cast lists. Still might not be true: another M. fabrication? But here I can recollect my own reaction, cf. long ago, above, and only suggest that we keep Miss Clio checking.

"Exactly," M. said, with some pride. "It *did* happen to her, in a way. Hazel may be dim, but never dishonest. And this was a long time ago, remember. We shot that scene just before she turned eight, since you seem so hungry for these garish chronological details. To get the expression I wanted, I told her to make a birthday wish, but not to tell me what it was. Came out perfect. More or less the same psychological way I dealt with her this picture."

"So you weren't . . ."

"Weren't what?"

"But her wish."

"I still don't really know what it was. Maybe she did ask for . . . that would have been precocious of her, wouldn't it?"

"But you didn't—you weren't. . . ."

"You think me that mad?" He shook his head. "No. Not then. Not with my little Hazelnut. With the mother. A ginned-up gospel singer who would do anything to get her daughter in the movies."

"Who was her father?"

"When her mother got drunk enough, she used to claim I was."

"You?"

"Retroactively. She had a strange sense of time. And an even stranger idea of sin. Combined, they made her very formidable."

"Formidable."

"Dreadful, really. Sing and drink, and pray and fuck.

'Roooooock of Aggges, beeennnd to meee!' "

"Why did you?"

"Why did I what?"

"Bend to her."

M. surprised. "Can't you see?"

"No."

"The daughter obviously had talent."

"Simon."

"Future talent. If it had ever really been developed, instead of wasted in silly films . . ."

"Simon, what talent?"

Annihilating skull grin. "Thought you'd just been through quite a display of it."

"So you *have*. . . ." I really had had enough. "All right, straight. What is it between you and her?"

"Best ask her."

Really had had enough. "Come on. Straight."

"I don't think I'm at liberty to divulge. . . ."

"You're both bleeding liars."

M. blinked: admit it was highly unjournalistic of me to phrase it quite that way.

"Are we?" Then very deliberately. "Or perhaps you just can't get a few simple facts straight."

"There isn't any simple. Isn't any straight."

"You give up too easily."

"I don't give up, Simon, but if I went looking for you Twenty Thousand Leagues under the Sea, they'd turn around and tell me you were Lost in Space."

Nice: Voyage to the Center of the Earth, and no Simon Moro. Sorry, he just left for Space-Time. But brings me up a little short here: same approximate mood and feeling in which, with which I began shoving ms. into this ragged envelope Monday. Stark, clear-day-see-forever perception of enfeebled . . . *diminuendo ad infinitum* . . . powers of
. . . perception. What is Truth? And P. T. Barnum re-

plied, "The greatest escape artist of them all!"

M. seemed to take a long, extra-close look at me. For once. X, *The Man with the X-Ray Eyes* (1963), Ray Milland able to see through walls, clothing, skin and bones, but M.'s cold, gray orbs peered deeper: saw down to what had crawled under the rocks at the murky bottom of my turbulent self-esteem.

"I wonder," he said.

"Wonder what?"

"What you'll write about me."

"I wonder myself."

"Though I don't really worry."

"No?"

"Not at all." Arrogance: Bourbon? "I can see you have high hopes of some integrity. Always. But you suffer too much from Rogers' Palsy."

"Rogers what?"

"Palsy. Very debilitating."

"What Rogers?"

"Your Mr. Will Rogers. Its first victim. The disease causes the sufferer to be utterly unable, ever, to meet a man he doesn't like."

"Just a goddamn minute."

"Publicly. Even semi-privately. Of course, privately, alone with his own thoughts, that's another matter."

First dumb thought that came to my mind: "Will Rogers really did feel that way."

"Perhaps. But do you?"

Said nothing.

"I know. Very sad. If *Esquire* assigned you Terry, you'd admire him immediately. You'd have to. Write paeans to his horror-realism, or some such foolishness, explain how he'd developed the cheapie into an art form."

"Terry's . . . okay."

"So are they all, all okay. If *Esquire*—no, *Playboy* gave

you Hazel to do, you'd love her on the spot. Make her out to be, let's see now, the liberated but still passionate female. Say she understood the new sexual freedom because she was . . . older, wiser, knew a trick or two. Am I right?" Then darkened. "When you know as well as I do, screwing isn't even really sexual to Hazel. It's the only way she knows how to 'communicate.' Isn't that what we say? Her way of yelling and screaming at you."

"Hazel has her points." Weak, weak.

"The only one I'd worry about you with is Quincy."

An out: I took it. "Never have cared for queers."

"I realize. You'd have to put him into context. As part of a more general, and enlightened, argument in favor of the homosexual contribution to our present day culture."

Stronger: "I hate queer art."

M. nodded. "But you understand its *importance*. Of course you do. You could present Quincy respectably to the readers of *The Atlantic* as a subtle popularizer of ambiguity. Not as intellectual as your Mr. Gore Vidal or your M. Jean Genet, but an advance over the late Nineteen-Fifties mother-centered, *piano blanco* perversion of your Mr. Liberace."

Had an idea there: hate to say it.

"So I don't worry what you'll say about me."

"I see."

"Only sorry you have to say it."

"Why?"

"Because for you, really . . ." M.'s most lethal grin. ". . . it must be horrible."

Recollected statement from last round of advice delivered at Breadloaf: "There sometimes occur moments of insight that are quite inexpressible. You see into character so suddenly, so penetratingly that no reportorial description is possible. The moment passes, unrecapturably, but never mind, it serves subconsciously to create a kind of mental midden, obscure, full of stench, but fertile, out of which the right words eventually come, grow, proliferate. Even if the right words can never be found for that particular moment itself." Now. What I would have gone on to say at that time, had I dared: "These moments, understand, are invariably moments of loathing. What you find is that you suddenly can't stand the guts of the man, or woman, whose guts you have been assiduously probing. Let me give you an example. I was sitting next to Simon Moro on the plane flying back from L.A. to New York. I'd finished interviewing him long ago. He just happened to say something to me, never mind what, nothing really very important, but it showed me in a flash what a mean, nasty, higgling, niggling, petty man he really was, what a drab, dirty inhumanity really lurked behind that high-bloody-mindedness he claimed for himself. Not the dignity of a vampire even, only the cravenness of a leech, & so forth, & so on."

But now to come round full cycle: even while these thoughts were stinking along down inside me somewhere, never, of course, to be expressed, I hit on a lead for my article. The words did indeed begin to rise from the midden, exfoliated: ironic-laudatory, and goodly, if maybe a little weedy. "Moro Man," I wrote in my head at 30,000 feet. "It's a curse, it's a bane, it's Moro Man!" Not great, but not bad. Exactly right for nostalgic, pop-love tribute to the anti-hero who rose to greatness in the Age of Classic Comics. Would've done fine and dandy if M. hadn't begun this mad-bad act, ranted and raved all over New York City like a goddamn golem, ruptured the subways, reamed the newspapers. I was home free, if he hadn't busted loose with his freak speeches, his porno fairy tales, his Halloween whoremongering, his transvestite banshee wails. Damn him. I wrote him up as the Greatest Thing since Gangrene. I made him a monsterpiece. Damn his x-ray eyes. I bugled him and boosted him and succored him and damn near sainted him. Simon Moro could have been America's last King of the

Creeps, the Man the Martians Come to See, but he crawled into town on his shaggy hams and positively shat on my copy!

TAG-LINE ITEM, since this envelope is supposed to contain all, be my own journal of record: last thing M. said to me as we lowered into Kennedy.

"Now I'd like to ask you something."

"Shoot."

"What is it that you'd really like to write?"

"About you?"

"No. Just write."

Whoops.

"And be honest."

Surprised myself. Didn't say my novel. Instead, I fumbled around. "I don't know exactly. I've got a novel started, but I wonder about novels. A lot of guys figure if you're going to be autobiographical, go ahead and be autobiographical."

M. interested. "Really?"

"I might like to write mine."

"Already?"

"Why not?"

"Then may I say that I sincerely hope—" Grin: right off the iodine bottle. "—that you soon find a halfway decent subject for it?"

II. *Certain Unedited Tapes*

Terence, this is stupid stuff.

A. E. HOUSMAN

Right. I don't do p.r. I used to do p.r., but now I do pictures. Simple as that. Only when I got a picture in trouble, I do the p.r. Also simple as that.

For openers, this is a lousy town for p.r. I hate this town. This whole country started off on the wrong coast. Next time Paul Revere operates out of San Diego, and we send all the wagon trains east. The Donner Pass is Holland Tunnel. The last place those who survive reach is New York City.

Some reporter asks me today—guy from *Esquire*, or the *Daily News* maybe—what about my maybe doing a horror film sometime in New York City? "It'd only be a travelogue," I tell him. Can you see it? Shoot live in the streets. Eight, what is it, going on nine million monsters? And all you got for a hero is Mayor Lindsay. He'd let them hold Werewolf Week.

"Nobody's safe," I tell them. "Why do you think Kong climbed the Empire State Building?" Watch that stuff. Need a good press. Maybe get up a luncheon for them with Simon? Too risky. All want to know, has he flipped. Who's to say? If he's crazy, he's a crazy crazy.

This afternoon, I go up there, first thing I say to him, polite but firm, "Before we discuss anything, better give me that finger."

"Oh?" he says.

"It goes to the lawyers," I say.

"Oh?" he says.

"For return to the rightful owner," I say.

"But I have possession . . ." he starts to tell me. The network people are all around us with spears, the whole country wants him tied down to an anthill, and he's telling me possession.

"Possession is going to be nine tenths of both our asses," I tell him, "if we don't settle this thing."

"I'm curious." He's curious. "In this country, does a man

retain a property right in his severed parts?"

"Got to have a signed release, same as anything else."

He gives me a look, a shrug, a laugh. "You can have it." Just like that. "I'm through with it." Starts patting his pockets. "If I can find it."

So we search around his suite. He goes into the bedroom, pulls back the cover, lifts up his pillow. "Had it under here last night," he says. "Maybe the maid . . ." I don't believe a word, but he's still making me queasy. He points back out into the living room. "Go check on the coffee table. See if I put it in the cigarette box."

I'm being cooperative. Above all, I'm cooperative. I go.

"The nail's loose," he says, "so be careful."

I pick up the top by its milkmaid-milking-a-cow handle, and only cigarettes. White filters. But look like a bunch of stuffed fingers. Only for a second.

He comes back out, pats all his pockets again, then says, "We'd better check behind the sofa cushions."

That I can't do. I'll look for it, but I'm not feeling around for it. He pokes under a few cushions, then remembers. Faking, any odds. Goes into the bathroom this time, and comes back out with the goddamn thing in a drinking glass with his toothbrush. "Must've left it in there this morning," he remembers.

I know what he's trying to do. I know. I just keep swallowing back, take out my handkerchief. He pops it on there. Stinking gray, almost black, but I wrap it up without really looking, stuff it in my breast pocket. I think what gets me most is knowing he's had his foot all over it. Send it off to L.A. tomorrow, registered.

"Sit down," I tell him. "We got things to discuss."

We both settle on the sofa, him smiling like death, me doing most of the talking from here on out. Looks a lot older. He really does. Getting fired by Papp must've been a big blow. But he's all smiles. "Nice of you to come by,

Terry," he says. "An unlooked-for visit."

I called him. He knows why I flew in. I point to the bulge in my breast pocket. Unsightly bulge. "That ends it," I tell him.

"Good."

"Good, bad, or indifferent, we're not discussing."

"It's been good."

I tell him shit. "What I'm here to discuss is getting you out of this town."

"Oh?"

"And out of this country."

"Oh?"

"We are, in fact, discussing your funeral."

That I catch him with. "You always seem to be offering me last rites, Terry."

"I'm not offering, Simon. You're having."

"Careful. Don't push."

"I'm pushing. You can call it the finale to this sick-o-rama you been running."

I'm getting to him. "You said we're not discussing . . ."

"We're not. It's done. All I'm saying, for the record—and there's going to be a record—is I didn't send you here to dry-fuck my picture."

"You didn't send me here at all."

"I am now."

"That we will see."

I get tough. "You are in trouble, Simon. Get that good. So we are in trouble with the picture. Even before it's opened. I'm getting us out of trouble."

"How?" Like he didn't think it could be done, and proud to think he'd fixed it that way. Damn near has.

"Through your funeral."

"When is it to be?"

Putting me on, but I act like as far as I'm concerned, everything is settled. "Here's the schedule. Monday you arrive by special air freight from Transylvania, in a sealed coffin, courtesy of the Rumanian government. Or we put it out that you do."

"Stupid. Everybody knows I'm here." Grin. "That's why *you're* here."

Am I ever. Because *do* they ever. But I say, "You got a contract. It says p.r. We do p.r. my way." Why didn't I talk to him like this on set? "I want a fresh start. We're reimporting you. From the source country."

"To where?"

"Out at Kennedy. From there you are taken by hearse to the Edgar Allan Poe House below Washington Square to lie in state Monday night, all of Tuesday, most of Wednesday. The public will be allowed in to view the body—"

"What body?"

"The one you're sitting in, right here next to me," I thumb at him. "Just listen, we'll get to all that. You're on view from dawn until midnight Tuesday, and from dawn Wednesday until the body's removed at eleven P.M. to the stage of the Pentagonal Theater on Upper Broadway."

"Whose body am I supposed to be?"

"Your own."

"Ordinary human?"

"Not the way you've been playing it. Whatever kind of dragon-assed zombie suck . . . you tell *me* if you think you're ordinary human." But I don't want to go into that. "We put it out that you're still dangerous. The public, for instance, will not be permitted inside the Poe House after midnight or before dawn because during those hours you are likely to rise and seek a victim. We cannot be responsible, right? I'm thinking maybe we release a bat out the window around midnight. To suggest to people you're maybe still out doing . . . the kind of things you've been doing."

"You're back to bats?"

"I'm not giving away a plot point."

"Tell me. Is it really Edgar Allan Poe's house?"

"He used to live down there. Carmine Street. We got a house near where he maybe was."

"Really?" He liked that.

"Now about the cortege. It winds up Lower Fifth Avenue, around Washington Square, over to Broadway, then up through Times Square to the Pentagonal. The coffin is placed on stage. You know the Pentagonal?"

"Not that well."

"It's been redecorated. Quincy did it. There's a small circular lip stage now. That'll be the catafalque. The audience will be supplied with small souvenir crosses to protect themselves against you."

"When I rise at midnight."

"Only you don't."

"No?"

"We give them better."

"What might that be?"

"We open the curtains part way. A clock is projected on screen, showing the seconds to midnight. At precisely a minute to, this madman rushes up from the first few rows. He's got a stake and a big mallet. He jumps right up on the coffin and drives the stake through the lid, you, the coffin, everything. Some Broadway lunatic. The police arrive. When they drag the madman off the coffin, break it open, there's nothing inside but your dry bones. Maybe a little dirt."

"How does that happen?"

"Two coffins. We switch them. I'll get to that."

He looks at me, ready to hoot, but gives me a slow zinger instead. "What happens when my avid fans tear the theater apart?"

I smile. "If they're that glad to see you gone, I can't object. I'm just as glad."

"Idiotic," he says. "But you know that. Why do you want to do this?"

"I'll be frank with you, Simon. You got to vanish from the face of this earth before we can get that film on screen."

He begins finally to see I'm serious.

"What is this now? The film is pudding."

"It's you. You know that. People are out for your blood. They think you're abominable. Nobody ever disgusted them more."

He beams. "Why should I desert such a triumph?"

"I think I can give you reasons."

"For disappearing? At this moment?" He stiffens up. "You don't realize how hard I've been . . . Wrong. Of course you realize. And you think you can stop me."

"I think I can give you better things to do."

"Do not mistake me."

"And somewhere better to go."

"Do not mistake me. I'm devoting myself, my sunset years to public service."

And he means it. He really thinks he's been doing good, by fanging the world in the ass. This is where I really smile. Above all, I smile. P.r. "This fits in with that, Simon. I'm offering you the best way. Let me break things down for you, and you'll see."

"I don't see."

"You don't really mind coming out to Kennedy, do you?"

"That I can manage."

"You buy Tuesday at the Edgar Allan Poe House?"

"Yes . . ."

"But what?"

"I don't like playing dead."

"You're good at it."

"Not that long."

"I can't play you live, Simon. You'd probably be killed."

"I don't like dead."

"Look. We can provide help." I'd gotten hold of a few of his old favorites. Tossed them down on the middle cushion between us.

He looks at them, like I stole them. "You would put me back on *these* to do this?"

"If they help."

"Never."

"Do you know that story about Raymond Chandler and how he wrote *The Black Dahlia?*" Love this story. "They started shooting before he'd finished the script. Still didn't have an ending. Chandler kept trying for one, but he had a big drinking problem. I mean, the problem was he wasn't drinking. Cold sober, brain dead. So he goes to the director and admits he knows he could find an ending, but it's going to take a big personal sacrifice, a lot of outside understanding. So the director helps him get back on the bottle. Kept him drunk for three days. Dead drunk. That's what saved the picture."

"Why do I want to save your pudding picture?"

"You're in it."

"To my sorrow." He glowers at me. "I've seen the cuts."

"But you're still in it."

"To what purpose?"

"To be seen. And if you're not seen, Simon, you're really dead."

That gets him thinking. He pushes the pills into a tiny pile, one at a time, trying to make them look smaller maybe. "Go on."

"Do you buy the cortege?"

"Yes. I like that."

"The coffin on stage?"

"Yes."

"The clock ticking on screen?"

"If I rise."

"The madman?"

"No madman."

"Why not?" As if I didn't know.

"And no stake. I rise."

"You can't, Simon. This is where you got to vanish."

"Don't tell me that."

"For a while. For your own good."

He gets angry. "You're worse than them." He is pointing to the pile of pills. "But you don't do me in either. I am fighting for my own. And I'm getting my own. You're only here because I am turning people pale in this city. Tomorrow the world. So why should I vanish?"

It seems about the right moment, so I tell him. "I have something to offer you."

"Nothing."

"Maybe you should hear first."

"Nothing."

"Another picture, Simon."

He laughs, real bad. "Another picture? A sequel? More you, more Quincy?"

"This is different. Your own picture."

"Like *Mouth of Evil?*"

Tough tootsie, Simon, but I tell him, "I'm talking all your own picture. Everything."

"And I'm to believe you?"

"You can."

"How?"

"Because you already made the picture."

"I already . . . ?"

"That's right." I let him think about it a minute. "That's what I mean."

"I do not believe you." But it takes him time to say it.

"I can get it released."

"How?"

"I'm a producer, Simon. I have friends."

"In Germany?"

"Some. But more here."

Now it's taking him even more time to say things. "They'll never do it."

"What would you say if I told you it's already agreed?"

"Why?"

"I convinced them it would serve our vital interests. In a roundabout way."

"It won't."

"It's however I make them see it. Our policy toward East Germany, all that wall shit."

"Brecht tried things like that with them."

"He didn't have my contacts. You can go back there, Simon. If you'll go quietly."

"Quiet as the dead."

"Only for a while. Until you finish editing whatever you've got."

I get tight now, counting on him thinking he has enough, hoping he thought he could still pull it together. Hoping big. Tense moment.

"Who'd distribute?"

Still tense. "My company."

"You don't have a distributing company."

"What's one more company?"

The longest time yet. "You would really do this?"

I'm nervous this close, what's exactly the right thing to tell him? "What do I lose?"

"Money."

"On an unknown early Moro classic?"

"It's too political."

"These days?"

"Then it's too religious."

"Same thing goes."

"Really?"

"It'll run for years."

He looks me up and down, finally says, "Break things down for me again."

I don't show a thing. I just go into details. "We're set at the Pentagonal. I got film of the last five minutes to midnight. Off CBS News. We're already moving stuff into the Edgar Allan Poe House. Manuscripts, some ravens from a taxidermist. You know they want three hundred dollars for a stuffed raven? And a big collection of old opium vials. We're not attributing anything, but some of them say 'E.A.P.' We can offer Kinney a deal on a hearse, get Western Union in on the flowers—"

"No."

"No flowers?"

"No Kinney."

"They're good. They're in the business."

"I'll get the hearse."

"You'll get . . . ?"

"And the coffins."

Fantastic. Too much.

"You're really with me?"

"I'm watching my end of it. Very carefully."

"You should. I want you to."

"Two coffins."

"Both the same."

"Twins."

"Identical. And both simple. Pine even. Something we can get a stake through."

That gets him thinking again.

"You understand?" I keep pressuring. "We switch inside the hearse. At the marquee. Quincy and the other pallbearers—"

"Quincy?"

"This is p.r., Simon. Not your friends."

He is still thinking.

"I'm making it easy for you. Quincy takes the one with the skeleton into the Pentagonal, and you go straight back out to Kennedy in the hearse. Then air freight to Tempelholf. No passport control, Simon."

"I see," he says, at last.

"You're an item on the cargo manifest."

"And everything else?"

"Will be arranged."

"Which Berlin?"

"Either."

"You can really do this?"

"You maybe don't dig my films, but they go everywhere."

He shakes his head. "The madman?"

"I'll get one."

"Where?"

"I got a call out for Saturday."

"A real one would be better."

"I'll come as close as I can."

He doesn't say anything.

"You got somebody already in mind?"

"No, I was just wondering. . . ."

"What?"

"Who would want to attack me like that?"

After what he's been giving the public. After all the zaps and zingers he's been handing this city, his one-man-show guerrilla theater, and that sick TV stunt . . . Curb Your Zombie. . . .

"Guess he'd have to be crazy, Simon."

"Perhaps."

"Anything else?"

"My agent?"

"I already talked to Robbie. There can't be a contract, but like I said, there'll be some kind of record."

"Where?"

"On tape."

"Money?"

"Either Berlin."

"One more thing."

"Give."

"How does this really help you?"

"What don't you believe?"

"None of it. All utterly idiotic."

I take him up on that. "You start something, you'd better end it, Simon. People want an ending."

"Do they?"

"A clean ending. Happy, unhappy, believable, fantastic, impossible—"

"Idiotic, absurd, stupid, ridiculous—"

"As long as it's an ending. End clean, Simon. Otherwise you make everybody feel dirty."

"Perhaps."

"That's what you're doing. In my view. All you're doing. You're being a dirty, wet, loose end. And I can't open the picture while you're still straggling around in public."

"I see."

"I want people to know they're rid of you." I go further. "Also, I frankly don't mind just plain getting the hell rid of you myself."

"I find I am similarly disposed toward you."

"Then we're agreed?"

"We're agreed."

Done. Makes me want to cut him in on things a little more. "You want to help me pick the madman?"

"No. I'll be gone the weekend."

"You will?"

"Getting the coffins."

"Let's say Monday then. Ten o'clock. Out at Kennedy."

"In a hearse."

"Come on around behind air freight. We'll unload you,

run you through customs, slap on a few stickers, then bring
you out to meet the press."

"Open coffin?"

"Closed. We'll open it two minutes for pictures."

"I don't say anything, do anything?"

"You'd better not."

He nods. "You want me quiet."

"That's the whole point. We've had your act. We want
your lifeless remains."

"Death's dreary sleep."

"Whatever."

He pushes at the pills again. "Another terrible role."

"You can win awards later. At the Berlin Film Festival."

"But a very hard role."

"Play it with those."

"All of them at once?"

"Hilarious."

He smiles. "On Monday, try to guess whether I have."

There's going to be a record, so that's the record so far.
To the best of my recollection.

Also, I'm keeping another record, my own record. Why
not? Whose tapes are these? Today, after I left Simon, I
crossed over to the CBS Building, got down into that dry
moat they dug all around the place, and did my first squeegee ever against a window of the Ground Floor. I held it
maybe fifteen seconds, and caught a lady right in the middle
of spooning up her chocolate mousse, maybe three feet
away from the glass. She was still staring when I pulled
back. But when I walked in to meet the *Esquire* guy, she
was reporting it to the head waiter. He interrupted her to
take me to the right table. They never think it could be
anybody they'd allow in.

Y OU WORKING NOW?"
  "Just finished."
"Doing what?"
"Spot. For Gillette."
"That why you got half a face?"
"I want you to see I'm a good beard."
"I see that. You can shave and start over. You still got four days."
"If."
"Okay. If."
"This likely to lead to anything?"
"It could."
"What?"
"I'm looking for types."
"I been types."
"You got any kind of a psychiatric record?"
"Yeah?"
"It'd help if you do."
"I've done therapy."
"What for?"
"A weak ego."
"Where was it weak?"
"All over."
"What kind of therapy?"
"Acting classes."
"Acting classes?"
"Too complicated to explain."
"Who with?"
"A real genius."
"I know most of the geniuses."
"Not this one."
"You like secrets."
"I keep some things to myself."
"No problem. I do the same. Your ego got all its strength back now?"

"It can hold its own."

"What about your physical state?"

"If you want me to run, the knees aren't too good."

"I don't need you to run. I need you to drive a stake."

"The arms are first-rate."

"Here."

"What's this?"

"What's it look like?"

"A big tent peg."

"Close enough. Try this for size."

"Yeah?"

"Go on. Heft it."

"Heavy son-of-a-bitch."

"Butcher's mallet."

"I don't know though."

"What?"

"I could drive this peg better with a hand sledge."

"You'd split it."

"What kind of wood?"

"Hawthorn."

"What am I driving it into?"

"Pine."

"Touchy. How thick's the pine?"

"Half inch, maybe three quarters."

"What else am I going through?"

"Nothing."

"If I take it slow."

"You can't. Very important."

"Why not?"

"Has to be done quickly. Five or six good, hard, fast blows."

"Maybe you better give me the whole scene."

"No. That's not how I work."

"My piece of it then."

"From the top."

"Vroom."

"You enter from the back of the theater, proceed down the center aisle, take a seat in about the third row. You're part of the audience. No different from any other jack-off."

"Carrying these?"

"Under your coat."

"What kind of coat?"

"Seedy."

"Vroom."

"On stage, there'll be a coffin."

"Whose?"

"Let that go for the moment. On screen, a clock is running. You watch it, begin to sweat, get dizzy. Maybe there's a buzzing in your head. You can't stand the whine, the ticking. At exactly one minute to midnight, you jump up, leap on the stage. You're waving the stake in your left hand, the mallet in your right, and you're screaming."

"I'm a lefty."

"Trade hands then. You straddle the coffin. Look for a small red circle we got marked on the lid. Set the point of the stake there. We've already started the pine, so pound like fury. You drive that stake straight down into the coffin, right through the splinters. You keep pounding until they pull you off. You never stop screaming."

"Who pulls me off?"

"The police."

"Where'd they come from?"

"Out front. Hired for the evening."

"Why am I screaming?"

"From the top again."

"Vroom."

"You're this failed actor, a real bum, a stewpot, and a little screwy."

"Beard, seedy coat, rotgut breath."

"You got it. This is a theatrical funeral for your great

rival you're attending. You half imagine. The two of you started out together, tried for all the same parts. He got them. But thank Christ, for two seventy-five, you at last get to see him laid away in his coffin."

"He's Barrymore. I'm me."

"But the funeral is only a trick. You half know this, you half don't. He's not dead. He's playing a sleeping vampire. At midnight he's going to rise again and be better than ever. He's maybe going to be one of the immortals. You're going to end up his dresser if you're blind lucky. Unless, wild hope, you can stop him. What is this mallet suddenly doing in your hand? Unless, mad thought, you can knock a stake through his fucking heart, and finish him off. Like forever. There's your motivation."

"I'm screaming blood."

"You are."

"Vengeance-is-mine crap."

"That's your piece of it."

"If."

"If what?"

"What's really inside that coffin?"

"Nothing."

"What nothing?"

"I'm not telling you."

"That's not friendly."

"It's how I work. I want a certain reaction."

"What reaction?"

"The surprise you're bound to show."

"When?"

"When you find out what's inside."

"You're worrying me."

"No need."

"I worry, I might miss and hit my thumb."

"Bang your thumb all you want. If you're really thinking murder, you'll still keep pounding."

"I don't know."

"It's five hundred dollars."

"But does it lead anywhere?"

"Maybe. If I see you show the right kind of surprise."

"No rehearsal, no nothing?"

"Total impromptu. I don't see you again until you go on stage. Read the papers, and stay out of touch."

"I don't know."

"I like what I seen of you so far."

"I don't know."

"Your yellow-bellying on TV. I got that in mind."

"Hell, this is just a peg job."

"How you do it is what's important. If you react, we'll all react."

"Tell me this much."

"Ask."

"Who's my great rival actor?"

"Didn't I say?"

"You're sparing me everything."

"Simon Moro."

"Vroom."

"Yeah?"

"Vroom, vroom."

Good thing too. He's the only one who answered the call.

CONFESS. Sunday in New York I don't know anybody. Monday through Friday I know everybody. Through somebody or other. Saturday I still got contacts. But Sunday I'm a power failure in this town. Nobody to talk to except this tape. Tape's Last Crap.

Earlier I put on the sneaks and went out squeegeeing. Nothing else to do. Fifth Avenue, not much of a risk on a Sunday. Stores closed, call it practice. I did the Doubleday Bookstore window at Fifty-third, all the book jackets, gave Jacqueline Susann a real thrill. Then I did one of the Saks window dummies in her p.j.'s. Then a pair of glass feet in T-straps at I. Miller. Then a giant Teddy bear in F. A. O. Schwarz. "Go on," I growl at him. "Report me." On Sunday you can even do Tiffany's, but it's only jewels blinking at your jewels. Not much in that, and the plate glass, like everything else in this town, is witch-tit cold.

I found myself following a route. Circling around St. Patrick's, thinking how some day I'm going to squeegee a stained-glass window. I am. Find some church where they're cleaning the stone, climb up the scaffolding, do it while the organ booms. But I'd quit on that for the day, pretty much. Wandered all the way over to Lex, then up to Fifty-third, then down Park, to Fifty-first, up to Fifth again. Where was I going? Guess. My last trip to New York, a few months ago. That line for Bobby. What else? I was following it again, down along the white police barriers, all those popped drinking cups, everybody in their shirt sleeves. A hot night, but nobody mad because they had to wait. Nobody. I never saw a line like that before. That long, that patient, that lined-up. That's what I want out front of the box office some day.

And if you think about it, they didn't even get to see the show. It was a good show, I saw it, Andy Williams was terrific, but they had to go all the way back home to the Bronx, Jersey, wherever, turn on the TV to catch it. What did they come for? The inside of St. Patrick's, free any day? A few celebs, McNamara or McGeorge Bundy if they were lucky, even knew one Mc from the other? The coffin? That coffin was strictly a black-box deal. No, you don't get to see what's inside, we *tell* you what's inside. What's more, the show's tomorrow, folks. Move along, we got to get you all through and out of here before it starts.

At least I'm not giving them that kind of a fast shuffle. Hell of a thought, though, to think where your thinking comes from.

Yeah, that Bobby thing still gets me. You better be part of your time, somebody said, or you won't have lived. But to be part of this time, you got to get yourself killed. Face it, that's where the line forms.

I'm anti-violence. I am. Violence is as American as cherry pie, the sambo says, but I'm just as anti-cherry-pie. I hate cherry pie. Nigger food. But if I were in the pie business, I'd make a lot of cherry ones. I would. I'd have to. Same thing if you're in the movie business. Got to give them violence.

With or without the pits though?

That's the question. That's where Simon and I differ. He's pro-, I'm anti-pits. Who's going to eat a cherry pie with the pits in it? But okay, this time, this once we try it pits and all.

Still worries me. Totally my idea, but he's got hold of it, and that worries me. Really does. You plan a thing like this, you got to be freewheeling, but if anybody's a hair off, it's a mess. It's like afterwards, everybody says, why did Bobby have to go out through that kitchen? Or, how come that crazy Arab ever got into the kitchen? But think of the poor guy, beforehand, who had to be sure both of them were in the kitchen at the exact same right moment. I don't mean there *was* a guy. I'm just saying that if there *was* a guy, he had one bitch of a job.

This thing is like that. It's so tight. That's okay, if I can get it set up right. But I can't play with it too much. No room, no time. What can I do? Make some notes? Who do I read them to? It's bad enough I'm letting myself talk to this tape. I should be erasing what I got down already. But if there's going to be a record, it's going to be *my* record. I don't mean I want anybody to know there *was* a guy, but if it ever comes down to that, I want them to know who the guy was, how it really happened. Shit. If I keep this up, I'm going to Zapruder myself.

Things can go haywire. So easily. And you never know who's looking at you. Just now. I'm coming back to the hotel, walking up Fifty-first past Schrafft's. Low windows all along there, a few people eating their three-seventy-five Sunday dinner. An old couple smack in the middle of nothing but empty tables, pretending it's as good as home. Or Europe. One girl alone, right beside the third window, just back behind the curtain. She's got big shields, a scarf over her head, and she's leaning way down over the steam from her coffee. I can tell she's letting it clear her head. Some hung-over broad, just got up from being sexually humiliated right up to noontime. I decide I can't miss this one.

I do it with a slide motion. I'm against the window, but still behind the curtain. Then I slip along onto open glass, so it comes up on her slow, like something live.

She bobs up from her coffee steam, sees it. Nothing happens. She keeps her shades turned on it, and I can see my . . . *its* reflection in the lenses. That never happened to me before. It looks like something on the side of an aquarium. Like some big pink snail's hairy ass. I'm stopped, stuck there. Then she pulls down the shades, no panic, never shows it's anything to her but just another guy's squashed bird, and it's Hazel Rio.

I think I got away. Maybe in time. You can't trust this fucking town. Save that stuff until I get back out to L.A.

That's where they should have kept Bobby. He would've had an even bigger line.

I'M JUST BACK from Kennedy in the hearse, sent it on downtown with Simon. I'm encouraged.

For a while there, though, it was close. A lot of press, even Leonard Lyons, and Simon is over an hour late. They're throwing it all on me. Especially the L. A. *Times*.

"I just checked over at the Rumanian Air Terminal." He points to TWA. "They say this flight is a hundred and seven hours overdue."

"He'll be here."

"They tell me it got hijacked."

"Yeah?" pipes up the *Hollywood Reporter*.

"Some fang is making them fly him to Graustark."

"You can't land a jet at Graustark."

"You can land, but you can't take off."

"He'll be here," I tell them.

"Maybe you should call around to the other airlines," says the *Hollywood Reporter*. "The last vampire I met came in on Albanian."

"I've been in touch with him," I lie. "They hit traffic. He'll be here."

"How soon?"

"Soon."

"I still got to file."

"You'll have time."

"Our graves open three hours earlier in California, remember."

"Get yourself a drink, Herb. We'll let you know."

But the *Famous Film Monsters* guy is worse. He's serious.

"This is a mistake. You are playing with many people's deepest beliefs." He's wearing this big flying-saucer ring, about a trillion-billion facets. Shine it right in some poor Venusian's eye.

"Let me reassure you," I tell him.

"Individuals need faith. Especially our young people."

"I agree."

"We have been planning a Simon Moro issue for some time. But no. Not if the present course of disquieting events continues."

"We haven't been doing a thing. It's all been Simon."

"He owes us an explanation."

"I'm with you."

"There are Moroites everywhere on this planet."

"Terrific."

"He cannot expect us to accept his more recent behavior."

"Tell him that. When he gets here, tell him that."

"We will communicate in our own way."

What gets me about these outer-space kooks is they're all such fucking snobs. Take you and me light years just to get a foot in their goddamn galaxy. I go get myself a drink, try to stay out of his force field, flack the New York *Times* guy a little. I'm telling him double what the gross is likely to be, maybe triple, when the hearse drives up. At last. But it's not supposed to drive up. It's supposed to pull around back. Right. So I start waving to the driver, try to turn him until I see there is no driver.

"How did you work that?" the New York *Times* asks me.

"I don't know." I don't know.

It's coming toward us, down on us, and there's only this spook in the death seat, in a wing collar, top hat, staring out the windshield, deadly mean, like when he gets to us, how badly are we going to cut the tires? Swerves right through, trying to take a life here and there, but doesn't get anybody. The guys bang a few fists on its fenders, yell at whoever the hell. The hearse stops, lets out a whopping big backfire. Didn't think hearses ever did that.

Then maybe I never saw a hearse before, if this is one. It's some kind of ancient Chrysler, very early gangster. Old enough to have wooden spokes in the wheels, some of them cracked, and the wheels almost up to your waist. The shades in the back windows are stitched, tasseled shade pulls. Up front the windshield rolls out on runners, knobs, and there's a finger vase on the dash with ferns in it and one dead white rose. On the front of the hood, this Grecian-looking silver thing is tearing her streaming hair out, and on the front bumper, there's Kiwanis, the Grange, Four-H, and a volunteer fire chief's emblem. The back bumper's got a rusty trailer hitch and a lot of hay stuck in it. It's as muddy as it is black, and there's still no driver.

It's this spook who gets out, and all I can think is, where did Simon find him? A real old country creep. When he's not working funerals, he must scare crows. In the same outfit. Looks like he keeps it hanging in a silo. Mud, no, red clay on the striped pants, even the cravat. The L.A. *Times* takes one long look, yells over to me, "Is the Rumanian ambassador prepared to answer a few questions?"

The spook takes off his top hat, reaches inside for something, and damned if he hasn't got a death certificate all filled out. Then he opens his mean mouth. Altogether maybe three yellow teeth hanging there, still on the cob. "Who gets this?" he wheezes.

I break through to him. "Inside there," I tell him.

"Which one?"

"Which what?"

"The empty, or the full?"

I catch on. "The full."

He turns, puts on his top hat again, signals a lot with his hands through the car window. The door on the driver's side opens. We can see it open. What gets down is about three foot seven, with a head like a field pumpkin. But somebody forgot to turn it while it was still on the vine. He is wearing regular gum boots, this trog, and regular suspenders, and the suspenders are either way down in the boots, or the boots are way up on the suspenders, whichever way you want it. He heads at the crowd, already kicking himself a path through, clomps around to the rear of the hearse.

"Hey, driver!" The photographers are yelling at him for a picture, but he doesn't seem to hear them, pulls open the tail doors, climbs in.

"One of the Little People?" the *Hollywood Reporter* asks me.

Shit if I know, but before I need to answer, he comes back out again, and he's carrying the coffin. Single-handed, on his neck along that flat side of his head, keeping it steady with his dinky little toothpick arms. He even jumps down off the back bumper with it. Quivers a little when he lands, but stays up. The spook aims him toward the entrance to air freight, and the flash bulbs really start popping. Great, couldn't be better. But they bother him, and when the *Post* tries to get too close, he takes a swipe at the guy. With the coffin.

Wild. Almost gets stuck going through the doors, like a burro. The spook backs him up, works him through. I guide them over to the right guy at the counter, pull out a bunch of stickers I want to slap on. The trog hefts around, slings the coffin up on the counter at a tough angle. The customs guy has to lean out over the counter to see who even put it there.

The spook comes up, snarls, "We're next of kin."

"Yes, very good," says the inspector, looking over the death certificate—from somewhere in Jersey, for Chrissake —also looking over at me since it's my fifty bucks. I'm licking fast, "Nach Deutschland" and "Via London," and pasting them down on the lid, which I wish I'd done before they got that trog doing his overhead carry. "What relation are you to the deceased?" the guy asks them.

"His only kin."

"I see. You're bringing your . . . relative into this country for purposes of family burial?"

"The sooner he's under, the better."

"Of course." The inspector looks at me again. "In this case, however, I'm instructed to make a brief inspection. There is some question about the cause of . . . you will allow me?"

"Who minds?" Then the spook gives another hand signal.

That trog is fast. He's got the lid off while I'm still standing there with a wet Trieste label on my tongue.

And there is Simon, eyes shut, out of this life altogether.

Shocks even me. Like he was found under some dunghill after the pigs had been at him. And mossy. Or moss over enough of him so they can still print the pictures.

Nobody moves. But the L.A. *Times* has got to mouth off. "Wow. Some jet lag."

That starts everybody. "Pictures. Let them up front," I yell, but the pencil press are on him already.

"You been in touch with the network since the show?"

"Mayor Lindsay said today you might represent a health hazard. Any comment?"

"Whose finger was it? You prepared to say?"

"Are you an actual practicing vampire, Mr. Moro?"

"Was it just that finger, or can we expect the rest of a body?"

"Hazel Rio told Earl Wilson you leave a real hicky. Anything between you two?"

"How much blood you drink a day?"

"When can we expect to hear something definite from you, Mr. Moro?"

"Hey, Terry, how much blood are you saying he drinks a day?"

"Louder."

"Did you really bite that woman on the subway?"

"Ask him to do his grin."

"Can't hear back here."

"What's the purpose of this visit, Mr. Moro?"

"Any truth to the rumor you're thinking about entering politics?"

"What do you consider your chances if you tried walking the streets tomorrow?"

"Louder."

They're shooting him close, all angles, and the spook is posted there with his top hat over his heart for some reason, and the trog is waving his six-inch arms, keeping off flies. I'm getting all I want. Simon hasn't moved a muscle. I can't even see how he's breathing. Back gills, or through his skin maybe. "Okay, boys, we're closing up." But before I can get closed up, I get something even greater.

The flashes don't bother Simon, not a reflex out of him, but out of nowhere, this terrific light zap hits him, right smack on his shut left eye. Focuses down, pinpoints like the sun through a magnifying glass, damn near burns his eyelid. He has to flinch away.

"Moro lives!"

It's the *Famous Film Monsters* nut, giving him super zing off that power station on his knuckle.

"Simon Moro! Rise and live!"

He gets squeezing-through room from the press, moves forward, leading with that ring, like his own asteroid. The worst type. A sci-fi Holy Roller.

"Return to us! Remember what you once were. The stern reptile. The vengeful moth. The whirring robot, and the honest strangler. Let us hear again a great stirring in your restless grave. Live, Simon Moro!"

Simon is trying to take all this zap, not budge once, and the press is getting on the kook.

"You wouldn't shit us now, would you, moon man?"

"Question, question!"

But he's still got half a sermon to go.

"Do not fail us, Simon Moro. Do not stay the false slave of earthling media. Rise. Leave the screen's prison. Youth needs your guidance. Rise, Simon Moro. The planet lies in shackles. Live! Lead us!"

I can see Simon is gritting his teeth, his whole body even, trying to stay dead. Tense. But then the spook waves once, and that's all it takes. That trog is damn fast.

Great pictures. He goes for the kook with his head down, gets him, at that height, right in the balls. The kook yells, real human, folds up, but the trog keeps after him. In the stomach, in the ribs. It's like he's kicking him senseless with his flat head. Brutal. Guys are shouting him away, but it's clear now the trog is a dummy. You got to pull him off to make him let up.

But time to get the lid on. The spook and I slip it over, bang it home, and the customs inspector smears on the paste, slaps down his declaration. Then the spook and I each take an end and head for the doors. We're trying to run, trotting, but what gets me is it takes the two of us, breathing hard, all our strength, full grown men, to heft that coffin back into the hearse.

I shut the tail doors from inside, and the spook goes back for the trog. The press come pouring out after them, those that aren't still interviewing the kook. The trog jumps behind the wheel. Under it, really. I'm watching through the little cab window, and he's really standing on the pedals and swinging from the wheel, when you come right down to it. The spook tells him where to head with quick hands, and we gun out of there, both gum boots on the gas pedal.

The empty is the only place to sit down. The whole back of the hearse is old horsehair, maybe even old porcupine. When we get out on the highway, Simon bangs on his lid. I open him up, help him out, let him have my raincoat, which he makes moss green all over the inside lining. We sit together on the empty.

"Who was that *Dummkopf?*" he says to me. "One of yours?"

"One of yours."

"Never."

"That's what doing for yourself gets you."

"He's none of my doing."

"Says he's a Moroite."

"A what?"

"You tell me."

"Whoever they are, I'm not one of them." He shivers, either cold or shaky, maybe just old. "But he is right about this planet."

"Is he?"

"We had better locate another one. For asylum."

"So now you don't like Earth."

"The new one would be Earth."

"What would this one become?"

"America." He shivers again. Age. "America hasn't got room for Earth any more."

"You better dress more warmly," I tell him.

"I plan to. Evening clothes."

"How did it feel to you?"

"Workable."

"Didn't need the pills?"

"Didn't need the pills."

"When do you breathe?"

"When nobody's looking."

"How can you tell that with your eyes closed?"

"I peek."

"Also when nobody's looking?"

"Exactly." He kicks across at his coffin, the one with the labels. "Plain, good, country workmanship. And cold as an ice chest."

"It'll do fine."

"You found a madman?"

"Not as crazy as the two you got."

He smiles. "Thought you'd like them."

"Can we keep them around?"

"They never leave my side."

I tap a knuckle on the lid of the empty. Very hollow. "I'll get a skeleton put in here tomorrow."

"That's half-inch poplar. Should give easily."

"Who made them for you?"

He nods up front. "Cosmo."

"Which one's he?"

"The mean one."

"Who's the dwarf?"

"Not a dwarf. Too tall. And keep away from him."

"Friends of yours?"

"I've worked with them."

"In what kind of act?"

"It's too long to go into."

I nod across at his coffin. "You could do with some cushions in there. Maybe a little satin."

"No. The starker, the better."

"At least for the trip to Germany."

"I'll take the pills for that."

"Good."

We don't say anything for a while. I take a peek out from behind the shade at the traffic, and it's swinging wide, passing us fast, avoiding us. Maybe only because of the way we're weaving, that trog and his driving, but it adds to the effect. We're a real midnight hearse.

"Simon," I tell him, "this is going to work."

"One way or another."

"And I hope you do a great film." Yeah, I say that. What's it cost me?

"Do you?"

"An epic."

"You understand. It is not a very family film."

"We'll art-house it."

"There is one scene in particular. You will be interested.

A very long one where I strap down this *Fräulein* and pull out all her teeth."

I say nothing.

"Very lovingly. One by one."

I still keep my peace. "You're in luck. I don't show that."

"No. You wouldn't."

"I show Quincy going out into the cemetery, a close-up of a pair of silver pliers in his hand. Then a psychedelic montage. Mostly a lot of big, red boulders rolling out of the mouth of this cave."

"You would."

"So it doesn't matter."

"Nothing does with you."

"We can still work together, Simon."

"Yes." He shivers badly. "Our cross-purposes cross."

A BOUT HAD ENOUGH of his shit, but we're getting the coverage, and we're getting a line outside the Poe House. Not exactly a Bobby line, but it's holding. When I left tonight, this morning really, there were even a few people starting to camp out on the street. Mostly hippies, some signs. "DON'T DIE, SIMON!" "WE ARE ALL SIMON'S SIMPLES." "SIMON STILL SUCKS!" One freak's got himself a body paint job like Ghoulgantua, and another one's telling everybody she's pregnant by him, slept with him as a bat in mid-air. Hardly your sedate crowd of mourners. They don't have to be there either, that's what gets me. I'm not paying them, and nobody's had to wait more than five minutes all day. But like the man said, the last sometime got to be first.

The big thing early today, yesterday now, is putting pennies on his eyes. I got down there a little late, wanted to read through the papers first. They mostly played it Martian Attacks Monster, Dwarf Fells Martian, but enough hard news to get people to get a move on. Lot of Macy's shoppers and mamas on the way home from taking the kids to school when I get down there myself. Cosmo meets me at the door, hands me a fistful of copper.

"What's this?"

"Twenty-seven cents," he says. "So far."

The odd penny is one somebody even put on his nose.

"How's he taking it?"

"Hasn't blinked."

The trog's been picking them off real careful, Cosmo tells me. We decide to move the ropes back so he's well out of arm's reach, but maybe we should've left it the way it was, because now they start pitching them at him. Finally I put up a jar marked "Donations," and get Cosmo to tell the trog to hustle any penny-slinger right the hell out of there. That's a risk too, but so far he hasn't put his head down at anybody.

You wonder, how does a thing like that get started? One guy does it, they all do it. Only I'll bet it wasn't any guy. Some blue rinse, a lot of loose change in her purse, but pennies is all she can spare. Reaches out, presses them down on his eyelids. Not too hard, but hard enough to pay her respects, feel to see for sure if he's really dead.

Opinion seems to be widely divided on that. We won't know how widely, of course, until this pollster who shows up around eleven gives us the final breakdown on his figures. Nobody I arranged. An independent. Comes up to me, "Do you mind if I ask your viewers a few questions as they come out?" Why should I? He stands on the sidewalk with his clipboard, and asks them first, do they *believe* Simon Moro is alive or dead in there, and second, would they *prefer* he were alive or dead? It's a four-way cut when you knock out the no-opinions. Dead–dead, dead–live, live–dead, and live–live.

"But it's all over the map," he tells me. "There seem to be more people who wish he were alive who believe he's dead than there are people who wish he were dead who think he's alive. But you don't really get that many people thinking he's alive who necessarily want him alive. You got significantly more people who think he's dead and are glad."

Somewhere in there is about the way I feel too, but I suggest to him that maybe he's talking to too many women.

"Opinion," he says, "is women."

They got strong ones all right. Some press are also hanging around, picking up goodies. One granny comes out shaking her cane, tells the *Daily News*, "Been dead for weeks. Swallowed that finger, and choked, and gone to hellfire, and serves him right."

Then there's one we have to pull out of there when she starts singing hymns over him. "Rock of Ages," real slow and weepy, and plenty drunk.

"We never married," she keeps telling us. Stuffed with

booze, but acting like she just came from choir practice, or maybe right from the church door. "Set my cap for him, but we never married."

The *Post* tries to get her name.

"Mrs. Simon Moro."

"Ma'am?"

"Should've been. Ask my daughter."

"I take it you think he done you wrong."

"He's gone to his rest. May it be a peaceful one."

"You consider he's dead then?" the pollster asks her.

"Been dead to me for years. But I still have a daughter. Praise be the Lord, I still have my daughter."

"Are you maybe saying she's his, lady?" the *Post* wants to know.

She raises herself up like a stack of Bibles. "How could I be? We never married."

The cops get her at the corner, but nicely, only for jay-walking.

Actually, we get a lot of them coming through in the morning who say they knew him. He used to be that strange janitor in their building, or the foreigner who was always trying to breathe on them in the Seventh Avenue. "You won't credit this, but I said to my husband years ago when we first saw him in the movies, and now I'm sure. He's the one that sold us that marriage manual with all the pages stuck together." But around noon, the crowd changes, and this big tub of guts comes through who sounds more like he's for real.

"Of course he's alive. This is all a silly stunt," he tells the pollster. "But he *wishes* he were dead."

"You prefer him dead?"

"Not I. He."

"Why do you put it that way, sir?"

"He was once a patient of mine. In Vienna."

The reporters move in.

"When I knew him, he was all but unable to function. He is simply trying to return to that state now."

"What would you say was wrong with him?" the *Times* asks, very seriously. "First the public insults, now this. . . ."

"Professional ethics, of course, prohibit me from saying. But I might comment more generally."

"Any way you want to say it."

"Actors are a peculiar psychological group. Theatrics are an excellent occasional outlet for most people. I employ them often in therapy. But actors become addicted to theatrics. And withdrawal can go very, very hard." He waggled a finger about the size of a shoehorn and put a lot of shove on what he was saying. "There is nothing more desperate in this world, gentlemen, than an exhibitionist who feels he can no longer exhibit."

But most of the noontime crowd is secretaries, a lot of them eating their lunch in line. Cosmo holds things up some by making each one finish before he'll let them in, but then they pretty much rush through and get out. A lot of no-opinions. Real irritated. "It was just something to *do*."

An hour later it changes over to the school kids, and a few teachers. The teachers are trying to tell the kids about the Great Writer whose home they're visiting, look at how careful his handwriting was. But the kids couldn't care less. Half of them can't hear through the rubber monster masks they're wearing anyhow. Gila Man seems to be the favorite, the Moth next. They're really there to scare him back. Begins to sound like a Coney Island ghoul-o-rama in there around four o'clock, and most of them tell the pollster they know he's just asleep.

But then, all of a sudden, the noise dies down, and kids start coming out with their masks off, a little shaky, plenty pale.

I get hold of Cosmo. "What's happening? He's not doing

anything to them?"

"Got his eyes open."

"Yeah," says a kid, on his way out fast. "But you can't see them."

I take a quick run through there myself, and I got to admit he's pretty gruesome. He's doing his backward eyeroll, nothing but the whites showing. How the hell he holds it for as long as he does, I'll never know.

I stop at the coffin, think maybe I'd better go under the ropes and say something to him. After all, it's my basic audience he's fucking with now. But you don't really want to say anything to him in there. All that Poe shit, and the crazy rainbows off the opium vials. Not much daylight, heavy curtains, heavy double doors, and big stand-up candles on both sides of him. Eerie. Movie-lobby eerie. He's got on white tie, with this red-lined cape underneath him, also makes a lining for the coffin. His boiled shirt's about three sizes too large for him, and wired up inside, so there's plenty of chest room for him to breathe without showing any movement. That's one way he pulls that no-breathing trick. But the touch that gets me is keeping the lid still halfway on, lengthwise and across the bottom, so it's like you're looking at him behind a crooked door. Looking *in* on him, and him looking back at you, only with no eyes. And if what you see is that bad, who knows what you don't see? Down at the bottom of the coffin maybe he's got bare feet and blood under all his toenails. At least that's his expression.

Also I don't say anything to him because right behind me, a couple of kids back, is this female phantom coming through. She's wearing a black lace mantilla down to her knees, but her skirt's right up to her crotch, black tights and big black shades. Mysterious mourning lady, right out of Poe maybe, but I know Hazel Rio now when I see her, and I don't want to see her right now.

There's a let-up after she comes out, looks over at me, lifts her shades, deliberately? Lasts until six o'clock when we start getting what I'd call the real horror crowd. Devotees. Mainly hippies, sure, but not limited to any one class of people. They all have this zonked look, like they're In the Presence, and the line slows down to a creepy crawl. I tell Cosmo to hurry it up, but he can't, or won't. Some of them have wild garlic when they go in, no wild garlic when they come out, and when I take a quick peek in there, wow, some whiff.

"What are they doing with the garlic?" I ask Cosmo.

"Rubbing it on themselves. For protection."

"You're kidding."

"The heads."

"You're kidding."

"They leave him the stems."

I go back and look again, and around the coffin are a lot of stems I missed, some on the lid, a few on his boiled shirt. I tell Cosmo we'd better stop it the same as the pennies.

"It's all right," he says.

"It is not all right."

"Go look at him."

So I go back in there once more. He's got his eyes closed again, and the room's darker now, but if you look very close, he's showing just a little bit of a shit-eating grin.

"I don't like this."

"It's all right," Cosmo says, meaner than ever.

What's all right? Outside they're giving the pollster answers that make me think you can get high on garlic.

Is he alive or dead?

"Either way, man."

"In this life, who lives?"

"He's the only one who knows, my friend. Really *knows*."

"It's like it is. He's living the dead life. Live it up, Simon baby!"

"Neither. He's in there getting born."

And some of them think they're here to help him get born.

"That's why we've come down here." No hippie, this one. A straight, working on his Ph.D. at NYU in demonology, he says, although he also says he has to work under the psychology department. "It's not that easy, you know, for a vampire to rise. He has to do everything for himself, and on most occasions, alone, and in entirely isolated circumstances. The traumas are similar to those you'd find after any unassisted birth. With the same catastrophic effects on personality. I happen to think that most vampires are, to a large extent, autistic."

"You believe . . . ?"

"Not a question of belief, is it? A matter for investigation, continued research into the occult." He looks at me with this screwy pair of eyes. "He shouldn't be here. He should be at the medical school."

I figure about then it's been a long day and I got plenty to do elsewhere, I'll come back around closing time. I don't dig this crowd much, where are all the people who hate his guts? You can't even call this crowd Moroites. They're too loose, elbows for brains, and it's bigger than that, and kookier. Doubt their Simon, they wouldn't try to argue. Just go for you with bare hands. Simon starts these things up in people, I don't care what he thinks he's doing, really. It's superglow fink-worship. And a lot of hostility goes right along with it. We're here to pay our respects, folks, and gang-bang the corpse. I see a good example of that, which I don't want to see, just before I take off. Lars Syndor—and what's he doing here?—comes through the line. I don't see him go in, but I catch him coming out, in a big huff with a nasty new beard. He winks at me when the pollster stops him, and he's very loud with his answer.

"Alive, and I'd like to see him dead, baby, dead. Vroom."

And the crowd starts hissing him. Like snakes and witches and warlocks. It's lucky he's a goddamn skulk, shies out of there fast, or we'd have had a scene. The commune would've divvied up his balls. I don't like it. I think he's crazy to show himself, but he doesn't know that much of it, keep in mind, and he's sure working on his piece of it, I give him that. But I decide to set it up a little safer.

"If he comes around again," I tell Cosmo, "turn him away."

"Been through twice."

"Okay. But not again."

"He knows he's not wanted."

I LEAVE IT, and head back here to the hotel. In my room I order up a ham sandwich and some lousy Brooklyn brew, sit there a while, wondering if I can keep control of it. Or is it going to be the goddamn ravens all over again with him? But no use wondering. Just thank Christ I got him playing dead, and not wild-ass. I pull out the suitcase with the skeleton in it, the same one he tried to ruin the picture by throwing a fuck at. Somehow appropriate, I think, that it's now going to be his. Then I taxi over to the parking lot on Eighth where they're keeping the hearse.

"Somebody's delivered these today," I hear right away from the attendant. It's the three bags of potting soil, leaning up against his shack.

"Yeah," I tell him. "Bring them along."

We take them and the suitcase back to where the hearse is parked. By just being parked there, that hearse makes the whole lot look like a junk yard. I open the tail doors, reach in and pull forward the empty.

"Who's in there?"

"Nobody yet. Tear open one of those bags."

We dump it into the coffin, then another. Two of them cover the bottom, but it takes the third bag to create any depth. Then I haul the skeleton out of the suitcase, lay it out straight, push the skull, some of the bigger bones down into the dirt far enough so it won't rattle.

"Now who's in there?" he still wants to know.

I give him a freebie. He reads it through and through.

"That guy I saw on Johnny Carson?"

"But so far," I tell him, "only you and I know."

"Can I tell the wife?"

I give him another freebie, and slip the lid back on. Then we both heft it to see how it handles. It's about the same weight as the full now, everything the same except the labels. But I can forget them. It'll look better on stage without.

"They'll be here for the car tomorrow night," I say. "Around ten."

"I'd offer you a rate, but they already paid."

"Just keep an eye on things."

He helps me shove the coffin back. He'll remember doing all this, some excuse if I ever need one. What excuse? *I played it straight with you, Simon. Ask anybody. I'm still ready to distribute. It's your Germans who messed up. But if you want back to America, swim.* Something like that.

I tip him big, then head over from there to the Pentagonal, just to check. The souvenir crosses have arrived, stacks of boxes in the lobby. But I wonder, do we really need them? People seem to have their own souvenirs. What if they all bring garlic?

By then it's eleven-thirty, and I figure I can face that gang at the Poe House again. But I can't find a taxi, so by the time I get down there, it's midnight, we're closed, and those hippies are staking out for tomorrow's opening at dawn.

"Don't go in there, man," says the Ghoulgantua paint job. "He's thirsty."

"Show him a little love," says the bat girl.

Reminds me I was going to release a bat. Out that window. Forgot to get hold of one. Can't think of everything. *Tried to think of everything, Simon. I can't help it if you Krautheads got lousy security.* Something like that.

The trog opens up for me. Only the hall lamp's on, over the copy we got of *Murders in the Rue Morgue.* Cosmo is standing in front of the double doors, back in the dark. They're closed too. I figure I'll just go in and say goodnight to Simon, show a little interest, then come back to the hotel and do this tape. But when I go up to the doors, Cosmo is very much in the way.

"The Master," he says, "will see nobody."

I look at him.

"He has retired for the night."

"What's this Master shit?"

Cosmo gets stiff. "I have instructions for you."

I look at him. Doesn't even talk the same. Still the old scarecrow, but with this dreamy, bugged look now, like somebody stuffed him with wet daisies and cowshit.

"You just stand aside there, Cosmo."

But he doesn't. He makes with the hands, and there's the trog, right behind me, in a crouch.

"Look," I tell him, "we're all friends here."

"You are to lay the skeleton in the empty coffin."

"Already done it."

"The lid is to be left open."

"Oh, is it?"

"The Master wishes to check everything himself."

Doesn't trust me. That's what all this is about. Dangerous, last-minute screwing around, and I don't like it one bit. "He's gonna nail himself shut? Or leave that to you two fuckheads?"

Cosmo stiffens even more, meaner.

"Do not come here tomorrow."

"You're kidding?"

"Until eleven o'clock."

"What *is* this shit?" I'm thinking maybe it's crowd infection from all those creeps coming through.

"You trouble the Master."

"Don't you guys *know?*"

"We will prepare him for you."

"*He's* not paying you. *I'm* paying you."

"He will be made ready for you by eleven."

"That's exactly how it just *better* be, Cosmo."

"He will be waiting for you. Outside, in the hearse, under the labeled lid. Ready for transport."

"Right. And you make damn sure about two things."

I get a lot of choke-weed eyebrow from him. "Yes?"

"That he's taken his pills."

"We will see that he takes his pills."

"And that he's emptied his bladder."

That ought to knock a little crap out of this act, I figure. Master's got a long way to go, I tell them to remember, we don't want Master to wee-wee. But Cosmo answers, and not a twitch. "We will empty the Master's bladder."

What in Christ-almighty-hell is Simon trying to pull with these two zilch-pickers? But I'm not about to rush in there and ask him with that itchy hammerhead behind me. Besides, I don't really see how they're harming my own plans any.

"You guys are a riot. Okay, look. I got plenty to do myself tomorrow. You'd be helping me out if you'd handle things down here. And if Simon wants it that way, we do it that way. Only just be goddamn sure you know who's really running this show, or I'll shit-list you from here to the Mummers' Day Parade."

Cosmo gets a little more straw-footed then, shuffles around, and the trog trots back off down the hall. Going to open the door for me now, real polite.

But as I'm leaving, Cosmo again.

"I've been told to ask."

"What?"

"Do you have any message for the Master?"

I turn around on him. "Tell the Master to go suck himself."

THIS is where it gets rough. There is where I win the Academy fucking Award for an on-the-spot p.r. original, or the whole thing falls flat as a dried kumquat.

Right now, right this minute, I'm talking from the back of the hearse, riding uptown, sitting on Simon's coffin. It's shut. And nailed. So's the empty, over there opposite me, with the skeleton planted in it. Those fuckheads do tight work. The trog bangs them in with the flat of his head, then Cosmo countersinks them with his best of three teeth, right? Maybe. Anyhow, this one's labeled, ready for shipment, and that one's ready to go on stage, just the way I told it to Simon last Friday. So far, and no farther. Like I'm not saying how far I'm really shipping Simon, or what he's going to find when he gets there. Never mind. Up front, they're now driving us past . . . when I peek out the window, which I hardly dare do, I see we're just passing Fourteenth Street. I thought we'd maybe get a few more blocks north before . . . no, the rabids are starting to pick us up, come after us, bound to happen. . . .

A goddamn pothead bike rally, that's what this is turning into. But it figured. Some cortege. They zoom up, work in close, pound the sides with their fists, even kick at us. That slamming noise in the background . . . I'll tell you what it's like. As if you couldn't hear, but I'll tell you what it's like anyhow. A long time ago I heard this old radio program. This U-boat is sneaking across the Atlantic Ocean, heading for Buenos Aires, with guess who for chief passenger. Only, halfway there, it gets mysteriously grabbed with a lot of thumping, and dragged to the bottom. Dead souls, on leave from the ovens, out to finish him. That's what this is like. . . .

Only they really love Simon, these bang-ass kooks. If I sneak back a shade even an inch, they spot it, bunch up, give me the finger. They give me the finger with their little fingers. That's the latest. A love token, a folk tribute to what is now called around the networks . . . Finger Night. Even I can't keep up with the latest shit.

Keep curtains closed, and a quick word about today. I spent most of it running around to the theater, to the cops, to the Mayor's office, trying to get ready for this. We should've known, we knew, but we didn't really, right? . . . I'm going on secondhand reports. It didn't come to bust at the Poe House, but almost. Word got out that his eyes were open. Really open, not just rolled back for the kids. They came in hordes, and a lot of them I guess after bad trips. Some of them anyhow. Enough of them. And Simon milked it for all it was worth. First one eye, then the other, but never, of course, both eyes open at once. Always leave them wanting more. The cry is, "Rise, baby, rise! Get up and get out!" The *Post* says, mid afternoon, there hasn't been anything like it since they tried to levitate the Pentagon.

My own opinion, Simon was druggy. They came to see his goddamn eyes, *eye* dilate. He's sure out now. When I bang on his lid . . . what's one more bang inside this kettledrum? . . . I don't get a scratch.

"The Master sleeps," Cosmo tells me when I arrive down there for him at eleven.

"Damn right, the way I hear it."

"The Master says from here on, we're in charge."

"He means I'm in charge." But I try to enlist him a little. "The Master get to see his skeleton?"

"We helped him sit up in his coffin."

"Then he saw?" Probably saw a whole boneyard, dancing on a marimba.

"Yes."

"And he approves?"

"Everything."

They had the hearse hidden behind A & P delivery, a block from the Poe House. They slipped him out the back to get him away from the rabids. Looks to me like that trog had to carry him over at least one garden wall, somehow. A cop is up the alley, and both coffins are lined up in the back, one on each side, ready for let's call it dispatch. I hop in and sit down on Simon.

"Listen," I tell Cosmo. "How about this time if somebody besides your short friend does the driving?"

Cosmo shakes his spooky head. "I have no license."

"And he *does?*"

"The Master said we are in charge."

Fucking hayseed. I give up. I tell him the route. We've got an escort anyhow, once we're down the alley and out onto Carmine, but I don't think enough of a one to handle what's closed in on us since Fourteenth. Not just bikes. On every corner, I swear I see three, four of his zombies, ready to rush us. Some friends he's got, where is the fucking enemy? You figure these things, but you never figure them right. If they ever head us off, it could be worse than Nixon at Caracas. Can't worry about that. My job is to . . .

THOUGHT we'd had it there for a minute. Wow did I. But count on that trog everytime.

They are lying down in front of us when we get to Twenty-eighth Street, two deep, all the way across. If it'd only been Cosmo, a good bet we'd have rolled right over them, but the escort chickened and hit the brakes up ahead of us.

What I can see of it is only what I can catch through the windshield from the cab window. Not much of a view, but I'm not about to pull up any shades. I can hear zombies all around me. There's even one up on the roof, banging on my head. It's like they're trying to bail the hearse by hand.

But that trog. So cool. Makes it look like a drill. He skins up over the steering wheel onto the dash and hunches down. Cosmo unscrews the knobs, pushes out the windshield just far enough so the trog can slide under, roll onto the hood. He stands up. Mighty Mite. Cosmo hands him through a bunch of something. He takes them, swings his puny arm around twice, then lets fly out over the zombies who are blocking the wheels.

Freebies. Maybe a hundred of them. Probably Simon's. They flume out, break apart, flutter around in the air a second, and then it's a zombie riot to grab one before your fellow corpse beats you to it. Good thinking.

Next the trog climbs up top after whoever's on the roof. I hear stomping around up there, and then the banging stops. Not just on the roof. On the sides too. He must've done something. Has he ever. I see when he pulls her down over the windshield onto the hood, head first. He's got her by her long dirty hair, twisting it around his wrist like a greasy rope.

She's maybe half again his size, clawing at him, wild, screaming, so are the zombies, but who hears? Not that trog. He just holds her out away from him, like a yowling cat, keeps working her along the side of the hood. You can't really tell what he's trying to do to her until he gets her around front, and then it's hard to credit. He tries to tie her to that hood thing, get her dirty hair knotted around its silver tresses. Drive right through the mob with her dangling over the grille, I guess. What a mind.

It's the cops who rescue her, hand her back over to the zombies. The trog shrugs, kicks at a few heads, slides back under the windshield, and drops behind the wheel again. No problem now. Nobody tries to stop us. Who wants anything more to do with us?

He's that bloodcurdling. He almost puts me off what I know I have to do. And there's only ten blocks left, chop chop, let's get cracking. . . .

DONE. An ending. You got to have an ending. And I've done all I can to set one up. Done all a man can.

I'm going to say, very quickly, just what I did. It's of interest.

I didn't go over to the empty first. No. First I lay down on this lid and stretched out full length. He's four inches taller than I am, the bastard, so I slide up a little toward the head of the coffin. We must be lying almost face to face, lying together like two loving queers except for the lid between us. Thin wood. Quincy would be jealous. I reach under my own chest, feel where my heart is beating against the wood. It's beating hard. I put my thumb on that spot, keep it there and sit up again. Then I shift the thumb about three inches to the right. My heart plus his own black heart, lying to my right, his left. The spot is on one corner of the "Nach Deutschland" label.

Then I say, right out loud, "If only it could really be you, Simon baby . . . with a big chopstick bunged through your stove-in, red-running heart!"

But you can't have everything in this world. So I move over to the empty. I mark about that same spot with a red pencil and draw a tiny circle in red around the mark.

Then I take out my pocket knife. It's got five different blades from the days when we were all Boy Scouts, and one of them is an awl. I turn the awl slowly inside the tiny red circle until it pushes through to the other side of the soft poplar.

Then I blow away a very small screw of sawdust.

That's all I do. It looks like a toy bullet hole. Took me six, maybe seven blocks. Only a few more to go now. What else can I do? When we arrive in front of the theater, I'll unlatch the tail doors from inside, but I'll leave it to Quincy to open them. Have to leave a lot to Quincy. He'll find me sitting here on Simon. He'll direct the pallbearers. He'll pick up the bones. He'll, he'll, he'll . . .

And then, Simon baby, we ship you out.

I'm getting too excited. Sound a little strange, even to myself. Got to stay contained. Plenty still could go wrong. The switch is on, but the switch is still to come. And if I let up for a moment, these last few couple of blocks, I know what I'd probably do. I'd rip up the shades, rip down the zip, and squeegee all of good old fucking Broadway.

I'M TALKING now from the balcony of the Pentagonal, about ten rows back, way over on a side aisle. The angle's bad, but the place is packed, and I'm trying to keep out of people's hearing with this tape. There's a runty little couple two rows ahead who've been staring back at me, but they're starting to argue. An old routine, you can tell. Why did they come, it's what he says she said she wanted to do, but she says he never says what he wants to do, why doesn't he say if he doesn't? They've got it memorized. Ought to last until the clock starts running, and if I keep it low, I should be okay.

I love this theater. Yes I do. The hell with that *Esquire* hack. Incidentally, he's down there. I can see him in about the fourth row front, squinting at the coffin, taking notes. Trouble is, I don't see Lars anywhere yet. But maybe it's the angle. That's the one thing wrong with the Pentagonal. You get a lousy view from the sides, even downstairs. But you can't knock the feel of the place, if you like a little decor. Black onyx mirrors in the lobby. Purple railings on the escalators. Moons in the ceiling for your house lights. Black seats, scarlet arm rests. And that wide-o-rama curtain, red with black sparks, yards and yards of it, but a lot of cute cape-play when it takes the out-curve around the lip stage. Of course that's Quincy.

Catching up here. First on Quincy. Didn't tell me what he was planning to wear, but when he pulls open the tail doors, terrific. There he is, head to foot, in a black domino. The peaked hood, the works, and three monks for pallbearers. Menacing. It cows the zombies outside the marquee, suits the occasion. With that hood, I can't see his face when he picks his coffin. Not that I'm looking. All I'm doing is sitting. What else can I do? But I'll bet Quincy is loving this. He's rid of the bastard too, and we can open *Mouth of Evil* next. Big. Wide enough to see its tonsils.

He takes the head, and the three monks take two sides and

the foot, and they're on their way through the lobby. Hazel follows along behind in her same get-up. The only mourner. Widow, bimbo, grief-stricken starlet? Who knows? At least she's got that mantilla pulled down over her shades, showing a little respect.

I don't see the rest of the procession because I've still got dealings with Cosmo and his pal. I hand the spook his seven hundred dollars in fifties and twenties, more than enough, and tell him how to get to Kennedy from here.

"You don't want us to wait?" he says.

"What the shit for?"

"The Master says make sure you don't want us to wait."

Cosmo is looking cow flop at me again, and I just don't have the time.

"You want the Master to get where he's going, or don't you?" I tell him.

"We'll get him where he's going."

I get secretive. "We're supposed to be shipping a stiff to another country, Cosmo. That's serious business. So get on it."

"Don't wait?"

"Hell no. Get on it, and then get lost!"

He smiles for some goddamn spooky reason. I'm getting nervous, everybody around. Can't control it. Then I notice the trog.

"What's the matter with him?"

"He's that way at funerals."

His tears are huge. Big blubbering baseballs.

"Tell him it's not helping."

Cosmo starts with his hands, but there isn't time.

"No. Just get him away from here. Move it."

"The Master says then to bid you farewell."

"Fuck off."

"Farewell."

"Fuck all." I nod hard back toward the shaded windows. "And the same to your Master."

The last I see of them, the last I ever want to see of them, is that trog weeping all over the steering wheel, then driving off with one hand so he can, Christ almighty, give me the little finger with the other. Him too, just barely up over the edge of his window.

I can't think about it, or I'll chase them with cops all the way out to Kennedy. Instead, I check the cops, and then once I'm inside, before I come up here, I check the audience. Not all zombies, a much better crowd. Like that Bobby thing again. For the real show, I guess you always get a different class of people. There's a lot of press, and some families, and even a few religious. Then again you never know who's going around as a nun these days. I tell the usher to watch the sister for any trouble.

"There won't be any trouble," he says.

"No?" That worries me.

"Not with the lights up."

So I get them turned down a little. Half moons instead of full.

That helps, but from up here, I can see the usher's got a point. Sure, there's plenty of ugliness down there, and not just the zombies. The good folk came to see the big, bad, nasty man too. With their jaws clenched. Some of them even picked up crosses. There's edginess down there, there's grinding of teeth, there's even real trouble down there. But it's all gone fucking sedate. They're sitting on it. This town will sit on anything.

Am I surprised? No, I'm pleased. I am. Leeway for good p.r. Means that Lars should make it to the stage without a lot of brouhaha, and then we're clear of Simon, and then everybody enjoys a good, clean, humping American movie, right?

Only I wish I could spot Lars. I'm standing up now and

scanning each row down there, trying to find that chin rubbish of his. Hell, if I can pick out that parking attendant in the seventh row, I should be able to spot where . . . *What the fuck is he doing in the balcony?*

I DON'T believe it. I do not believe it. He actually wanted to *try* it from the balcony. Knew he couldn't. It's a hundred-foot drop, and he's still got on the overcoat. But he's up here blocking out a whole John Wilkes Booth scene for himself.

"Why the fuck aren't you down front?"

So he has to tell me, from the top, vroom, how he leaps on the stage, *sic semper tyrannis*, how great he could have been.

"You realize," I hiss at him, "Booth broke his fucking leg."

Then the clock hits the screen.

"Vroom," he says. "We do it downstairs. I still got five minutes."

"Only four, less than four to get there. Remember?"

"I'm going, I'm going."

Why can't I get rid of the geniuses in my life? It's Simon all over again. You hire a nothing for a simple, walk-on stunt. You hire a nothing because he is a nothing. You tell him to stay a nothing. And he turns up Raymond Massey trying to be Mighty Joe Young. . . .

I DON'T see him yet, and honest to God, I don't know if he can make it now.

Don't know if I can make it myself. I'm so goddamn up-tight and nervous, finally. That clock is coming up to two minutes, and this shitbrained audience is too much. A few zombies are big and loud for him to Rise, Baby, Rise! . . . you can hear it. . . . but most of it's this incredible, stupid, *polite* moaning. Why are they being polite, when he's nothing but *disgusting?* But I know the last time I heard that same type moan. That New York moan. Only time I was ever in Times Square for New Year's Eve. That same goddamn sick-sad, scream-mutter-mumble, piss-it-away whine that gets going under all the good-cheer farting when it's almost midnight, because who the hell knows whether it's going to be a happy new year or just another three-hundred-and-sixty-five-day lifetime hangover?

And these bastards are pulling the same heartbreak shit . . . he didn't break your hearts, you goddamn morons, he knocked out your brains! . . . for a sadistic, washed-up, toothless, bone-fucking, eighth-rate, Nazi vampire . . .

THERE's Lars. Thank Christ.

Don't try to find a seat first, you fuckhead! Just go on up and do your thing. . . .

I know what this is like. This is like shooting a quickie, five days straight, and it's been five days straight too, this one, exactly, and all that comes back from the lab is the audio—

Jesus. That usher.

And what the fuck good's the audio? You can't hear that coffin on stage. Bet I haven't even mentioned it. You can't hear Lars's too-goddamn-big overcoat. You can't hear that usher's uniform. You can't hear the straight faces on the zombies, or the crazy faces on the goodies, or, Jesus, the face on that nun. All you can hear is my mouth, and them starting to count that fucking clock backwards.

Deck him, Lars. Just deck him, drop the coat, take your tools and get up there. . . .

GODDAMN but it's the goddamnedest thing, he's got himself caught in the sleeve of his coat, but he's still pounding. He's pounding like a jackhammer, and it's splitting up like kindling, but it's going in like a fencepost, and the cops are coming in like vultures, but he's still banging away like a madman. It's working. The arm whipping, the overcoat flying, but whack home everytime! Go it, Lars! Drive it down! What you can't see is the cops grabbing him, the zombies climbing over the seats, the goodies kicking the zombies, everybody, everybody in the aisles, the moons blinking, great, great, just great! What you can't see really, I can't see yet, soon, soon, is where that beautiful, beautiful stake went down, down, down. . . .

S O BON FUCKING VOYAGE, *Simon baby! This part of the tape is specifically for you. You'll be hearing more of it, the parts I want you to hear after I edit, but this much, when Robbie sends it along to you, wherever you end up in the world, you can believe is straight. . . .*

Which, remember, Simon baby, no matter what you're thinking, is how I played it right along. I said I'd distribute. I'll still distribute. Bonn agreed to release. They've released. We left nothing standing in your way, including the U.S. government.

Only first, you better find the fucking film, right? Try either Germany. That's arranged too. Wander all of Europe. Tour the Mediterranean. Visit Africa, Russia, China, Mars. And tell you what. If you can find even three feet of that film, any three feet, Simon baby, any three scratchy, out-of-focus, over-exposed, piss-ass feet, I promise you a week-long festival at Lincoln Center. And a promise is a promise.

Meanwhile, I hope you're finding work in somebody's Bavarian home movies for beer and sauerkraut, because the word is, and no p.r. this time, the word is you just did your last picture. For me, or anybody. And I am going to help spread that word because it's going to help the picture. People will love going to Your Last Picture. In fact, we're going to roll it right now, you shit, just as soon as they get the lid off down there on stage and dump you out!

That's what I don't want you to miss, Simon baby, even though you can't be here. This wonderful moment. I am here in the balcony for the pleasure of telling you, firsthand, exactly what little is left of you. You, your career, your menace, your goddamn fad, your anything at all but a few freaky stills in some fag critic's old movie album. Down there is your finish. Your bleached bones. Do you dig? No more flesh to flash, Simon baby. No more make-up miracles, not on dead bones, baby. And no more fucking artwork with your goddamn eyes. Down there they are holes. What we are about to see, Simon baby, is your dried-up fossil in a busted-up German cigar box, with a big pin already stuck through you for a goddamn Has-Been label! And you know something, Simon baby? It's going to be so goddamn awful . . . they're pulling off the lid now . . . so goddamn awful I hardly dare to look almost as much as I'll bet you can hardly bear to listen. . . .

III. *A Final Manuscript*

Better to end in horror than a horror without end.

ADOLF HITLER

THERE COMES to mind, on this first *nacht* of nights, *Walpurgisnacht* minus two, something someone once said about your own career, E.A.P. It was your sunshine enemy and midnight friend, Mr. James Russell Lowell, if memory serves, and it goes, "He squared off blocks enough to build an enduring pyramid, but left them lying . . . (something) . . . and unclaimed in many different quarries." I like that, for the both of us. Though to make it better suit my own case: "Some of his blocks were of pumice, light as those great feathery stones carried by blacks atop their heads in Nepenthe. Others were of chalk, or sea-wracked shale, or petrified sponge. Still others of old adobe, of frozen peat, of pressed slag, even of fly ash reclaimed from blue-belching smoke stacks. S. Moro quarried where he could." But there is still a pyramid there, somehow, wobble-sided, apex askew, struggling like Venice not to sink. I believe that. I do, and am only held back from watching it build fantastically anew in these last nightshade thoughts . . . by *this* thought. Concerning pyramids. When the slaves are all dead as dung from hauling hard, sun-baked, Egyptian ass up those manmade slopes, after the blocks have been inched up three spans of Nefretete's thirteen-year-old instep every chiliad, and the engineers have the whole thing up, the square of the millennial hypotenuse equal to the sum of the squares of the two blood-drenched legs, every grain of granite in place, and the tippytip point right there, Osiris, massively hard and desert-erect between the crocodile hairs, guess who they put inside?

*

Rudy keeps wanting to make me more comfortable. He is in and out of here, nodding his crocodile head at the desk, or trying to get me over to the sofa by giving its corner leg a meaningful kick. A leg as bandied and swart and scarred as his own crocodile leg. Poor Rudy. I do my best to ignore him, but when he grows too distressed, I placate him by signaling for another pillow. And another. He has already stuffed four from the sofa into the coffin, three behind my back, one under my butt. They keep me fairly upright while I write this. On the lid. Set across here, lengthwise, it makes a passable lap desk. Lit by two floor-standing candles on either side of me. Each unwinking. Like a Pharaoh's wall-eyed stare out of the Book of the Dead. I am cramped, stiff, aching, but peculiarly sensate. I am beginning to feel the part. My own inchoate rigor mortis.

*

These asterisks indicate noddings-off. I admit. They mark where an old man momentarily dozes, exactly where the true north of his anciently vein-mapped nose drops that last half inch and stars the page.

Snapping out of it, my skull seems full of stale lightning. From a repeated white blitz of sulphurous dream jolts, their last thunderclaps still in my ears, like static. That old radio program, *Sturm und Drang*. I stare, and yes, I can almost believe I am inside my tomb. But it is not the way you wrote, E.A.P. So brilliantly, but I am sorry, all wrong. There is no telltale smell of moldy earth, odor of stripped bone. There is only the most ordinary locale. Concerning sepulchers. If they are whited on the outside, they are far more elaborately painted on the inside, by clever and talented worms, to resemble our utterly flat surroundings. Ingenious topiaria. To fool us into living, even when we know we lie interred.

I am using all this. I am getting there. I may make it yet. Though I could use more time, a morbidly slow clock. In less than six hours, I go on display. My bier opens free to the public. No admission, free bier. By then, what? By then, hopefully, I should be in the arrested grip of a last, gruesomely prepared death rattle, ready to meet them, face them down with exactly the right curdling . . . expression. One that will finally . . . *finally* freeze their goddamn blood. I plan to clear off this lid, but still leave it ajar, so it partly hides me, forcing them to peek round, look in to see for certain "Is that *him?*" Him, hell. These cerulean lips, fossilized teeth, this yellowed skin of dried mummy's buttocks, one sunken, puckered-up ass-hole eye—"Is that *it?*" Even worse. That is not him. That is not it. That is simply, mortally *that*.

*

Lonely work, sitting my own death watch. I could do with some intelligent company, somebody to cue me occasionally. Yours, E.A.P. We understand each other. Your revenant, my rot. We understand each other only too well. The gist of it being a shared esthetic. The only true art— and it is lost—the only true art for either of us was to take fright, and give freely of it. To take great fright, and to give magnanimously of it. But for you it was so much easier. Your readers had not yet been granted—Mr. Franklin Delano Roosevelt's one big mistake in the Atlantic Charter —freedom from fear. My audiences have. The same horrible things keep happening, of course, over and over and over, but they are accomplished now without any knowing horror. With—and hear, play with every syllable of this baleful word—*fear-less-ness*. Allow me a brief declamation on your prose and poesy:—"You lived, sir, and wrote during an earlier, simpler moment of darkness when a drunken Fortunato had to be bricked into a wall by an individually skilled artisan. Now we immure whole neighborhoods in one day's urban renewal. You must realize. The Fall of the House of Usher only cleared the way for another highrise. The Descent into the Maelstrom is the daily ride to work. The Pit is one of our two major political parties, the Pendulum the other. The Masque of the Red Death is held annually for combined interfaith charities. The System of Doctor Tarr and Professor Fether has been medically approved. Though we are more hesitant now about rushing the Tell-Tale Heart to transplant. The MS. is Found in a non-returnable bottle. The Purloined Letter is junk mail. The Bells are recorded. The Black Cat has been 'fixed'. . . . Everywhere there is an odd blood, with no taste to it. None. It comes in a pop-top aluminum can, with a non-fattening lymph substitute, and an enriched plasma base, plus artificially added hemoglobin. It leaves a strange film on the tongue, and hardly fizzes. . . ."

*

Where there is no spine, writes Mao Tshin-Bone, the people feel no tingle.

*

A need. A grousing need to explain why I have been menacing the nerves, and late evening news, of this paraplegic city. Why I have felt compelled to wander up and down, even at my age, barely galvanic of body, much naphthalated in mind, as the Imp of the Perverse. Yes, E.A.P., the imp himself, struggling to communicate some small pixie piece of the horror to this madding crowd. Through the blank newspapers, over deaf-and-dumb radio, blind TV, and now, live, from this oblong box. . . . America! O beautiful for specious skies, for amber waves of pain! From every mountainside, let freakdom ring!

*

But to tell coherent tales. One tale, first, of the grotesque. Set this down for epigraph. *You taught me language, and my profit on it is, I know how to curse!* Said by Caliban, who never found his way to Central Park, who has reason enow to curse the day he came to Manhattan Isle and fell among Joseph Papp's resident—and evil—company. A tale entitled "Livia."

*

Livia!—thy lucent name lives on in far reaches of lasciviousness, thy lap and lithe limbs, but most of all, my Livia, in livid memory of thy elongated lacteal lugs. Like targes, they were. Great, leathery shields, crudely stretched, a giant boss at each protuberant centrum, yet fretted with the most delicately haired rosettes. I had never viewed such enormity companioned by such truculent promise. With each effulgent breath, in every luxuriant rise and fall, I sensed a subtle, limpid strength, a stout battle-readiness. They would—o breastless Amazons!—turn aside your spears.

She was to be, among the dramatis personae of our thespian joining, Miranda. She, my Livia, was to be Miranda because my Livia's melancholic, half-crazed consort was the director. Papp's dramaturge. He had grown his hair long, but long after it had grown gray. From every dormant follicle, renascent whorls of matted shag linked earlobe to nostril, pate to chin, until he was mangy as a mammoth, and equally tusked.

"Understand," he addressed me that first time in the drear rehearsal hall. "It's a very dirty play. It's all about this dirty old cod Prospero. 'I'll break my staff.' Shit he'll break his staff. It split on him years ago. Why's he got Ariel? To hype his sex fantasies. Wouldn't he like to be bouncing our Mr. Caliban's big rocks? That's how I see Calibaby. He's out to ball Miranda, sure, sure, but really for Old Prickless. *Who can't admit it.* So you do your monster thing, great, but get a little senile lust in there too. It's a mix. You're your own horny bastard, but let's see something else in you. Some-*body.* Daddynuts. Trying to throw a fuck at her *through you.*" His wink dripped a fell lubricity. "You're right for it if you're up to it, Gramps."

My Livia's lord, then, suffers from a malady of birth, satyriasis of the brain, and alas, it has touched her own lumined soul. Would that their flesh had never crossed! But the perils of any orgy are never what such as my limber Livia may do there, but whom she may meet there. "He wouldn't get off me. There were other guys hanging in there with us, but they all shot and left. He stayed hard. I couldn't bring him off. He just got harder. I was left there all alone with him." He worked his deliberate wiles upon her. "Sometimes he can talk so dirty that, like, anything you really *do* feels clean?" They married. Or, as my Livia says, they have, are in possession of, maintain a marriage.

"We have a pretty good marriage," she bespeaks herself.

"Where do you keep it?"

"What do you mean?"

"You have it. Where do you keep it?"

"Back at the apartment."

"Could I possibly come see it sometime?"

"Look. It's for the kid."

"I see."

"A kid when she's young doesn't care that much. But when she gets older, she wants you married. I've seen how it is with our friends' kids when they're not."

"I see. Kids don't help a marriage. Marriage helps kids."

"Well . . . you don't want it interfering."

"With what?"

"Your adult life."

"Of course not."

"I mean, it *stays* in the apartment."

My Livia, though she was not quite yet my Livia, lay atop my bed in the Warwick, while explaining these conjugal vows to me. Capriciously nude, though I had seen her often enough that way throughout the week. The storm, as her husband conceived the opening scene, tears every last button and stitch off both the courts of Milan and Naples. "It's

called *The Tempest*, right? It's not called *The Cloudburst*."
But she was this way now, and here, here and now, all on
her own. I had asked for my key at the desk and simply been
told that it had already gone up. This was, Livia, a most
unilateral assignation.

"Suppose I tell you," I said, "that you're married, you
have a child, maybe I don't want your adult company."

She sighed, lissomely sighed. "He warned me you'd be
blueballs."

I did not ask who then, my Livia, and strove to elevate my
thoughts above your sordid imprecation, but I had learned,
long ago, never to let loose talk like that circulate backstage.
So, with sad heart but soaring ballocks, I accepted your lustful challenge, allayed your every dire doubt, with nibble
and nudge, bite and brawl. I turned you two times over, and
three times round. You grew dizzy, then faint, but I was
kind. I rendered you justice with mercy, while you wept
at your folly and error.

"I got to tell him about you."

"Who?"

"Who do you think?"

"None of that."

"He's got to *know* about you."

"Why?"

"He won't mind. Why should you?"

"I don't like even friendly sexual rivalry."

"He's not that way."

"We're all that way."

"Lionel and I aren't."

"Then I am."

"He'll want to be here himself next time."

I dispatched detailed written orders to the desk, counter-
manding any such possibility. Let my Livia flop her fill in
some other fishfry, but he must have raped the maid to get a
key.

"Liv tells me you're pretty good, Gramps."

He had her fleshed across the arm of the divan, white but-tocks spread on high, their snow coving his cruel rowl. But he pulled out in gentlemanly fashion, to turn and converse with me, still wet and wicked as an icicle.

"Take over for me."

"Out."

"Gramps . . ."

I searched for the proper phraseology. "I swing my own ass."

He raised a sly, gray eyebrow, up and away into his matted forelocks. "You don't like this kind of relaxation?"

"I don't like your Don't bang us, we'll bang you."

"But we're working together." How his satyr's grin em-braced us! Kama and Sutra and Pinch-Me-Tight. "Let's get to know each other a little."

There was a piteous stir from my Livia. "One or the other of you." The couch arm quivered. "Shoot the bird, let's shoot the bird . . ."

He callously ignored her. "I don't want anybody along who's not with us all the way."

"What way?"

"I don't think the cast has really settled down, Gramps."

"I do. Very nicely."

"We'll have to wait and see."

"Say what you mean."

"It's not two weeks yet, Gramps."

"Nobody said two weeks to me."

"Didn't they?"

"And I don't read for parts."

"Don't need to hear you read, Gramps. You're a great read." How sponged and empurpled and cloven-tipped he stood, this proud hard man. . . . "But let's just see how well you can relate to Miranda."

"Shoot the bucking bird!"

I temporized. Yes, I begged off and left him to lift my Livia out of her immediate distress, turning to my own thoughts, while he slipped and slid down her deep and ferny ravine. But on familiar footing, I could tell that, even as I undressed. Inevitable. The husband always knows the best, the quickest way down.

"Now," he asked, "what would *you* like to do?"

My thoughts had strayed, far afield, back into the Wienerwald, behind a dark pine where I had once had my way with a frog-legged maiden, while her own tongue hopped like a horned toad in the grotto of another. Perhaps, even here. . . . "I would prefer to straight-fuck Livia," I said at last, in the vernacular of the day, "while she eats your cock."

To him, nothing that much out of the ordinary—a man of my years, he seemed to say, should boast more recondite kinks—but he would go along, out of politeness. Livia settled herself in splayed abandon, then ingested him all the way up his long, rigid shank, but with her soft, winsome gaze still on me. I told them to begin, proceed, I was certain I would be readied in a moment. That enlisted his sympathy. "Poor old dads," he said, and my Livia gave me a silent thumbs-up.

I waited until they were more enmeshed, less observant, then went down on my hands and knees. "Go it, Gramps," he encouraged these tired old bones, even reached out to help me up into her open mount. But I waved him aside and entered under my own power.

Half a minute later I had that nap-balled bastard.

"Livia!"

But you did not heed his cries, my loyal Livia. They did not reach your love-stopped ears as your jaw firmed, your teeth met in carnal ecstasy.

"Livvvia!"

You heard him not as he doggedly howled, sought in desperation to free himself, but only clenched the more, riding

the last shuddering waves, my Livia, my fire-breasted
Valkyrie, of a clitoral *Götterdämmerung*.

"Liv!"

"Who?" she said dizzily.

"I'm bit through."

She touched him. "Who?"

"You bit hell out of me, you little bitch!"

"I never."

"You did, Liv."

"I wouldn't *do* that."

"Look."

Where now was its pluck and ambition and fine spicate
form? Who now would recognize this poor, pulled, pink
piece of taffy for the organ of tyranny it once had been?

"Honeybaby."

He only moaned, took tender hold of himself.

"I would *never*."

Then his appalled regard sought me out, where I still lay
like a lambkin in my Livia's lap.

"A folk secret of the Lower Danube," I said, "but it takes
the right kind of girl."

Without one more word he gathered up his clothes, both
their clothes, a motley, clanking pile of chain and leather,
and hurried into the bedroom. She hesitated, my Livia, but
then pushed me off and followed him, as a good wife must. I
heard sounds of frustrate passion, as if he were trying to
have a bit of a go at her, but found it all still too painful.
When they came back out again, dressed and shackled, she
was carrying his heavily studded belt for him over her arm.
A poor, bent, graying man.

"I'll see you," he threatened through his agony, "at rehearsal."

I looked longingly after her as she stayed her moment at
my door, and our eyes embrously met, my Livia, though I

failed to note in them the first secret luster, alas, of your lurid betrayal.

*

But all, astonishingly, went well, or so I ignorantly believed, that next hastening week. The rest of the catamite cast stayed far away from me. An unlooked-for boon. They too had been hovering, communal maenads and bacchantes, ready to fall upon my venerable, liver-spotted sex. I do not exaggerate the peril. They had a game they played of eve, lolling about backstage, grass-bent and yoga-sprung. Blindman's buff. Eyes covered, both hands behind your back, no peeking or touching, can you tell who is blowing you? One guess only, and you have to guess before you come. Guess right, the man or woman caught blowing goes in the middle. Guess wrong, stay where you are, get blown again. Or eaten, as the case may be. My Livia confessed to having once tricked her own noble lord with a false Vandyke, but she no longer cared to play, and in fact, circulated word that I might do grave sexual harm, so that I too would be excused.

Merciful respite, time gained in which to arm and strengthen my Caliban against Lionel's miscreate staging. He was militantly scabrous, sapping whole scenes for the most dragged-in titillation. Ferdinand and Miranda do not engage in a chaste game of chess. They engage in a fierce copulation, throwing tangled shadows on the thin scrim of her tent walls, and cry out, "Rook takes Queen!" He cut Ariel's lines down to the rawest graffiti. "Where the bee sucks there suck I," sung in sibilant tremulo, as if written above a phone number on an Eighth Avenue steambath wall. My own battles were with Stephano and Trinculo, who climbed each other like two Airedales, tried floppily to climb me until I began wearing quills.

Yes, quills. And gutter slops and leprous cankers and a

horsepiss, Liederkranz stench from across the street at the Sixth Avenue Deli. Whatever would keep me unpalatable, untouchable. That, of course, is the true way of the monster. His credibility. But here it was also a personal stand. I imagined my Caliban as that fearsome abort, a monster of principle. Grosser than thou, O regurgitating mankind. One of my better cosmetologies, my Livia, thy delicate touch helped open every sore. Also, essentially what I employed this evening for my arrival at Kennedy. The hope now is to dress it up in white tie, tails, evening cape for formal lying-in-state. If it works—and it must, it must—I shall be wished away, Monkey's-Paw-fashion, by all and sundry while remaining utterly unapproachable.

What should have alerted me, if not my Livia's strangeness, was her lord's acquiescence. He appeared to drop his threat, approve apace my insurgent beastliness. "Terrific," he bleated. "Repulsive but terrific. I want you to do something for me. Slur your words even more." I was striving for a speech defect, a birth injury that had left my mooncalf Caliban hare-lipped. Pitiably nasal but banked with gut-chewing, tongue-tied fury. "And you're right, Gramps. He has to stink. He *likes* to stink." I fell down epileptic on stage in a squall of spittle one day, came in deliberately drunk the next, but no luck. I had hurt him once, but could not now manage to disgust him, even though Livia was my ally— false even then?—in every debauch.

"More monster, less man," she warned me.

"Still?"

"Always."

"How?"

"You got to get ahead of where he is."

"Explain."

"Know anything about living in this city?"

"You tell me."

"It's the Congo."

"I see."

"The Congo with elevators."

"Go on."

"You got to be what we go around thinking—"

"Fearing—"

"Maybe even hoping . . . will leap out at us."

"On the elevator."

"Stuck between floors."

"You go too far."

"Keep going. You'll get there."

I ruminated that, and yes, I let a little of the Dark Continent slip into my Caliban, let these eyes begin to drip an aboriginal rheum, let this sly old head turn fuzzy-wuzzy, a little bit Zulu. And you were there, my Livia, to heap on kinks and curls.

"Farther."

"What?"

"You're almost there."

"Where?"

"Hundred and twenty-fifth and Amsterdam Avenue."

"Too far."

"You're already past Ninety-sixth."

"Far enough then."

"No. They'll catch you."

"Who?"

"We will."

"They don't come near me."

"Lionel will make them."

"Stop it."

"He told me."

"He can't."

"They're getting used to you. They're not afraid. Lag one step behind, and they'll all fall on you."

"Ridiculous."

"Fawn on you."

"Impossible."

"Love your demon dong," she wailed nuttily, "worse than I do."

Did I actually realize then what I was doing, what was being done to me? All I can plead is that I still trusted my Livia, that I was determined to save my Caliban from their foul, liberated clutches, Lionel's tumescent approach, that I went to a savage blackface to defend my honest monsterhood with reawakened rapacity.

That was toward the end of the week, my Livia's own fingers assisting at the burnt cork. On Saturday, our last day in rehearsal hall before going up to the Park, Lionel announced, "I want to try something here. It may not work, but I want a look-see. Let Calibaby drink the whole bottle. The way you came in here last Wednesday, Gramps, that's your own business, but I think we can use it here. And slur it up. You're shitfaced, so let's hear that cleft palate." Livia touched my darkened visage. "Go far enough," she whispered.

We ran through Act Two, scene two. Stephano and Trinculo, much as my Livia had predicted, set themselves to goosing each other, really trying to get a grab on me, while putting more edge on their sneers. ". . . this puppy-headed monster! A most scurvy monster! . . . The poor monster's in drink. An abominable monster! . . . A most ridiculous monster . . . A howling monster! a drunken monster!" How they do add up, those stinging epithets, and all straight Shakespeare, but I gave back as good as I got. My Caliban wallowed in a belligerent drunkenness, with a nasty, threatening slobber, seething underneath. When I went to kiss Stephano's foot, I bit it instead. Rabidly. And on my final outcries—"Freedom, high-day! high-day, freedom! freedom, high-day, freedom!"—I let them all know how rebelliously my black heart still beat. It was a brutish scene. Low comedy lowered to real bedlam. I must admit. Not since

Ghoulgantua had I felt that old hellfire glow of roaring menace and inner misericordia.

I was, how woefully! even touched with pride. I rose to search for Lionel, spotted him back in the rear of the hall talking with some irate stranger. Whoever it was kept pointing at me, jabbing his finger stiffly, in sour anger, without ever once looking at me. He was clearly saying what damn well was going to be what from here on out, to Lionel, who was acting pleased!

My Livia crept to my side. "Guess who that is," she murmured in an unfamiliar, nay, unhallowed voice.

"Who?"

"From the Mayor's office."

"Cultural Affairs?"

"Human Rights Commission."

O my Livia!

"Lionel thought maybe we just better check everybody out."

Right then, I plumbed the deepest bottom of treachery as she pulled forth the tiniest of pocket mirrors.

"Like a peek?"

It was cracked across, its silvering badly scaled, almost scrofulous, but in the random reflecting flakes I caught hideous sight of what deed had been done me, what wrong I had, yea, wittingly! done myself. A gaucherie of Negritude, a deformity of racial leer and cake-walking coonhood, a Stepin Fetchit in the guise of Othello. The bleakest blackamoor in this showboat city. I turned to you, my Livia, in dismay, and there fell from your harsh labia, in rude-tongued tones that I can scarce still credit, o my libeling Livia!—"You went far enough this time, niggerlips."

*

Imitating again. Endlessly imitating. Stealing your style, E.A.P., nothing but the very best for me, of course, but as always, making off with only the most worthless amounts of substance. My chiefest crime has been petty mimicry. And why, *why* have I never been caught at it? Years ago, let's say I stole a cheap Austrian accent from Franz Lehar's overcoat hanging unwatched in some *Heuriger*, and to this day, somebody like that *Esquire* sneakcock, bright enough otherwise, is willing to believe I am truly Viennese. And even if I were, there *are* no true Viennese. The Viennese, "we" Viennese are all veneer, smiling human stucco. Though perhaps that makes everybody truly Viennese. Only you, E.A.P., and the hallucinations you raised to elegy, to history —and we gigglingly pretend are apocrypha—remain solid, the very best. Let me say it. Let me confess how utterly I admire you, how hard I once tried to emulate you. When I first got into pictures in this country, when I finally returned from my Old High German fantasy life, came out from *unter den Linden* and tried to stop being a closet American, the first thing I did was . . . attempt to grow your moustache. I did. But couldn't. Not enough facial hair. How I envied you that black, lush, Frenchified, almost pubic bush of a lip! And when I found out that you had once, in Philadelphia, in a fit of paranoia, asked to have it shaved off, to escape your killers . . . I *believed* in your killers. I still do. But they did not want your life, E.A.P. They sought your moustache, and have succeeded. I wish I could have carried it on for you. Immortally. But understand what has happened. Even if I had it now, if my arid lip had been brought to bristling blossom, it would only look now, and alas, only feel, like Ben Turpin's greasy nose-tickler.

*

I did not wait around. I walked straight out into Forty-second Street just as I was, markedly putrid, and did a drunken, hambone stagger all the way back uptown to the Warwick. I created at least one incident I am aware of, maybe others, along my route, with some spade selling the

Black Panther newspaper. "Walk proud, you mother-fucking minstrel!" he yelled at me. "Or we gonna cut yo'r banjo balls!" I answered him in hare-lip-ese. It made better copy than the official complaint against racial stereotypes lodged with the Mayor. "William Shakespeare's respect for minority groups is already too well known through his moving, civic-minded portrait of Shylock the Jew to require further documentation from this department. We see no reason to open the public theatrical facilities of our park system to this distorted and unbalanced characterization, one that not only insults our black citizens but perverts Shakespeare's own humanitarian treatment of what would now be recognized as a socially disadvantaged late-learner." I heard first from the *Times* that I'd been fired. Had I been unaware all these years of the racial sensitivities of the people of this city? I thought of pleading a stubborn Germanic ignorance, if only to heighten the absurdity, but I finally said I only hoped an actor would be found who could deal with Caliban's brutal ethos within the American traditions of fair play and broad liberal understanding. I suggested Henry Fonda.

*

Sullied. Euchered. Never trust a husband-and-wife team. Their dirty little secret always turns out to be they are really married. I was once almost myself. I thought very seriously of it. But I know now that marriage to her mother would have destroyed all that Hazel and I have since had together.

It would have been equally wrong to have married Hazel. Though for the sake of her poor, dear, destabilized mother —floating somewhere out there in the dark, like a grapeskin in a wine vat—I would like to see her settle down.

Marry then, Hazel. Beget children, and tell them how you once knew a circumspect old man who, throughout a long, long acquaintance, never—I think this is fair to say—never

once, as close as he was to you, forced you to choose between father and lover.

*

I propose to set down here the entire text, which I believe
I can give from memory, of what I said on the occasion this
year of Edwin Booth's Birthday, when Miss Julie Harris laid
the annual wreath at the foot of his graven image in Gramercy Park. Press coverage was scandalously inaccurate,
and editorial commentary benighted. But a word or two
first about the Club, since its members have taken such um-
brage at my remarks. Frankly I had not been there for years,
fearing lice and communicable eld, had simply sent in my
dues, my library fees, and ten dollars every Christmas for a
bartender who never poured me a drink until that very day.
A dodging, pudgy, noodle-nosed gin-sneak who had the
nerve to say, "Welcome back, Mr. Moro," and claim to remember I always drank sidecars.

"You never saw me before in your life."

"You're a tradition, Mr. Moro," he shrugged.

"Right, boy. I used to come in here and write witticisms
on F.P.A.'s napkin when he was drunk. Do you remember
that imitation of a cockroach I did for Don Marquis? Or the
night I whipped Mark Twain four straight games of Eight
Ball and he damn near broke his damn cue over your idiot
pate? That's it, right there on the wall."

The Club's vice president had more tact.

"Oddly enough," he snorted through the clear half of his
cancer-eaten nose, "I don't think we've ever formally met."

"I never come here."

"A shame."

"I don't like mausolea."

"Then it's kind of you to fill in for us today."

"Who dropped dead?"

"Dennis had a small cerebral accident, affecting mainly his

right side. . . ."

"But why me?"

"To tell the truth, we'd been thinking of honoring you with a Night here. But after this Papp business . . ."

"Bad business."

"Yes, I'm afraid."

"So this will just have to do."

"We still all admire those early films. Some of us, I'm sure you know, were in them."

"Refresh my memory."

He snorted again, the bad side this time. "As I said, we've never formally met, but you did smother me in *The Moth*."

"Did I?"

"Yes. I was one of that group of young entomologists sent to capture you."

"I remember now."

"I expired, it must be said, after the briefest of agonies."

"But you've been dead then for nearly thirty years."

"Wouldn't put it quite that way." He struggled to put it another way. "We're trying to become a younger club."

"Women."

"What about them?"

"You'll have to admit them."

"We admit them. We do indeed *admit* them. But whether that means, except on these very special occasions, they can be allowed simply to burst in here off the street . . . at noontime, particularly . . . Come meet Miss Harris."

We got through drinks. We got through lunch. We even got across the street. Miss Julie leading her flock of wheezing old pigeons over to the park where I was to crumble up my slice of dried bread and throw them a few memorial crumbs. Nothing makes me feel older than a bunch of old actors trudging along in tragedy's high-button shoes, comedy's sagging socks.

Miss Harris stooped pertly to lay the wreath. Laurels on

verdigris. Her haunch touched her Achilles' heel, and a lock of loose red hair strayed from her, like a wisp of ruby smoke. Only Edwin Booth and I really saw.

Then I said:—"Fellow players, we are gathered here today, many of us in the seventh act of our own lives, to honor one who long ago made his own sad exit. We have spoken here before of how nobly he left this earthly stage, though still burdened with a deep personal sorrow. His grief over the death of Abraham Lincoln, for whose murder he felt he disgracefully bore some consanguineous guilt. We understand and respect this grief. Indeed, we hesitate to disturb that ennobling silence upon which he himself resolved, even at this distance of years. But do we, in the end, best serve his fond memory when we fail to give voice now to what we have come so painfully to know? Should we continue to bear this grief with him when our hearts can conceive, out of the terrible events of more recent years, some consolation?

"I will speak therefore today in the conviction that sorrow, even gone off into the wings, may yet be assuaged. And asking your forebearance, I will speak more of John than of Edwin. I will speak of John for the sake of our dear Edwin.

"John Wilkes Booth, whatever pall now falls upon his name, was also once our fellow actor. He is not so often thusly embraced, but before he ventured out into a darker drama than could be contained within our feeble footlights, he showed great talents. Perhaps far greater than those failing abilities we muster here today. He was horseman and swordsman and pistoleer. He was, above all else, a striking stage presence, with black hair and the blackest eyes. He had both daring and fancy. Even in his youth, we hear of him driving a sled up and down Maryland's dirt roads in the middle of July, and shooting down any stray cat on sight. He had, during a meteoric career, the most excellent of notices. Boston attests to his Romeo, New York to his Antony.

He knew fame. He knew women. A certain Miss Henrietta Tree is reported to have tried stabbing him in Madison, Indiana, only to turn the dirk upon herself. He may have even known madness. His father, Junius Brutus Booth, was in no wise free of it. He failed only to know himself.

"Though in that, he has not been alone. We have all, including his brother Edwin, failed equally to know him. That is the terrible tragedy. When he stepped into the Presidential box on April 14, 1865, and fired point black at the President's head, it is clear he ceased to be an actor. He had thrust himself most bloodily upon reality, and must have known as much. That far we may assume he understood his own destiny. But he did not know—nor did his brother Edwin know before he himself died here within sight of this lovely park—nor did the Nation itself know for another hundred years—that John Wilkes Booth had in fact founded what has become our most enduring political institution.

"In the fullness of time, we have grown wiser. We have at last understood, after the similar ventures of admittedly lesser men, of a Leon F. Czolgosz, of a Charles J. Guiteau, of a Lee Harvey Oswald, what it was that John truly achieved. And perhaps it is the ultimate tribute to his unique genius that his single deed, thought utterly mad at the time, not only profoundly altered the course of the Nation's history, but has now become almost a commonplace of our political life."

This is about where I began to get their real attention, though a lot of their silly sheep's heads were actually nodding in agreement.

"So I would propose to say to our dear Edwin, across all these past bitter years, if I might be so bold as to prompt eternity: 'Raise up your head. Your brother's terrible deed can no longer be called an aberrant act. It has struck a kind of true norm, a bench mark by which your own great country now measures itself, its present direction and future hopes. He cannot be forgiven, but perhaps you have reason, at long last, to feel a touch of fraternal pride.' "

By this time, even the dimmest of them were on to me, so I worked abruptly into my peroration.

"But if these words sadly cannot reach our dear Edwin, there is still much we can do here, among ourselves. It is a fact that John Wilkes Booth did not escape. An even more chilling fact that few apparently ever do escape. The record of assassins caught, though marred by constant rumors of undiscovered conspirators, is still a long one. Here we might be of some usefulness. Could we not collect moneys among ourselves, in memory of Edwin, in honor of John, to provide for the future? Remember, the best and worthiest of the lot, our own fellow actor, was left alone at the last to shoot himself through the head in a burning barn. Could we not have helped him? *Would* we not have helped him? Is it beyond us now to turn over that annual Yuletide bar tip to the Edwin Booth Memorial Presidential Assassins' Escape Fund to allow—"

I could have gone on a bit longer, but Miss Harris, to her credit—though I am well aware it is not at all her ordinary ladylike behavior—started a pretty good action, I guess you'd call it, by actually throwing her right shoe at me.

*

I am very, very tired, and one reason is that I have been masking my own moral fatigue. Like most people, I took America as a stimulant, when it is really a depressant.

*

I had, of course, during times between these grander contretemps, begun to cruise the subways. In full regalia.

The trick was to keep walking through, never stay too long in any one car, but pretend I was really looking for a seat. I would take along an old newspaper. When I spotted somebody, usually a midmorning shopper, since I had to avoid the rush hours, I would swerve over to the seat next to her and pat it with my leprous hand. That was usually enough to put her to serious flight, but if it wasn't, if she froze, I'd pull apart the newspaper and start spreading the sheets carefully over the seat. The idea that I myself thought I was so foul that I didn't want to soil anything was the real shocker.

Once or twice, however, I did meet with unexpected kindness.

"You'd better get yourself to a hospital."

She was a good old soul, alone in the car, with a Bloomingdale's shopping bag, a straw purse, and a net full of artichokes. I raked the air in front of her smiling face.

"I can recommend you a good hospital. My sister works up at Columbia Presbyterian."

I shot out my green fingers to within an inch of her throat, quivering them, but didn't dare do much more.

"This subway goes there."

So I sat down.

"You got three more stops."

"You're afraid of me," I hissed at her.

"My sister'll see you get cleaned up."

"You're afraid of me."

Then her jolly face did finally collapse. She stared away from me, out at the rushing darkness.

"Aren't you?"

But the train slowed, and she got back her smile immediately, began pulling together her packages.

"I'm always scared I'm gonna miss my stop, but I never do."

When she got up to get off, I made a menacing, just-short lunge at her.

"No. You want a Hundred and Sixty-eighth. Stay on two more."

The other time I was followed by two Haitian-looking black kids on the Lexington Avenue. The whole length of the train and back. I thought they were trouble, and faced around on them when I reached an empty car up forward.

"Mister."

I half crouched.

"You want chicken, mister?"

I growled, but he was a brave lad.

"We get you a chicken, my brother say you bite its head off."

His brother pushed him in disgust. "Where we gonna get a fucking chicken?"

"We get it, he bite it for us."

"Get his own fucking chicken!"

"You don't want to see him bite no chicken?"

"He ain't no voodoo man."

"You say he was!"

"Up close he ain't no voodoo man."

"What the fuck you think he is?"

"He's a fucking mummy."

"He ain't no fucking mummy! He ain't wrapped!"

"He come unwrapped!"

"Mister."

I let him move another step forward.

"You a fucking mummy, or a voodoo man?"

I bit the air viciously with long teeth, and he stepped back.

"You see that?"

"What I see?"

"He want chicken."

"Shit he want chicken!"

"He eat chicken head!"

His brother pushed him again.

"Shit he eat chicken head!"

"We get you chicken, mister."

His brother pushed him almost off his feet.

"We can't get him nothin' but *fried* chicken! He gotta have *live* chicken!"

And they turned around and ran.

Otherwise it was very much as reported. I spread terror on the IRT, panic on the Shuttle, but never really enough to bring down upon myself the full weight of Transport Authority justice. This was gesture, not assault. Their tactic of trying to force me off as a matter of public sanitation was adroitly conceived, but needed more proof. "If it looks like a syphilitic, walks like a syphilitic, talks like a syphilitic . . ." the health officer tried to argue.

"You still have to catch him spitting on the platform," said the magistrate.

"He drools right in front of us," I had the pleasure of hearing him admit in open court, "but it never drops."

∗

O my Manhattanos, I meet you in your streets, and you meet each other, and we all look askance, aside, away, and I am reminded of a young man I once knew in Berlin, a bitter isolate who collected snakes. He did not even like snakes. But he knew other people feared them, especially his dear mother, and so he found relative contentment among the twinings of his boa constrictor, the rippling scales of his adders and vipers. They slithered around his narrow room like exposed ganglia.

But ironically, they began to force a kind of society upon him. Other herpetologists. Such seem to meet together even more often than other fanatics, deep in the cold bowels of natural history institutes, and I admitted one day that I was pleased for him, thought it fortunate that he had found their company.

"Why?" he said.

"Now you have other people to talk to."

"We never talk."

"At least you share something in common."

"Do we?"

"You come together and sit together and—"

"Everybody sits two seats away from each other."

"You don't, in some way, commune?"

He sighed. "When I have to meet anybody at these affairs, face to face, I can think only one thought."

"What's that?"

"I know why *I* collect snakes, but why does *he* collect snakes?"

*

The odd part is that I really had forgotten about that finger. I'd stuffed it into the purse Mike T. gave me, no idea really what I thought I was going to do with it, then packed the purse to take along with me here to New York. One day I was looking around for something to put a lot of candy in, for the prostitutes along Broadway, like the Marquis de Sade with his poison bon-bons. I thought of the purse, hauled it out of the bottom of my suitcase, opened the hasp, and caught a whiff. I had to turn it upside down to shake the damn thing out of there.

I got it into some formaldehyde, in an old jelly jar, in just about the nick of time. Hate to think how long I'd had it around by then. Still don't have the faintest notion why I wanted to hang on to it. Just interested.

Actually, a couple of fascinating things I discovered about that finger when I held the jar up to the light and really studied it, joint by joint. I must've counted at least nine different and distinct old scars, plus other blemishes. His jackknife slipped, he slammed a car door on it, he cut it clipping his hedge, he put his fist through a window, he fell down in the bathroom while changing razor blades, one guess is as good as another, I suppose. In any case, that finger was marked for severance, bound to go sometime. He'd also chewed the nail almost down to nothing but a speck of shellac. The nervous type, as well as accident-prone. Most fascinating of all, there was still the trace of an indentation running all the way around the flesh above the first joint. Very tight, like a banding. So what was a ham-fisted clunk like him doing with a pinkie ring?

It gave the damn thing a personality. Been through the wars, come out with scuffed knuckles, but still a bit of a dandy, even a sybarite. I started thinking of it as Pinkie.

*

Another tale. Several. In fact, all the tales of the arabesque I told them at the day-care center, down in that church cellar near St. Marks Place. Some parts of the City remained desirous of my services longer than others. My free services. This was the Library Reading-Out-Loud Program. The thought I presume was that I would do a Boris, read the kiddies fairy tales to prove I wasn't the Big Bad Werewolf at heart. Columbia Records was interested, sent along a representative, Miss Flopsy-Mopsy, who I hope got her Cottontail full.

But without Martha, I don't think I could have gone as far as I did. Into the Secret Memoirs of the Little Match Girl, and other such Grimmnesses. Martha Williamson. A beautiful brute of a woman, built slowly, like a reef, into a blissful maternal isle. Part Jamaican, some Irish. A lovely tropical brogue and a strange streak of Caribbean blarney. She was being rehabilitated into a children's nurse, under threat of sterilization, after a career on welfare as Chelsea's leading Soviet Mother.

"Won't let me have my own," she told me, "but they still keep bringing me more." They tumbled about her, shoeless and filthy, and she smacked them down like monkeys into a flea-picking circle at my feet. "Storyman's here. Settle ass.

He's gonna tell it like it 'twas."

"What would they like to hear, Martha?"

"Ask 'em."

"What would you like to hear, boys and girls?"

" 'Goldilocks and the Three Bears'!" was first.

"But you've already heard that one."

"Sure."

"Hundreds of times."

"Sure."

"How the Little Bear comes in and sees Goldilocks and says, 'Somebody's been sleeping in my bed, and . . .' "

"And she's still in it!" said a baby mandrill.

"That's right. But do you know what else the Little Bear said?"

"Tell us!"

"He said, 'Goldilocks, you can't sleep in that bed. That's the only bed we got, and there's three got to sleep in it already. Mama Bear when she get home from work and she is dog-tired, and Papa Bear if he do come home, and hope he ain't too drunk because, if he is, he take up most of the room, and me, Little Bear. We can't put *four* in that bed, Goldilocks. I get crowded out enough. And if Papa Bear come home after Mama Bear asleep and he spot you, you ain't gonna like it, Goldilocks, and I ain't gonna can help you none. So haul out of here, Goldilocks, I got enough trouble. And was it you or the damn cockroaches ate my porridge?' "

A hushed chittering.

"Wow. That how it happened?"

"More than likely."

"I thought they giving us the wrong story."

Some heads nipped around to look at Martha, but she was just fine. A big calypso smile.

A little girl chimpanzee stood up and whispered, " 'The Little Match Girl' . . . can she be next?"

"You *know* what happened to her," I said.

"Yeah. She lit her last match."

"And then . . . ?"

"Don't know."

"You don't?"

"Nobody told us yet."

"Well, *then* . . . a really *big* man stepped out of the alley and said, 'You dumb cunt!' "

They laughed, but I wasn't sure until I saw Martha laugh too. Deep, with no ripples, like a lagoon.

" 'You ain't burned down nothing. You scratched off your last match, girl, and this whole block is still standing! Now you get out there and hustle me some fire. I show you what to do with it. They's still Woolworth's. They's still the A and the P. And you better hustle hard, girl, cause goddamn if you look to me like you even worth a damn match!' "

Over their happy screaming, Miss Flopsy-Mopsy cried out, "You mustn't do this!"

I turned Weimar on her. "I believe your Mr. James Thurber has already said about Miss Red Riding Hood that little girls aren't so easy to fool any more."

"You're unspeakable!"

"Shall I stop, children?"

There were loud protests, and a call for "The Emperor's Nightingale."

I was surprised. "You know that one too?"

"Martha told us."

"Well, if she already told you . . ."

"*You* tell 'em, storyman," Martha chuckled. "It wasn't no jewels and gold, was it?"

"I'm afraid not."

"Tell 'em."

"It was plastic. Fourteen ninety-five, as advertised on television, and when the emperor got it home, the warble busted. The second time he played with it. He took it back to the store, and they told him it only needed new batteries, and wouldn't give him a refund. That's why he went looking for a real nightingale."

"Man," said a lemur down in front of me, "they hard to find."

"He's still looking."

"Listen." He really had something he wanted to ask me. "Listen . . . what really happened to the wolf?"

"Which wolf?"

"The one that was after the pigs."

That one was too easy.

"The pigs got him."

"Yeah. They did, didn't they?"

"Once they had him inside that little brick house, he never got out."

"Boiled him. That right?"

"That's right."

"But I mean, what did they *finally* do with him?"

"Really want to know?"

"Yeah."

"Ate him."

"He'd of done the same to them." Martha didn't ever seem to stop laughing. "Done the same to them."

"Martha's right. Do you know about Hansel and Gretel?"

"Yeah, sure. They cooked the witch."

"Baked her."

"But that's not *all* they did," I insisted. "When they found out how much fun it was to cook a witch, they went and got another one. They cooked her, and then they caught two more. Baked them both together in a casserole. But after that, they had trouble."

"Ran out of wood for the stove," said a baboon.

"No. Lots of wood. But ran out of witches. Weren't any more around. So Gretel said, 'Let's get somebody and pre-

tend she's a witch.' Hansel didn't like that much, but he
went along. They caught a fairy next, and put a peaked hat
on her, and broiled her quick without looking too close.
Then they cooked more fairies, and elves, and nymphs, anybody and everybody."

"How many?"

"Millions."

"How many millions?"

"Oh maybe six."

"Go away, storyman," Martha joshed. "Two kids
couldn't cook that many folks."

"They had help." I smiled around the circle. "You'd've
helped, wouldn't you?"

Uproarious assent.

"Did Martha ever tell you about the City Mouse and the
Country Mouse?"

She had, but this time some of them didn't want to hear it
again.

"No?"

"Don't want to hear about no stupid mice!"

"But I tell it about rats."

Sudden awe.

"They listening, storyman."

"Once upon a time, the City Rat went to visit the Country Rat, and—"

"He take the subway?"

"No, he took the sewer."

"Long as he got there."

"He did, and it was a drag. So he brought the Country
Rat back uptown with him, to show him some excitement.
The Country Rat was going to go right up the front stoop,
but the City Rat took him around back and up through the
wall. 'You gotta cozy it around here,' he told the Country
Rat. 'We wait for dark.' And when dark came, the City Rat

crawled out with the Country Rat hanging onto his tail, and
there, in an empty frozen-orange-juice box, was a little
baby."

Miss Flopsy-Mopsy got up with an appalled look and left.

"She thinks she knows the story," Martha said, "but too
bad she don't."

"Then the City Rat said to the Country Rat, 'Go on.' 'Go
on what?' said the Country Rat. 'Bite the baby,' said the
City Rat. 'You crazy?' said the Country Rat. 'That's what
we come for,' said the City Rat. 'I'm not biting no baby,'
said the Country Rat. 'You no fun at all,' said the City Rat,
and he climbed up on the edge of that juice box and leaned
down toward the little baby's cheek and . . ." They were
hanging on my every word. "—and clicked his big rat teeth
once, twice and then—"

But even I couldn't do it.

"—and then the light suddenly snapped on—"

"There ain't no light." Martha laughed.

"—and the City Rat was knocked right smack dead with a
work shoe—"

"You lie."

"—and the Country Rat ran all the way back to the country, and found an old feed pail to chew on, and said, 'I don't
want no part of any city.' "

"Amen to that," said Martha. "But you shitting us, storyman. You ain't—"

"Let's play a game."

Gibbering assent drowned her out, and so she had to go
back to laughing. Still no ripples. Calm over the whole dark
sea.

"Girls first," I said. "The boys can watch this time. Does
everybody know Drop-the-handkerchief?"

"If you got one."

There was room enough. I got the females into a circle

with Martha's help, then pulled out my handkerchief, twirling it taut and untaut. "Now we're all going to close our eyes, and I'm going to go around and around in back of you, and drop this hanky behind one of you, and—"

"She chases you!"

"That's right, but nobody's to open her eyes until—"

"—You say you dropped it! We know, we know!"

I started off with just a wee bit of a skip. "A tisket, a tasket—" I figured I still needed some small incident to go with the tales they would take home, spread abroad. "—a green and yellow basket—" I picked out the most jutted behind and, a little more than softly, snapped my taut handkerchief at its high cheek. The girl giggled. "I took a present to my love—" So I picked out another, and snapped harder. More giggling. "—took a present to my love—" I wanted something besides a giggle. On my next circle round, I saw some trembling here and there, girlish nerves, especially in one tiny, dirty derrière, bare as a baboon's under her dusty skirt. I whipped it one but good. A real yelp. "—and on my way I dropped—"

But I never got to drop it. It was yanked out of my hand.

"Get his butt!"

Martha was waving them all into the fray with my handkerchief. "Boys too! Get that butt-pincher!" I started to back away, but quickly thought how silly, and stood my ground. They were serving my own purposes. Some of them really tried to pinch hard, but their fingers were just too small. Nibbles. Guppies attacking flab. Still, I squealed, rubbed a few of their heads sweetly, pretended excruciating ecstasy, and it was all a great laugh, especially to Martha.

"We on to you, storyman!" she chortled.

"You won't report me?" I pleaded, quaking in my dirty old man's shoes.

"*That's* how come you know so much about children."

That caught me off guard a little.

"We gonna report this ol' butt-pincher?" she said to the apes.

"Please," I made moan.

"Tell you what. If we reports him . . ."

"It's something I can't help!" I laid on.

"Then we ain't never gonna get him back again."

The monkeys howled.

"Keep him! Keep him!"

"Now just a damn minute," I blurted.

But she was gleeful. "I got your hanky, storyman. I'm the one that's chasing you now."

And she was, in a manner of speaking, did, right back to her barrow on Eighteenth Street after the other mothers came for their own. But a goodly number of them still went with us.

"All yours?" I asked.

"All *mine*. None of 'em *his*."

They loudly booed whoever, or how many, he might be, in happy unison.

"I been telling 'em those stories. But I been telling it like— who was she?—that Singing Lady—remember her?"

"I do indeed. Your Miss Irene Wicker."

"Man, you got her beat."

"But you see how I *am*," I tried to insist.

"I seen." She looked at me very wisely across her tremendous bosom, that outermost reef. "You a rare man. You understand children. Turn your back on 'em, they kill you with a coconut, but they only doing it for love. And if you don't show 'em how cruel they is, they just gets crueler. We ain't got time in this world to pretend nothing to nobody. If you love a child, you better let him know what's hateful in him. And love that part of him just as much as the rest. You don't, he's gonna take it away from you, and hisself right along with it." Waves could beat against her, but they only set her another hand-slapping rhythm. "And I ain't lost none of my own yet."

"Martha, you've got to report me."

"Who says?"

"I shouldn't be allowed near children."

She roared. "You big on getting reported, ain't you?"

"Martha, it's your duty."

"Tell you what, storyman. I maybe do my duty, if you do *me* a little duty here."

This involved locking all the children in the kitchen with a giant jar of peanut butter and a spoon each, then helping her roll out the daybed on its sprung and rusty crutches. She shucked her dress and lay down heavily, turning herself over so that all that island majesty rose up into new boulderous heights.

"Let's see what kind of a buttman you really is."

It outweighed her bosom manyfold. I approached it with some trepidation, feeling very old indeed. But she reached back between her legs and pulled me strongly into her. A plunge down a swift race between those two giant boulders, and higher than I aimed to enter.

"Wait," I said.

"You just stay where I put you."

"We can come to that, Martha."

"I got my reasons."

The boulders began to move, sweetly crushing me.

"If we gets bedchecked, they can *see* I ain't running them no risks."

*

Dwelling upon moody death tonight, E.A.P., I think of your own sad end. Five days you were missing before they found you in that Baltimore tavern, beyond drunkenness. A shivering mind covered with only the barest threads of consciousness. And that day—when Dr. Snodgrass rescued you for four more days of what passed for life, most of it a suicidal delirium that I well recognize—was Election Day. That is the touch that appalls me, that you may have been kept those five blank days in some foul "repeaters" coop, drugged and made mummy-ready to be taken to the polls. Over and over again. To vote until either you or the municipality corrupted, whichever first.

My God. Concerning the vote. It is the addiction of this country. We cannot kick the habit. We will vote until all our treasure is spent, the national will exhausted. Yet after a big vote, such as this hallucinating nationwide high we get on every four years, what withdrawal symptoms! The stark, cold, rucking truth that seizes us, the chills that wrack us when we realize whom we have actually sent to the White Halfway House. We should quit cold turkey, but no, here we are, about to do it again. I was serious before. The choice is, in fact, exactly as you described it, E.A.P. A man who has become a deep, fatuous, and knived pit into which the walls are forcing us—in order to escape the other man who swings back and forth above us, from coast to coast, scything the air, who has been lowering toward us for years, clanking, razor-edged, whetted and ready, if he can only reach us at last, to cut us all right in two.

They have names, you know them.

*

When that *Esquire* snoop got after me about politics, digging into my supposed pinko past, I finally told him that in my ultimate view, there is only God and man.

"That's religion," he said.

"I'm very religious about answering all political questions."

"All right, Simon. What about God and man?"

"As far as politics goes?"

"Whatever."

"Well, I'll say this much. I am perfectly willing to see God made elective. It might even help somewhat. But I am opposed to all these modern changes in the terms of office for man. They're extremely shortsighted and often very cruel."

"I don't follow."

"If you'll recall, his was originally supposed to be an appointment for life."

*

Among my other depredations, I tried to do what I could, my small share at least, to stop the vote. As somebody who finally managed to quit voting, I thought I might be able to help others to help themselves by becoming a poll watcher.

I was naturally refused by the Board of Elections, but did talk to some interested press about the matter.

"What was your purpose in seeking to become a poll watcher, Mr. Moro?"

"Admonitory."

"How so?"

"My thought was to challenge everybody."

"Indiscriminately?"

"Yes. Some, of course, would still have to be allowed to cast their votes. But by and large, only the most hopeless cases. Those who've been voting a straight ticket for twenty years, that type. There's really no point in trying to rehabilitate these lost souls. But the so-called independent voters, for instance, those who still feel they are making some real choice, they could be turned away. And should be. This sense of exercising choice is the most dangerous thing about voting. Most voters become hooked before they realize it is a delusion."

"Anybody else?"

"The young. Those who will be voting for the first time, unless stopped. They're very important. My feeling is that if

they can be warned off, voting might very soon die out altogether. In other words, I don't think the situation, though
desperate, is irreversible. It is largely a matter of educating
people, and particularly our young people, to recognize the
inevitable self-abuse, the tax on their own intelligence that
voting demands."

"You ever voted yourself, Mr. Moro?"

"Of course. Often. You can't be moralistic about a thing
like this, especially when it's so deeply woven into our society. I approach the problem strictly as an ex-voter who
understands the attractions that voting has for certain dissat-
isfied people."

"Who'd you ever vote for?"

"I'd rather not say. And in taking that position I realize I
am contributing to the secrecy already connected with the
ballot, a secrecy that I also know to be a large factor in the
rapid rise of the vote. I realize that, and I am opposed to that
secrecy. But as long as the secret ballot is the law of this
land, I will respect it, however unwillingly, even in my own
case. This is a highly complicated problem. Voting, of
course, can't be outlawed. You already in this country tried
Prohibition. But private individuals certainly have the right
to abstain from this vice, if you will allow me to call it a
vice. And above all, we can certainly insist that it be made
an open and aboveboard affair. To put it another way, I am
for fully, not just partially, legalizing the franchise. I would
think that, as a first step, we might begin by removing all
those silly, opium-den curtains from the polling booths—"

"Mr. Moro, I don't think you understand our democratic
system."

I grew wroth. "That excuse has been offered time and
again. You're as well aware as I am that voting has crept
perniciously step by step into the system by which this
country first Constitutionally arranged to govern itself. Voting, as we have it now, is an abuse of that system, and your

Mr. George Washington would agree with me."

And so on, & So Forth.

I'd have to admit that this adjunctive campaign did not catch on quite as well as my subway junkets or my revised fairy tales. The City still thinks of me primarily as a child molester, not a political maniac. It only goes to prove that people, even in the nature of the evil men do them, don't want change.

*

Then there is this business of handing out candy to the whores, my own *affaire des bonbons*. None of them seemed to have much of a sweet tooth, though great talents for invective. I took abuse that would have shriveled Priapus. Finally, outside the Americana, a tough little puss-puss, about five foot two in her poofed henna wig and punishment heels, yelled so loud she brought a cop.

"Okay, dads," he grabbed me. "Let's give back the purse."

"That's his purse!" she yowled.

I got all his Irish eye. "His, is it?"

"He's freaking me, him and his purse!"

"You always carry a handbag, dads?"

"No harm," I said.

"Maybe, maybe not."

"It's full of lemon drops!" she screeched.

"Is it now?"

"For my fair ones," I wheezed. "Sweets to the sweet."

"And who might they be?"

"No harm if I want to give treats to my little girls."

"This one of your little girls?"

"I got nothing to do with this candy freak!"

"No harm." I opened the purse. "Have one."

He poked the purse right back at me with his nightstick. "Let's see you eat one first."

Of course I hesitated.

"Go on," he nodded. "Treat yourself."

I kept my jaw tensely set, and the whore muttered, "Tol' you, tol' you."

"Plenty there, dads."

"They're for my sweet little ones," I crowed nervously.

"Something in them," she snarled.

"What's the name, dads?" He had out his notebook.

I clammed up again.

"Come on. You got a name."

"Sade."

"The full name."

"Mark D. Sade."

"Live in the city?"

"No."

"Where you staying?"

"The Bastille."

He didn't seem to know that hotel.

"Got any identification?"

I put the purse behind my back.

"Come on, Mark. Let's have a driver's license or something."

"No harm."

"Otherwise we take a little walk."

I started suddenly shaking, pulled the purse around in front of me again, tore it open. Then, with a very good crazy snicker, I fisted up a big handful of lemon drops and jammed them into my mouth, wrappers and all. They were damn hard to swallow. I almost gagged on the cellophane twists, but the choking added conviction.

"No harm," I laughed hysterically. "No harm."

He knocked the next handful out of my hand and blew his whistle. The whore ran. I staggered, dumping lemon drops all over Eighth Avenue, tried to pick them up and cram more into my mouth. He tackled me and was struggling to put his finger down my throat when the squad car roared up.

I took it as far as they wanted to go, even let them stomach-pump me. To insure my effect, but also because I didn't really fancy trying to digest all that crinkly cellophane. I then spent a restful night at St. Luke's under close observation, found myself very big in the newspapers again next morning. The nice part about the *Daily News* story was that it connected me with "a long series of previous incidents involving Moro that have increasingly annoyed New Yorkers." I was beginning to establish myself.

Though exactly as what kind of a poor flimflam—yes, still!—I didn't find out until that cop stopped by at St. Luke's, to decide if there was any way he could press charges. I thought he gave up pretty easily.

"They were nothing but lemon drops," he said, "as if you didn't know."

"No harm."

"Right. You really don't mean anybody any harm."

"Don't be too sure."

"We're sure."

"The papers aren't."

"You're the kind of nut, if we catch you making an obscene phone call, it's always to your wife."

"I'm not married."

"I'm talking about the way you're trying to scare this city."

"Out of its wits."

"People are that way already. Everybody's scared, but nobody knows what he's really scared of."

"The blacks, crime in the streets, their apartments being robbed, police brutality—"

"Too much to be scared of. That's the trouble."

"Add me."

"I am. But everybody's really better off being scared of you."

"What?"

"You're a safe way to be scared."

I was outraged. "I intend to strike terror, absolute terror into every heart!"

He smiled. "We'd be happy to cooperate."

*

That's when I knew I was going to have to use Pinkie. Somehow. Maybe this was even why I'd kept that finger back so long. Always in readiness, but never publicly committed. Once or twice I'd taken it along with me in my pocket, on the sly, to push elevator buttons with, or stir a cup of coffee. But it didn't work on those square-lit panel buttons. They operate on body heat. The finger has to be live. And I couldn't drink the coffee, too much formaldehyde. Besides, I knew these were furtive horrors, wasted on my dull-witted fellow passengers or a few drifters in Nedick's. There had to be a right time, a moment when I could, with maximum exposure, stick that finger right in everybody's eye.

Grisly of me, yes. But necessary. Concerning all this. People are much more frightened by pieces of people than they are by actual people. The foot still in the dead soldier's boot, the head on a pike, the lopped limbs in the Grand Central baggage locker, the testicles stuffed in the mouth, the string of ears, et cetera. It is once again the part for the whole. We blanch and shiver more at what is missing than what is there. We remember the dismembered. Ghoulgantua. I had it all together back then, as they say. That once. Every bit and piece of me was really *somebody*. The problem here was how to create that same fear of rampant carnage out of not even so much as a man's hand. Easy enough to drop the thing in somebody's Caesar salad, but how to make a little finger go a lot longer way, the whole way?

*

Luckily Terry was beginning to take a panicky interest, started calling me from the coast.

"What are you doing to us?"

"How are you involved?"

"The trades got you in Bellevue."

"St. Luke's."

"Molesting prostitutes?"

"And kids."

"Kids?"

"And old ladies on subways."

"Simon!"

"Life goes on."

"Listen careful."

"Speak."

"We've got you on the *Tonight Show*."

"Excellent."

"But you'd better behave."

"Watch me."

"I will, and I want to see Mr. Nice Ghoul."

"I'll tell them fairy stories."

"Don't shit me, Simon. We're already hearing some of those out here."

"Then I'll tell them how I made the picture."

"How *who* made the picture?"

"A family picture about family people with family problems."

"Well . . . in a way . . . it *is*."

"I quite agree."

"How come you agree?"

"I'm family myself. The black sheep of the Family of

Man maybe, but still Family."

"I warn you, Simon. Any more trouble, and I'm coming east."

*

So the right time had come, and for the occasion, since I would be wearing my Ravenswear, I decided to put Pinkie in costume too.

"A ring for my lady's finger," I sang at the salesgirl behind the Woolworth jewelry counter.

"What kind of ring? Engagement? Birthday? Anniversary?"

"Anything that will get us into a motel."

"You want a wedding band, then. And you probably want it adjustable."

"No. We can try it on here."

"She's with you?"

"She couldn't come, but I brought this along."

We tried three before we found one that really fit that old groove. That is, I slipped them on and off the finger as she handed them to me, standing very far back of the counter. Then she said she needed to call her supervisor if she was going to make change for my dollar. Altogether it made a nice little preliminary stir.

*

So then, the night Mine Host, whoever he may be, met Pinkie.

I've always hated these talk shows. Hated them. Rhetorical *fellatio:* You've been around a long time, haven't you?— Yes, a long time.—Do monsters ever grow old?—I think they try to age gracefully, like most of us.—How old would Ghoulgantua be now?—A lot of him would be practically senile, but some parts of him would still be fairly young.— That right?—Yes. His left ear could hear a pin drop, but he'd probably need trifocals for his right eye.—This is some conversation we're having, isn't it?—Yes it is. It is indeed. —Do you enjoy playing monsters? I mean, do you really feel monstrous yourself?—I think most of us feel pretty monstrous most of the time.—You think so?—Oh yes. I've been wandering around New York a lot lately, just on my own—You certainly have, haven't you?—Yes, and I notice there's a lot of mayhem, in people's faces.—How do you mean?—It's the way they look at you. The same way I used to look at Fay Wray. Or Hazel Rio in our new picture.— Fay Wray. Whatever happened to her?—I don't know.— Married King Kong and had six little princess apes.— Maybe.—Hey, we're having Hazel Rio on the show next week, you know that?—I heard that.—We'll have to ask her just how *do* you look at her. But you've been getting lots of looks yourself lately, haven't you?—Quite a lot.—What kind of looks?—Oh . . . nasty, mean, bitter, angry, desirous.— Desirous?—Rapacious, really.—But tell me this, despite all that, I mean, despite everything, haven't some people been *kind?*—A few.—How have they been kind?—They've tried to get me to a hospital, or asked a policeman to help. The ones that haven't run away.—A lot of people run away from you?—Quite a few.—Why do you think they run away?—I think it has a great deal to do with themselves.—They're not just afraid?—They're afraid, but afraid of themselves, really. Like I just said a minute ago, what I see in them is myself, and what I think they see in me is themselves. At least that's what I want them to see.—But you're such a *nice* guy, or are you?—Well, you know what they say about nice guys.—Finishing last, you mean.—Yes.—They do say that, don't they?—They do, but it may not be the whole story.—How do you mean?—Let's say it's all finished, whatever it happens to be, and there's this one last guy, all alone.—Yes.—Why shouldn't he think he's a nice guy? Who's around to tell him any different? He could be a very bad guy, the worst guy who ever lived.—You think there

are a lot of really bad guys who think they're nice guys?—
That's one definition of a monster.—Who's around now
that's that kind of a monster?—Well, there's Richard Nixon,
he's been last a few times, and Chiang Kai-shek, and Hubert
Humphrey, and—I'm not sure I like how this conversation
is going, do you?—And maybe you could include yourself.
How's your rating lately?—Hey now, I thought you were
supposed to be the monster around here.—Yes, but I'm a
monster by intent.—That's better?—Much.—All right.
What makes me a monster?—You're a monster through circumstances.—I can't wait to hear this.—You can't help
being a monster when millions of people give up what used
to be their own quiet times together, all their small talk,
maybe a good two hours of sleep each night to watch you
mouth—What's that you're wearing, Simon?—This, you
mean.—What do you call that outfit?—Ravenswear.—I
want to ask you about that, just as soon as we hear this word
from . . .

*

Hate them. Oral onanism: Simon Moro's been telling us
here how he turns into a Raven. What are those back there,
wings?—My dark pinions.—What happens when you
moult? That's a bird-brained question, isn't it? Let me ask
you something else about the picture. Who directed it?—I
did.—You did?—Largely.—Why does it say Terry Cowan
here on the card?—Terry worked as my assistant. A very
bright lad too.—He's coming along?—He's coming along. I
predict quite a future for him. But he's got one problem.—
What's that?—He's squeamish.—Squeamish?—Sight of blood
sickens him.—Doesn't that make it a little hard for him
to do a horror picture?—Yes, and it shows in his work.
Somewhat.—Kind of like being Busby Berkeley with two
left feet, isn't it?—Almost.—He's not going to mind our saying that, is he?—Busby might.—Let's see here, the script is

by?—Myself.—You wrote the script?—I collaborated.—
With?—Your Mr. Edgar Allan Poe.—Who else? I guess I
just tear up this card, don't I?—Hasn't been right so far.—
This is pretty much your picture then?—I think you could
say that.—I know you've done some great pictures, *Zeppelin*
and *The Moth*, you have, and those lizard ones—who was he
again?—Gila Man.—Right. I knew that. Classics they've become. But it's been a long time.—Yes. Eight years since *The
Shoplifter.*—I saw that one. It was great. But eight years,
you say?—Eight years.—So how does it feel to be back in
this one? You happy with it?—I was when I left Hollywood. But we've lost some good things in the editing.—You
know, you hear that all the time, but does it ever really happen?—It can easily. You play a great, long, torrid love scene,
and it ends up a last-minute handshake.—Did you play any
love scenes for this picture?—Oh yes. Several. Ravens are
terrific lovers.—Who do you make love to?—Lenore.—
Hazel Rio?—That's right. Hazel.—Tell me, how does a
raven make love?—You better see the picture.—Anyhow,
it's a horror picture, not a love picture, isn't it?—Both,
really.—But will it scare people?—Petrify them.—Really
and truly?—Yes. Particularly the love scenes.—Did I hear
him right, audience?—They're some of the best horror.—I
guess I did. So it's a horror love picture. Have I got it
straight?—Yes, if you realize that all horror is erotic.—I
didn't know that. Did the audience know that?—Very
erotic.—Now that I know, I'm not sure I *want* to know.
Should I take my wife to this picture?—Yes.—I *should?*
What do you think's wrong with my wife?—Take everybody. It's good, clean family eroticism.—Whoops!—They
don't always turn out that well!—It can get *worse?*—Some
horror films go off in very strange directions these days.—
Do we want to get into that? I guess not. How do we get out
of it? Let's talk about Quincy Adams.—That's not going to
get us out of it.—It's not, is it? But isn't he in the picture

with you?—Briefly.—He was on our show once. Briefly. I
don't mean that. He stayed a long time. What's he do in
your picture?—Equivocates.—He does what?—Equivocates.—That sound as bad to you out there as it does to me
up here?—He's very good at it.—But do we dare ask him
back on the show again? I don't mean that either. Is he going
to mind our talking about him like this?—I don't think so,
really. He equivocates pretty openly.—In the picture too?—
Throughout.—You actually show him equivocating?—In
extreme close-up.—Wow. Listen. You were going to tell us
something that happened on set, weren't you?—If you'll
allow me a few liberties here, I'm even going to demonstrate
how it happened.—What sort of liberties? *You're* not going
to equivocate, are you?—Not in the least.—What is it you
want me to let you do?—Take off my shoes.—Go ahead.
While Simon Moro is liberating his feet here, we'll return
you to your local stations. Don't go away, folks, we'll be
right back. . . .

*

Still crap, but bringing me closer, very close: Simon
Moro's got his shoes off here, but you can't see his feet because . . . what do you call that skirt thing?—A caftan.—
Okay. His caftan, as you can see, he's practically tripping
over it. Let's move along here.—Well, we had this quite
wonderful live raven on set named Rupert.—You're going
to be Rupert the Raven?—I'm the raven, that's correct.—He
mind you stealing his part?—We're still good friends.—Go
ahead. I'm interrupting.—We went through a terrible morning, Monday, the first week of shooting. A lot of fracas.
Rupert's stand-in was injured, and the scene wasn't working.
Everything a disaster.—Like every night on this show.—
Anyhow, one of the grips lost something fairly valuable to
him in all the confusion.—What was it?—I'll get to it. In
fact, I brought it along with me tonight.—Good.—Nobody

could find the thing, everybody hunting high and low. But Rupert spotted it.—Where?—Way up in some spider web-bing.—A real spider web?—No. Fake. No spider. Part of the set.—I see.—And when Rupert saw how high up it was, realized he was the only one who could reach it, he took off.—You were telling me they've got very keen minds, ravens do. Am I right?—Yes. He flew up, picked it right out of the web with his beak, and brought it back to me.—Why you? Why not the guy who lost it?—He knew me better.— Or he knew you were going to be on tonight's show. Smart bird there, Rupert. Okay. You're going to do it for us, that whole bit. When? Right now?—I'm ready whenever you are.—Then here we go. Ladies and gentlemen, Simon Moro as the Raven, in a moment of . . . what's it say here? . . . a Moment of Recaptured and Reiterated Horror? You got me. . . .

*

Finally, after all that horse prattle, I switched raucously into ravenese. I waited for the trumpeter to quit, then flut-tered out of my chair in a jabber. I pulled Pinkie out of my pocket, but too high over my head for focus.

—What's that? Looks like a sausage.

I tossed it away quickly, out past the cameras into their cables, call that the web, so they couldn't get a shot of it yet. They stayed on me instead, as I leapt into a flight pattern.

—He'll never get off the ground, that raven.

Then I was out there in the cables, on top of the finger, covering it with the skirts of my caftan. I did some blinking and burbling, until I had Pinkie between the big and second toes of my right foot. The cameras caught up with me again. I lifted the caftan and slowly brought talon to beak, feeling the tendons in my leg tighten with age, but still yield, stretch all the way to my mouth.

—Isn't *that* some trick?

There was a spattering of applause around me. Like tossed bird seed, I remember thinking.

—Some of our viewers probably remember Simon doing that in one of his earliest movies. I do, I'm here to tell you. Boy. Fed himself soup with a spoon, and never spilled.

I turned, very much on the wing, and swooped in a gyre twice around both cameras, twisting them into each other's lenses.

—All right, Rupert, let's see what you've got there. Hey, how do you call a raven?

I screeched through my teeth, past the stench and sponginess. He screeched back at me in proudly silly imitation.

—Too much parakeet?

I plummeted down on him.

—Do I take it from you, or . . . *Christ no I don't!*

But the cameras had already moved in tight, and for one slight, bright, shining moment, I think I actually unified this country.

*

Though possibly I exaggerate. Here, as perhaps in much else I have claimed for myself so far. Not all parts of the country got to see it. Some local stations balked, cut to their "Please Stand By" opticals. And only the studio audience saw all of it as I've described it. The tape was trimmed, keeping attention during those last few seconds on Pinkie, not Mine Host. The network wanted its man absolved. Its attitude toward me was one of rough justice. "Since you're never going to appear on television again, Moro, we're willing to show why." I suppose, by its own lights, that was magnanimous, even daring of TV.

But am I wrong, or did there rise at that moment, as parceled out across the land as that moment had to be, a wave of universal revulsion? At long last? After all my efforts? I think so, and will not pretend modesty. I have not been unaware of my increasing fad, nor ignorant of the reach it could give me, despite its shallowness. But please, my only real conceit in it has been the chance it offered me to make just such a meaningful gesture. And frankly, I believe I brought it off.

I feel that wave still. It supports me yet. It makes it possible to lie down in this coffin and press forward with Terry's ridiculous scheme, though, as you will ultimately see, very much in my own fashion. For I am not going to let that wave subside. In fact, I have resolved upon a dire stratagem that will bring it to tidal proportions.

Concerning this revulsion. If I were to analyze it, I would say that it extends outward from that tiny finger, if only subconsciously, to all the great bestiality we have undertaken as a nation. I certainly hope so, in any case. Much can be attached to that finger. I will not bother to list the horrors we have known lately, and indeed done. What I have really tried to do is show, by vivid and palpable example, how they must, *must* be taken between our teeth.

*

But I have to prepare now for the day's doings. Rudy will be in here soon to dress me, jury up my starched shirt with chicken wire to hide breathing, whiten my visage with a bloodless face powder, and so forth. People are coming to see what has revolted them, and they must continue to be revolted. Otherwise, all this self-torment, to what end?

*

Sunlight strikes the facets of your vials, E.A.P. I approach the first dawn of my popular death. Its rattle shakes my pen, and my words, for the nonce, expire.

*

If there is a God, by god I hope he is a professional. . . .

WALPURGISNACHT minus one. After what I must admit has been a very defeating day. Pennies and garlic. The riches and breath of this city. The good folk came first in rivulets, then in washes to cleanse my body with their tears. Not really. Not at all. Only to stare. To stare and stare, with no commensurate reaction. And another worry. I've always said I never lost a staring contest. But did I today? I did not stare back. As the unseeing dead, I suppose you could say I was hardly required to. Excuse enough to keep my lids lowered, or turn aside my eyes, upward into my head. To disengage. But I'm not satisfied with my performance. Not satisfied. I've played this whole first reel with my back to camera. *Tour de force*, yes, eternally, and old tricks from *Zeppelin*, but how do we know if I'm really any good? I must find some way tomorrow to turn around. Open my eyes. Play dead straight.

*

I wish to note here the visit of only one mourner. My dearest Hazel.

"I know you can't talk now, Simon honey, but there's a few things I have to tell you. I found out about Terrykins. He does it to windows! I caught him at Schrafft's. When he was outside, I was inside. So I don't think I can do much with him, baby, I'm not glass. But I've been to the German consulate, and they checked. They say sure they're willing to release your film, but they don't have it any more. They could be just saying that. But I did one of them, and he says it's very embarrassing, but some Israelis stole it. To make a documentary about the prison camps for American tourists. I'm sorry. They used your work, but they lost most of you. It's not fair, is it? My German says they think it's even more unfair to them because the Israelis took what you made up and pretended it was real. Anyhow, it's all gone. I wish I'd at least seen it. Also, mama may be coming through the line today. I know there's not much you can do, but think about her. She always said she wanted to see you dead. So you don't really have to go much out of your way to give her a little treat."

*

So much for Terry's integrity. It is like my Hazel's chastity. Not quite. I doubt if it ever required even initial violation.

As for her mother, she'd already been through. Assaultingly weeping and tunelessly wailing. I tasted one of her tears on my lip. Gin.

*

Rudy, Rudy, Rudy, Rudy. You are such a strange device upon this scarlet field of human endeavor.

I remember when I taught you how to make the sign of the cross. Touch forehead, touch heart, touch shoulder, touch shoulder. So simple. Another signal you could make with your hand. This one will let you in the church.

But your eyes kept asking me, what does it mean? What am I saying? And why does everybody else make the same sign? Head, heart, shoulder and shoulder?

It is an admission, Rudy, that if God is really present, we must all be deaf and dumb. If He is speaking, we do not hear. If He is listening, we cannot speak. We can only gesture with our hands, like you, and look for His. In everything, they say. But I do not see it myself.

Your trouble is that you were born a stump with an abstract turn of mind. But try, please try not to philosophize. I am being concrete. When I butt my hands together and close them palm to palm, I do not mean prayer. I mean my notebook. And when I make cursive motions in the air with a tightened fist, it is not the revolution. I am only asking for another ballpoint pen. Bring me one.

*

I am going to write about My Trip to the Country. The account will contain essential information. Perhaps a little stale. Some of it, in fact, fifty years old. But I have kept it all buried too long. These things also must rise and walk in the open sight of men.

When I cover my eyes with my hand, Rudy, it does not mean I am thinking. It means I can hardly bear to look.

*

Last Friday night, then, I rode wildly down the Jersey Turnpike in a Hertz Mustang on a complicated mission. First through the thick, chemical fogs and marshy luminescence of the Elizabeth refineries. On all sides of me, oil ominously cracked, and hydrogen sulfide burned off at the wick of a tall, laddered taper, like an ignis fatuus. Once I saw the tail of a lurking tiger curl around a storage tank. Billy Blake Enters Heaven.

But soon I had left all that, and the city's stinking moat, far behind me. I swung down the ramp at Exit 8 and roared off into the desolate countryside. The roads were still vaguely cement, but more and more broken, soon scabrous with tar, then tar altogether, then tar mixed with sand. I passed lonely outposts. The Citizens Rifle and Revolver Club, and the snip-snap sound of small arms emptying their chambers in the dark. Gert's Meats and Groceries, shut for the winter, open next famine. An abandoned pick-up truck, its front end buried in red clay, emblazoned "We'll Haul It For You!" The Au Fait Decor Design Center, advertising a special on Venetian blinds, along with "Plastic Flowers— Reduced." They were all somehow familiar, or if not exactly these hulks of enterprise, certainly the sandy, piney miles and miles between them. I only worried about the frequent and flaky signs—"For Sale, Eckmann Realty"—that my headlights picked up along the roadside, in stubbled fields and eroded front lawns, on falling fruit stands.

I came to Mabel's, though I had never known any Mabel ready to offer me Fried Clams, Chicken-in-the-Basket, Music, Dancing Sat. Eve., Liquor, Seven-Up Time, Rooms for Rent, Pottery, Snacks, Live Bait, Souvenirs, Free TV. I pulled up to her single unmarked gas pump and honked. I waited several minutes, listening to her sign hiss and tick. It was a long-stemmed 1940 cocktail glass, slightly tipsy, in pink-elephant neon. Somebody who was not Mabel, at least by sex, came out to say they were all closed up, and he didn't have the key to the pump.

"Can you tell me if I'm anywhere near Vienna?" I asked.

"Where?"

"Vienna."

"Never heard of it."

Was I that far off the track? Then I realized. After all these years, I'd absent-mindedly slipped up on the local pronunciation.

"Sorry," I said, and then enunciated, "*Vi*enna."

"Oh. You want old Vi Town."

We were agreed.

"Half mile straight ahead, first left."

He hurried back inside Mabel's and turned off her pink gin fizz.

Five minutes later I was at the sign the Volunteer Fire Department had put up at town's edge in 1911.

WELCOME TO VIENNA

And then the rhyme line below it.

Why-enna where else?

I was back.

*

I drove straight through, not stopping, only checking on one or two places. We still seemed to have the only decent house in town, three down on the left from the fire house, still right opposite the General Store. Our whitewashed wishing well still stood next to the storm cellar doors. How many wishes I'd thrown down that hole, I remembered, but quickly looked to the right, for Eckmann Realty, next to the General Store. Double empty, and maybe it was only the night, but I could hardly make out Eckmann's peeling name on the old signboard over the transom.

But there was a much newer placard in the window. "Sold by C. Moro."

Ah so. To himself, most likely. He'd turned realtor, then, too. There always had been a certain skulking prosperity in the town. All you had to do was keep jumping it coming around every corner.

But I was already outside Vienna, going toward the Jersey shore. The beaches were a good ten miles distant, but the real sand began here. A windy swirl of it churned up in the road ahead of me, and spattered the car windows like hard rain. When it cleared, I was at the brick gates of the Austro-Hungarian Picnic Grounds. The old chain was dropped down so low and rusty that I drove right over it.

I stopped and got out at the first fireplace. There seemed to be more fireplaces than I remembered, as many as sixty, but then we were always building more fireplaces. Every summer, another barbecue pit for the new folks in town, though the architecture never changed. And hadn't, from what I could see. Still the same low-hearthed, double-grilled, wood-burning, soot-blackened family units. All summer long, the pitchy smoke of charred hamburger and scorched chicken legs, or sometimes a flank steak, hung in the burnt air. The bricks never cooled, and my father played stubborn, beery piano hour after hour over the popping grease.

I wandered over to the music shed. Its roof must have been replaced sometime during all those years, but it was still corrugated tin. I remembered its resonance, whomping out his thumby chords in schmaltz booms. The piano here now was still an old one, its keyboard locked up for the season, but a new one, of course, to me. It had been a Player Pianola in my father's day. He'd mastered the instrument by running the rolls over and over, following along the keys with his hammy hands, memorizing their plunks and dips downward. He could have played those slaughterhouse Strauss waltzes of his blind as well as deaf and dumb.

Something of all this, however distortedly, had gone into my work, and I had come here first to be alone, to dredge up those long-ago summertime fancies. My mother's mad Tyrolean dances. Eckmann and the alphorn he built out of stove pipe. The frenzied, clog-footed cotillions that everybody flung themselves into, linking steins and rear ends. Comical, chimerical, but some noisome stench of the future here. Odors of the *Anschluss. Ah so*, that weird, almost Ruritanian evening when my brother followed the toast to the Emperor Franz Josef by rising to propose they also drink to the Kaiser. Strange to think of him rebelling that way, yet still staying on, a crypto-Prussian, to become a town father. Stranger still to think of that opera bouffe gesture as any kind of a rebellion. He must have been all of fifteen then, barely old enough to drink schnapps.

I walked back to the car with perplexing geopolitical thoughts. Why had my parents come to this country if all they wanted to do was refound that same farcical principality all over again? Gaiety travels no better than wine. I had been raised as a miserable sprite in the New Jersey Vienna Woods, had tried to escape all the way across the sea to the real Transylvania. It occurred to me that I probably couldn't have gone a longer way around to never leave home.

*

As I drove back out over the chain, I noticed a new structure across the road, and back in a ways. A drive-in theater, in fact, the top of its screen curving just over the pine trees. The marquee, built of brick in that same fireplace style, had last July's feature still listed in hanging letters.

S. MORO
in
HITLER'S CAMPS

I wondered if I might have become a local war hero.

*

Back in Vienna again, I stopped first at the General Store. Frankly, to see if anybody who might be up that late would notice me. The deep, buckling swells in the floor hadn't changed. I remembered my father once joking that this was the farthest inland the Jersey surf had ever reached. A huge roller, still carrying the candy counter at its crest.

There was only one lone codger tending the store. It took me a moment to realize it was Eckmann. Eighty if he was a day. When I asked him if I could buy an American flag sticker for my car, he didn't seem to recognize me.

"Have them in again Monday maybe," he said.

"You're out?"

"Been a run on them."

"Town must be livening up."

He didn't say anything. I sensed he was lying.

"This your store?" I asked him.

"I mind it."

"Who for?"

"Man across the way."

"With the wishing well?"

"That's the war memorial."

"It's the what?"

"He give it to the town."

Eckmann's eyes had gone bad on him. He was hand-fumbling his way down the counter toward me.

"Important man around here. Owns most of us when we're dead too."

"How so?"

"The cemetery's his. Made his mark in life out of that cemetery."

He'd almost reached me, would once he got around the horehound candy jar.

"Had a business myself. Next door. But got to be too much for me. So we kind of traded real estate."

"Watch you don't bump that jar."

"Traded even. My holdings for one of his plots. And I get to hang around here until I need it."

I was about to say Eckmann, you always were a damn fool, go blow your horn, when somebody came in the door. It looked like somebody too small to be up at this hour. Before I had that idea out of my head, he was hugging me around the knees, like a small bear.

*

Rudy in tears. Rudy trying to say everything with his hands, but needing them to wipe away his tears. So I wiped them away, and tried to catch up with all his fingers had to say. How good it was to see me, how long it had been, how old we were getting! Did I think he'd grown? Did I? Did I know he could still lift over twice his weight easily? Did I know he could drive the hearse now, if somebody was with him? Did I want to hear him play the piano? Could we go right out to the picnic grounds and he'd play and I'd dance, the way our folks always did?

I tinkled piano keys in the air, then twisted a key in a lock, and then shrugged.

He understood. He'd run and get the key.

I hauled him back before he escaped and shook my head.

He understood. But why not?

I pointed across the street, walked my fingers, indicated both of us, and drew a face as long as I could remember my brother's being. I meant we must.

He understood. He kicked me.

But I understood, and hugged him hard, rubbing my cheek on the balding flat of his head.

"Look out for that little runt," Eckmann said. "He's got mean toes."

I realized Eckmann still didn't know who I was.

*

We didn't go to the front door, but around to the storm cellar doors, which Rudy flipped back like shutters. Harsh light and a chill rose up out of the cellar, still as whitewashed as the wishing well.

Cosmo was working over a corpse, and wearing a green eyeshade. It was my father's eyeshade, or one exactly like it. I'd forgotten how much our parent had tried to pamper his one best remaining sense.

When Cosmo saw me, he yanked it off in acute embarrassment. Hadn't seen me in nearly fifty years, and here I'd caught him wearing it. I'm sure Rudy meant that to happen.

He didn't say anything for quite a long time. Then he said, "We'll talk in the morning."

"Where do I sleep?"

"Rudy will show you."

"All right."

He pulled up a strand of the corpse's stringy gray hair. "She's got to be ready for church by eight."

"I said, all right."

"All right then."

"One thing though."

"Talk to Rudy. You were always good at talking to him."
"When we go out, don't put it back on."
He ground his snaggly teeth.

*

We went out into the cemetery together the following day, just before noon. To check on the grave Rudy had dug for the old gal, who'd owned a beauty parlor over near Point Pleasant. Which was why she had to look extra nice, Cosmo said. But also to talk things over, and for him to point out to me one headstone in particular. It was already somewhat weathered, lichened, with the Imperial Death's Head and the slogan, GOTT MIT UNS FÜR KÖNIG UND VATERLAND, but incompletely inscribed.

SIMON MORO
1900–

"This was where I was going to put you," he said, "if you'd come back to us with any honor."
"It wasn't my war. It was your war. Why didn't you go?"
"I had all this to worry about."
He stretched his knobby hand out over the far-reaching graves. We were standing in the original family plot, a good distance out back, but still the dead nearest the house. He'd fenced it off, but where were the sheep, and my mother with her scythe? The sheep had long ago become mutton, and my mother . . .
Her grave was next to our father's, right behind my own premature memorial. I'd remembered them as being very much alone out here, but now they were all but lost in a great, green-rolling, anonymous crowd. I guessed the place must draw from at least three counties.
"I served, Cosmo."
"But you didn't win."

"Nobody did, really. It was a bloody circus, and they killed all the clowns."

"You just set it up for that friend of yours."

"What friend?"

"Hitler."

"I hated Hitler."

He smirked at me slyly. "Didn't look that way in your last picture."

I tried to keep my patience. "You wouldn't understand, but I had to run from Hitler."

"Just like you to."

"You don't know."

"I know when the family name's been disgraced on the field of valor."

"I didn't even use our name. I used Eckmann's, if you must know."

"You went as a Moro."

"I went illegally, remember? American citizens weren't supposed to be fighting for the Kaiser. I fought and I deserted—"

"*Deserted?*"

"Both bravely, Cosmo. As somebody called Rudi Eckmann."

"Rudy? You think he'd be proud of what you done?"

"Yes, if he could ever know."

"It's worse than I thought."

"You don't know."

"I know what you did to our good name. Couldn't defend it yourself, so you let a bunch of monsters do it for you!"

I tried to change the subject.

"When did you force out Eckmann?"

He squirmed a little. "He was a charge on the public rolls. I got him off last year."

"And left him with nothing."

"I left up his signs."

"His land?"

"It ain't much, but I'm holding on to it."

"What for?"

"I got my reasons."

"We're old men, Cosmo. You, me, even Rudy. And none of us has any family. What good is your damn greed?"

"You don't have any family?"

"None I'm tied to."

"Legally?"

"That's not the real point, but it's the case."

He was pleased by this, felt freer to talk.

"The land's for more of the same." He waved again out over the stones already raised, and the profitable grave sites beyond. I could see now what he'd turned into. A quick-buck land developer on death duty. "Nothing here for you," he went on, "except maybe this." He patted the skull on my headstone. "If I even let you have that. So now, how come you're back?"

"I need your brotherly help."

He snorted. "I disowned you after Versailles."

I got angry. "I had a lot to say about Versailles myself. And I said it. Out loud, publicly."

"Where?"

"In the real Vienna."

"Didn't reach us."

"How would it? You just do not know. I've spent years, trying to shock people out of making mistakes like that. And worse ones. Every way I could."

"That what you think you've been doing?"

"That's what I *know* I've been doing. I'm still doing it."

"With your spook tricks."

"With my life. What have you been doing with yours?"

"Don't get high and mighty with me. Remember I seen your last picture. You didn't even stick up for your Nazi friends!"

Useless. I was trying to reach him across too many piled-up decades. It gave me pause. I realized I still clung to my old Marxist habit of trying to get aboard the train of history. But to Cosmo, to most people, history is only a ghost train. They hear its wail far down the tracks sometimes, but never see it go by, don't even want to ride the rails.

"All right, Cosmo, all right. Suppose I say that I need your professional help."

"Who for?"

"Myself."

"Yourself?"

"Yes."

He grinned. "Now that might be arranged."

I explained at length what was going on, what I needed from him. It seemed to appeal to his streak of connivance.

"Pretty complicated."

"That's why I want you and Rudy along."

"You really going back to Germany?"

"That's the plan, but I don't trust the plan yet. I don't think I can really depend upon anybody involved in this. Except my family."

"Your family."

"Especially if I have to change plans."

He squirmed at this too, but seemed to take my point.

"Well, I got a new hearse."

"No, I don't want that one. Rudy showed me the old one this morning, back of the firehouse."

"That's the town ambulance now."

"I don't care. I want it."

"And two cheap coffins you want."

"Just as cheap as Father used to make them. Thin. Out of old scrap wood, if you've got any."

"I got some pretty thin pine, some old poplar."

"Then pine for the sides, poplar for the lids."

"I could do things a lot fancier, if I had time to order."

"Don't have time to order, and I don't want fancy."

"You don't." He sharpened up his sharpest look. "You really in trouble up there in the big city?"

"Enough people think I am."

"Why?"

"I want them to think I am."

"You always did go looking for trouble. That time you played Satan in the church play?"

"King Herod."

"Herod, was it? Looked like Satan to me."

"I played it that way."

"Chopped every damn doll in town right in two."

"But then Eckmann stopped stropping his daughter, and our father quit going after Mother, and . . ." But it was too complicated, or just too long ago.

"You were a hellion, all right. Whole town glad to see the hind end of you." He considered. "And I guess what all this boils down to is us seeing it again, don't it?"

"For the last time."

"Never thought you'd come back. After the Armistice maybe, but not after that."

"With your help, I won't need to again. One way or another."

"Guess I got to be for that, don't I?"

We started walking back toward the house, but wide around through some of the older graves. I passed one pitched-over stone with a big chip out of its side that I recognized as my mother's work. It gave me a momentary pang.

Cosmo was full of himself, pride in his calling, how big he'd gotten, how much the buried population had expanded since our father's sparsely settled days, but something else was still puzzling him.

"What kind of trouble you get yourself into up there in the big city?"

"Don't you have television?"

He smiled hard money at me. "When we get to wanting it, we ride up to Mabel's."

*

He put on his overalls after lunch, worked hard most of the afternoon, down in the storm cellar, sawing and hammering. I sat outside a while on the edge of the wishing well, mulling him, Rudy, the town, other things over. The well had been converted into the war memorial by simply chipping out of its uneven stones a badly spaced tribute that ran all the way around and caught up with itself.

BATTLE TO OUR HONORED DEAD IN

When he came up once for a little fresh air, I asked him about this unwonted public-spiritedness.

"Sure I give it," he said. "But I didn't tell them which war." He poked the lettering with the claw of his hammer. "And I didn't tell them which side neither."

*

Later on, I decided to go in search of Rudy. "Out back," Cosmo yelled up to me from the storm cellar, "digging another grave."

I found him already three feet down in the tough, red clay, in front of my own headstone.

I stood there at its wintry marge, and Rudy looked up at me with a miserable, thoroughly astonished expression after each shovelful, but kept on digging. It was back-breaking labor, the clay unyielding when he spaded into it, wet when he lifted it. This must be what has kept him so strong all these years, I ruminated.

When he stopped to rest, I squared off a long box with my hands, then lay my head on my open palm with my eyes peacefully closed, and then did a quick, very cheerful skeleton dance, smiling broadly.

Rudy still didn't understand, but saw at least that I didn't object.

I went back to Cosmo to find out just what he had in mind. He scooped up a handful of loose sawdust, let it sift out of the bottom of his fist. It made a small pile on a pine knot, like sand in the bottom of an hourglass.

"I'm sticking by my word."

"What word?"

"To the town."

"In what way have you oathed yourself to this town?"

"I promised them I'd only let you back here to be buried."

"How much you must have missed me."

"Somebody might recognize you."

"Not so far."

"If they do, I'm at least covered."

*

I took a walk through Vienna around five, once again to see who indeed might know me. Along our sandy, little, gutterless Ringstrasse.

No face was particularly familiar, though some of them I knew I'd kissed, and one or two I might have struck in a schoolyard fight. But none of them seemed to know I'd ever been anywhere near any of them before. Even the several ancients stooled up over their cups of coffee at the Rexall drugstore. Our Café Mozart.

I also looked in at the Seahorse Dinette. Our Demel's, where my mother had once, to save us all, slung hash for six months. The present waitress, reading the Asbury Park *Evening News*, told me she'd be right with me, or I could get a plate and help myself. I asked her if I could bring her anything.

"I eat at home," she said, leaning nearer the newsprint.

I said I would do the same, and left, unnoticed.

Changes everywhere. The old gaslights were gone, of course. There had been three, their nightly tendance one of my father's bounden duties. The church was still the same denomination, but locked up and gray, instead of Easter-white with its doors forbiddingly open. Our own St. Stephen's. The school was now the post office, and the post office was now the B.P.O.E. I couldn't even find the one-room Public Library. One summer I read it all. By the middle of August. That got me in trouble too. I was too quick for my own good, and there were better things for a growing boy to do than sit around all day and read, and if you take them out again, you'll wear out the bindings before others have had a chance to borrow them. . . .

But learning, I guessed, had been moved regionally out of town. You reached it now by school bus. Though I didn't see anybody school age either. It looked sadly like a place where there wasn't even any Halloween any more.

When I stopped to pet the Dalmatian lying in front of the fire house, our Belvedere Palace, the dog was abruptly called to come back inside. By a man standing with one foot horsed on the fire engine fender, who I was sure used to deliver eggs to us when he was a boy.

"You tell old man Cosmo at least that dog's life is still his own."

I dropped by the General Store again. Eckmann's face seemed to light up the least little feeble bit.

"I ain't forgot. You're after a flag sticker."

So I went back down the Ringstrasse to Cosmo again, who was just setting aside work for the day, one coffin half nailed together, the boards for the other sawn and laid out, like pants pieces.

"There seems to be a stranger in town," I said.

"They'll remember you someday."

"When?"

"After you're gone."

"But not fondly."

"That time you drove all our sheep into church."

"The Lambs of God, Cosmo. I was showing how each living creature is—"

"They'll remember that."

"I see they've locked the doors."

"Come on. We got to go help Rudy."

"He's doing fine on his own."

"Not toward the end. He gets six feet down, he can't pull himself out."

*

On Sunday, while Cosmo finished work on the coffins, Rudy and I test-drove the old hearse down to the shore, with Rudy at the wheel. Between us, me shouting, him shifting, we made it.

Once there, I tried to give him a treat. I took him on the indoor merry-go-round with me, two on a horse, gave him some change to waste on the prize machines, bought him a candied apple that he tried to put in his pocket, half-eaten. Then we went for a long stroll down the almost empty boardwalk. He insisted on walking right next to the row of closed concessions, his shoulder hugging their boarded-up fronts, his eyes turned away from the sea. Finally I pulled him over to the railing and made him look. He was trembling.

From his hands, though he always kept one or the other tight to the rail, I got the idea he didn't know how something like the ocean could exist. Too big. Where did it all go?

I tried to show him by making a boat with my hands, then an airplane, then even swimming strokes that it could be crossed, that it did have another side. That I'd been there myself, might go again.

But he couldn't follow, and we were both soon way over

our heads in a discussion that lacked all finger dexterity. To end it, I cupped my right hand, reached way far out with a giant scooping motion, and brought the whole sea carefully back up over the railing for him in my palm.

That reassured him. He clearly thought it was marvelous that I could do a thing like that. He wanted me to take it back to the car, and all the way home to Vienna, but since I'd decided to do the driving on the trip back, I let it all dribble out between my fingers.

By the time we returned to town, the coffins were done, and there was a fresh corpse in the storm cellar. Eckmann's.

∗

"Heart attack. But he can just wait a couple days," Cosmo said. "I'm too interested in your good riddance."

Rudy had the old hearse drawn up to the storm cellar doors, and was loading the coffins in back for the next day's journey. Cosmo and I went across the street to close up the General Store. There were still a few horehound drops that hadn't been picked up out of the troughs of the undulate floor. Eckmann had been struck down still just short of rounding that candy jar.

∗

Later that evening, a lot of the town gathered in front of the General Store and stood staring across at us while we were inside eating our dinner.

Cosmo told me there was a rumor around that Eckmann had met with foul play at the hands of the stranger, whom some of them were beginning to think they recognized as somebody they knew something about from somewhere.

He waited until we'd finished dessert, then went outside and spoke to them from the porch. He didn't explain who I was. He just told them I'd been at the shore all day, and Rudy could verify that.

"You'd best stay inside the house until we're right ready to leave," he smirked. He whiled away the rest of the evening, writing me out a death certificate.

*

We left the next morning as soon after breakfast as I could get my make-up on. But it was an elaborate job, took some time, so a lot of the town was out watching again, even more suspiciously, when I climbed into the back of the hearse. As quickly as possible. The waitress from the Seahorse Dinette still let out a very slow scream.

But mostly they seemed to be down on Cosmo, dressed in his damn mourning like a hick Fred Astaire.

"Who's your house guest?"

"Some stiff you short-changed come back to get you?"

"That thing don't belong in this town, Cosmo."

"Scared old Eck right out of his ticker."

"Just couldn't wait for your one and only friend's natural end, could you?"

"If you didn't have Rudy, we'd take both you and it."

"We may yet."

"Don't bring that thing around here again, Cosmo."

"No sir."

"And you know we don't ever forget a face."

Rudy backed us out of the driveway, then wrenched us brutally, yawingly into ratchety forward motion. As we rolled down the tarred ruts, Cosmo grinned back at me through the cab window.

"You get everybody into trouble!" he yelled.

"Could have told them who I was!" I yelled back.

"Who are you?"

"The only one of you who ever did enough wrong to make good!"

He pointed at me, gleefully. "Can look at you and *see* that ain't so!"

"I'm *known* for looking this way!"

"Nobody *we* know is."

I felt absurdly disconsolate. Behind me, in the seat of my often harrowing childhood, an angry populace and my own open grave. As we chugged out of town, we passed the back of that sign.

YOU ARE LEAVING VIENNA

And then the other rhyme line. A civic challenge.

Try-enna, where else!

*

I had them in here earlier tonight, both of them, not just Rudy, together for a conference. A story conference, to settle how we're going to handle tomorrow, and I seem to have matters very much back in hand. Cosmo has been a lot more pliable since I got him to the big city. A lot more, especially after what he has been seeing today. My crowds frightened him. I thought Rudy was the one I'd have to watch, who might shatter, maybe very badly, but I guess Rudy figures if I can pick up a whole ocean in one hand, I can hold off whatever scares him about New York with the other. It's Cosmo who turns out to be the coward under all that small-town meanness. Soon as things start to get a little urban, panic. Yelled we were going to blow right off the Goethals Bridge, and damn near jumped himself. Probably did the same thing at the Verrazano, though I was under my coffin lid by then, and couldn't see. If I'd known Rudy was going to be that stalwart, I'd have had them go through Lincoln Tunnel instead. Very, very slowly, to give Cosmo a real claustrophobic taste of just where he puts people.

But I don't want him to lose all his starch. I brought him in here tonight, snarled at him, right in front of Rudy, a piece of policy, and told him, "I want you to start acting more like family."

"That so?"

"I want you to start treating me the same way Father used to make us treat him. Never mind why. I have reasons. From now on, I'm the master."

"That so?"

"Yes, that's so. Tonight the master sees nobody. Not even Terry. Rudy will bring the master any messages. The master doesn't want any messages Rudy can't bring. And you're on guard for the master."

"Yes, Master," he sniggered, trying to make a joke of it, but the joke was too thin. He was too distraught. It makes him look meaner, but I can tell his real meanness is losing substance. I was really trying to shore it up some.

"Say that again."

"Yes, Master."

"Father was deaf. All he could do was watch your mealy lips move. He couldn't hear your real churlishness. But I can. Try again."

His lip curled.

"And get it right."

His lip hid its curl.

"Yes, Master."

"Much better."

Then I went over what he was to tell Terry, and carefully explained how all that fit into my own plans for tomorrow night. Which are, indeed, quite, quite settled, now that Hazel has done her intelligence work so well. It is another sure sign of Cosmo's weakening meanness that my plans actually shock him.

"I thought they'd suit you," I smiled.

"When did you decide this?"

"I've had it in the back of my mind right along."

"Terrible."

"Why?"

"You could've told me."

"Do I have to tell you everything?"

"I'm involved."

"Are you?"

"I'm your brother."

I laughed, and then noticed Rudy's flat head was going back and forth between us, wondering what we were laughing at.

I froze. "Whatever you do, don't tell Rudy. Don't even look at him right now."

"Yes, Master."

"Only tell him after he can't do a thing about it."

"All right."

" 'All right, Master.' "

"Whatever you say, Master."

The forced servility was galling him, and therefore bucking him up considerably. I was glad I'd thought of it.

"Now get out of here. I want to talk to Rudy."

"Immediately, Master."

I made Rudy a big parade with my hands, then spun a steering wheel to show him how he was going to be driving in it, and then laughed again to prove how much fun Cosmo and I thought it was going to be.

Rudy frowned doubtfully, but dutifully took me at my word.

Concerning lies. It is extremely hard to tell them with only your hands.

*

Rudy has since been in here with one message. From Terry. He delivered it by putting his thumb in his mouth, sucking very hard on it, then pointing to me. When I looked puzzled, he repeated it. Then we both shrugged at each other. I suspect that somewhere along the line—from what Terry said to Cosmo, to what Cosmo signaled to Rudy, to what Rudy tried to pass on to me—something has been lost. Though I doubt if it is important enough to be regretted.

In fact, tonight, incomprehension comes to me as a distinct pleasure. Almost a giddiness. There is so much now I have no need to know. Perhaps never have had. It even strikes me that a way to pare this world of its meaningless is to resort to simple dumbshow. Kisses and blows, wild gestures and timorous twiddlings, & so forth. Doesn't everybody agree that the movies lost something when sound came in? Exactly. And tomorrow I return myself bodily to those former, happier days. To epic-making silence.

*

But of course it is already tomorrow, and I'm not going to, cannot go on with these scribblings. I'm far too tired. A big performance ahead of me. Tomorrow. Tonight.

Yet I still worry about a critical point that has often been attacked in your own work, E.A.P. How close the horror sometimes borders on the ludicrous. Cosmo and Rudy and Simon. Will we turn out to be as diabolical as *The Unholy Three*, or as comical as Chico and Harpo and Groucho? The Moro Brothers . . .

So I wonder about tomorrow. Tonight. It's settled, but no prices are good until paid, said the cheat, no promises are good until kept, said the infidel, no deeds are good until done, said the undoer. At this point, and at my age too, my whole career is—*wunderbar*, precisely!—at stake.

W ALPURGISNACHT. It is here. Very little to say about to-day's events. Like yesterday's, just more of the same. I did try one eye open. Then the other. It only seemed to bring a worse class of people. Maniacs, Moroites, mummers, marrow-eaters, multitudes. If I'd opened both, Cosmo and Rudy couldn't have handled the crowds. They are out picking up the hearse now, so a few random notes before departure.

*

Only one note, really. A philosophical memory, away from all this clamor. About a coach lamp. Its mantle used to burn all night long at the side of our house in Vienna, over those storm cellar doors. It wasn't there when I went back this time. I only remember it now. Or did I, telling baroque stories to that *Esquire* scribbler? Anyhow, gone. My suspicion is that Cosmo sold it for some outrageous, antique-inflated price to buy more embalming fluid.

It was black, with little, round, golden knobs, each threaded to hold a long pin in place for six delicately bevelled glass panes. Old glass. Gorgeous and clear, like that first winter skim of pond ice. It gave off a scarifying light, but that's what attracted the bugs all summer long. Clouds of them. Moths, mayflies, earwigs, mosquitoes, even those big June beetles. I never did understand how quite so many worked their way inside the lamp. There were holes, of course, to let out the heat from the gas flame, but they were so few and so small that the lamp was like its own closed world. A dusk-to-dawn nova. It was like gaining entrance to a star. But they crawled in there, and died in a fiery instant, and piled up until I could see the rising white level of their dead even from down on the ground.

Then it was my job to climb up a ladder and clean them out of the lamp. I'd have to take it apart very cautiously. The mantle was even more fragile than the glass. So were the dead. And there they would be. The brittle beetle carcasses, the moths burnt to brown dust, one or two charred crickets, the immolated gnats. And I could see everything. Thousands of little legs, furry faces, torn wings, turned-up bellies, severed antennae. A mass grave. Yet they lay so lightly upon one another that I could pick them up one at a time if I wanted. A mosquito by its shriveled, tiger-striped body, or a mayfly by its stiff, iridescent web.

And often I did, by way of delay, because I knew what I would eventually find underneath. As I pulled away the corpses, pinched slowly down through that insectal pyre, I gradually—and it was always a gruesome sensation—came to the *living*. Tiny, squiggling things. Vital mites and feisty larvae, snuggled away under all that pall and quietus. It was terrifying to see a snapping, twisting shape suddenly pull itself up over a tangle of dead limbs, across a disintegrating sphinx wing, and *thrive*. Inside that lamp, where bright death reigned perpetually, and dropped myriad cadavers down into the pit below, life still went on.

But that's how it is. Just how it is.

*

Quickly now. I am writing this still from my coffin, but the coffin is now in the back of the hearse. Rudy is up front at the wheel. Alas, Rudy, I wave good-bye to you here, handlessly. Cosmo, in an error that is unlike him, has had to go back for the hammer.

Though his meanness is muchly recovered. Consider the following last request he has just made of me, smiling his fell desires around his three rotten teeth.

"You're going through with it?"

"No question."

"None?"

"None."

"Then I got an idea."

"Make it quick."

"I want to bury the other one. Back home."

I gawked at him in sheerest admiration. "So you can keep your word to the town."

"As soon as Rudy and me get back to Vienna. It's got the skeleton. Everything. Your grave's dug. We just pop it in the hole."

"Baroque."

"That so?"

"What about . . . you don't care what's going to happen here?"

"None of that'll ever reach us."

"Probably not."

"If it does, they're wrong, we're right."

"Of course."

"This way," he smirked, and it was a grin as good as my Ghoulgantua's, "we're rid of you, in a way, but we also got you back home."

"In a way."

"All right, Master?"

"I'd be honored."

I told him he could even have a little fun with Terry. Badger him with farewell blandishments, and then skee-daddle. Yes, Terry, even our double-cross-purposes have finally crossed. But I told Cosmo he was all on his own there.

*

I'm on my own here. Or almost. Closing up now. Cosmo is coming up the alley with the hammer.

We simply switch lids.

Nothing could be simpler. Or rather Cosmo will switch lids. Take this labeled one—and farewell, o faithful lap desk —over to the empty, and bring that one over here. And I will watch from inside as he lowers that one down over me.

I am now taking Terry's pills, one by one. Only because I do not want to scream out and bring an unwarranted halt to the proceedings before they are done. In truth, I would like to see the whole thing as it happens from inside here, but I do not trust myself to hold my tongue. For similar reasons, Terry, as per your request, I have also emptied my bladder.

This notebook will be found under my staked corpse. I hope not too blotted by . . .

I have no farewell words. Hands are better than words.

I have only a last question.

After you bore witness to this climactic and totally egregious little horror of mine, my beloved voyeurs, did anybody bother to stay for the movie?

IV. *Remains*

Hazel Rio
MERRYMAKING
As told to Warner Williams

The off-beat, revelatory memoirs of a not-so-well-known screen actress who, as she writes, "stayed a starlet for thirty years." Miss Rio describes her strife and hard times as the ingénue victim of innumerable horror films, and recalls her long and poignant relationship with her mentor, the late actor Simon Moro. Her narrative throws new light upon the possible artistic reasons behind Moro's self-immolation. "He was a man who knew when to end his own epoch," she suggests his tragedy, "and somebody who always preferred the appalling to the appealing." But Miss Rio also knows a happier Hollywood, and is cheerfully frank about its present sexual mores, her own escape from Puritan torment along "the thorny path of virtue." Whence her career, and hence her title. Lavishly illustrated.

MARCH / NON-FICTION / 320 PAGES / $7.95

—FROM *Spring Books from Atheneum*

DOUBLE HORROR FEATURE

S. MORO IN RAVEN

Q. ADAMS IN MOUTH OF EVIL

FAMILY NITE WED.

—*from the marquee of the Peace Gardens Drive-In Theater, Minot, N.D.*

THE SCAPERELLI LIVING ROOM. *Baronial style that still fits a family budget. Aged oaken furnishing, heavy velour drapes, medieval to Renaissance artwork. Also canopied bedroom suites to match. Darkened floors included, slate or vinyl. Mullioning of windows optional. Another new décor from Quincy Adams Associates, Hollywood, Calif.*

—FROM *Sears Catalogue*

. . . *find no record of delivery on that date. Our files indicate that air express had been arranged by you for a coffin on our 4:39 A.M. flight to Tempelhof, but that no bill of lading was issued that day, or the preceding night.*

We are sorry that we cannot be forthcoming with further information. We would suggest that the matter be settled by your check for $100.00, covering solely our immediate expenses for previously ordered special handling, with no additional charge for other unused services.

SINCERELY,
(*Unsigned*)
for Frankfurt Air Freight, Ltd.

—FROM *letter in files of Maliproductions, Inc., Malibu, Calif.*

COWAN ACQUIRES RITES
TO MORO HORROR BIOG,
FLETCHER TO SCRIPT

—HEADLINE IN *Variety*

. . . will drop its present spot commercials featuring character actor Lars Syndor. An agency spokesman described the conduct of Mr. Syndor as "brutalizing, and detrimental to the tradition of clean, cool shaving." Apparently the agency wants nobody thinking those kinds of thoughts with a razor poised that close to a man's throat on nationwide television.

—FROM *Advertising Age*

"The Auxiliary Ego as Counterplayer in a Senile Case of Morbid Exhibitionism."

—*title of lecture delivered by Dr. Horst Yost to the Horst Yost Institute of Psychotherapy*

. . . that suicide, anciently understood as *felo-de-se* or "self murder," may in the Moro Case have to be redefined as a tort. Certainly it depended to a great degree upon various forms of contributory negligence. Mistaken identity, suppositious intent, the engineering of public response, to name but a few conundrums. . . .

—FROM *The Columbia Law Review*

Unentitled ms. Holograph. 89 pp. Undated. Damaged. Hardboard cover broached, pp. 1–71 penetrated, pp. 72–89 heavily scored and dented. Stains throughout, compromising legibility. Designated a prompt book, and attributed to Simon Moro, 20th-cent. German actor.

—*description in Rare Books Collection of New York Public Library*

"In the main, I think we're all saddened, regretful. But I also think we can be somewhat grateful that this fair city was never subjected to his interpretation of Caliban."

—remark of Quincy Adams to Joseph Papp
on The Mayor Lindsay Show *over* WNEW

"They're very gentle birds. People get the wrong idea. They don't go around pulling off people's fingers. Look, I'll show you. Bite, Rupert. Go on, bite. See? Didn't even break my skin. You could let him bite you the same. Bite Johnny, Rupert."

—extract of interview with Gregorio Tarkas,
bird trainer, on The Johnny Carson Show

GOTT MIT UNS FÜR KÖNIG UND VATERLAND

SIMON MORO

1900–1968

—from an old gravestone in family cemetery
near Vienna, N.J.

Brock Brower

Brock Brower was raised in Westfield, New Jersey, graduated from Dartmouth College in 1953, and later attended Merton College, Oxford, as a Rhodes Scholar. Besides numerous political articles, he has published a previous novel, DEBRIS, *a collection of his reportage,* OTHER LOYALTIES: A POLITICS OF PERSONALITY, *and a recent children's book,* THE INCHWORM WAR AND THE BUTTERFLY PEACE. *He was Lecturer in Creative Writing at Princeton University in 1968–69, and presently makes his home in Princeton, with his wife and five children.*